ThE pOWER ANd ThE GLORY

INVICTO

BOOK THREE

—•——◦∾◦——•—

CHRISTINE WASS

Romaunce Books

1A The Wool Market Dyer Street Cirencester Gloucestershire GL7 2PR
An imprint of Memoirs Publishing www.mereobooks.com

978-1-86151-967-2

First published in Great Britain in 2020
by Romaunce Books, an imprint of Memoirs Publishing

The address for Memoirs Publishing Group Limited can be
found at www.memoirspublishing.com

The Memoirs Publishing Group Ltd Reg. No. 7834348

Typeset in 10/16pt Century Schoolbook
by Wiltshire Associates Publisher Services Ltd.

TO ROGER
WITH LOVE

CHAPTER ONE

Flavius Quinctilius Silvanus breathed a sigh of relief as he looked up at the massive structure of the Appian Aqueduct towering over the Caelian Hill. It had been an arduous journey from Caesarea, but, thanks to the gods, he had reached Rome safely.

He had been serving as a Tribune Staff Officer to Pilate, Procurator of Judea, in Caesarea when he had received a communication from Senator Claudius Marcellus, an old family friend, requesting him to return to Rome as quickly as possible as his father was dead and his mother was in danger. Marcellus had not said how his father had died, nor why his mother was in danger. These were things Flavius would have to find out for himself. Tired and hungry, he rode up the Hill towards the Silvanus Estate.

Flavius entered the perimeter of the vast estate and

looked around. Something was wrong. The flower beds were filled with wilting flowers and weeds. The grass had not been cut for many days. Where were the slaves who tended the estate gardens?

He rode closer to his family's villa and quickly reined in his horse. Saturn protested at the sudden stop, but Flavius calmed him by patting the black stallion's neck, saying softly, "Easy, boy".

Flavius frowned as he saw some Praetorian Guards standing outside the main entrance to the villa. Hoping they hadn't seen him, he turned Saturn around and left the estate. Why were Praetorians outside his family's villa? He rode to Claudius' estate to try to find answers.

The huge estate of Gnaeus Claudius Marcellus was close to the Silvanus family's land. Claudius and Flavius' father, both members of the Senate, had been friends for many years. Flavius had known Claudius for most of his life and had been best friends with Claudius' son, Aelianus Claudius, whom Flavius had nicknamed Claudio. Flavius did not remember much about Claudio's younger sister, Claudia Marcella, as she had not been allowed to play alongside her brother and his friend.

Flavius was two years older than Claudio. When they had reached young manhood, they had gone their separate ways; he had led a hedonistic lifestyle whilst Claudio, who was always more obedient to his father's wishes, refused to join him in his immoral activities. Claudio was more of a home-bird who was content to confine his activities to the occasional celebration with his family on important religious festivals, but mostly to studying for the day when he would follow his father into the Senate.

Flavius hoped they would rekindle their past friendship, if Claudio had not yet joined the Legions, as his Senatorial ambition would force him to do. If he had joined, he hoped life in the Legions would not change Claudio as they had changed him.

He looked back over his shoulder, making sure he wasn't being followed. Satisfied that he wasn't, he entered the Claudii estate. He tied Saturn to a tree, then took his saddlebags and approached the villa.

Hearing insistent knocking on the villa door, the door porter opened the grille. When Flavius identified himself, he quickly unbolted the door and let him in. Before he closed the grille, his eyes scanned the area outside. Satisfied Flavius had not been followed, he closed the grille, making sure that the sturdy door was securely bolted. He called for a slave to take Flavius to Claudius.

Claudius greeted Flavius with surprise and mixed feelings: sadness about why he had returned to Rome, joy at seeing him safe and well, and worry about how to tell him what had happened to his father.

"Where is your horse?" he asked Flavius.

"Outside, tied to a tree," replied Flavius.

Claudius called for a slave. When he appeared, Claudius said, "There is a horse tied to a tree outside. Take it to the stables immediately." The slave bowed and did as his master had commanded.

Claudius looked at Flavius and said, "Your horse is easily recognisable as the finest and most beautiful horse in the area. If he is seen, the Praetorians will know you are here. Now, come with me."

Flavius followed Claudius into his private office.

"Leave your saddlebags over there, Flavius." Claudius pointed to a small marble table set against a beautifully painted wall, then watched as Flavius laid them carefully on the table. Bidding Flavius to sit down, Claudius clapped his hands. Another slave quickly appeared and bowed before his master. "Bring wine here," ordered Claudius. The slave bowed again and left the room, soon returning with a tray of wine and two wine cups. He set the tray down on a small ornate table close to Claudius.

"Leave us, I will pour the wine," Claudius said stiffly, "and close the door behind you!"

Left in private, Claudius poured the wine into the wine cups and handed one to Flavius, then sat his tall, lean body down on the couch opposite. Seeing Flavius' expectant face, he knew he had to tell him the whole sorry saga concerning his father's death. He drank deeply from his wine cup and began.

"I am so sorry about your father, Flavius, he was a decent man, and my friend." He ran a nervous hand over his greying hair. "I have to tell you his death was not through illness." He saw the puzzled expression on the younger man's face and knew he had to tell him the truth. "Your father took his own life."

Flavius jumped up, crying out "No! My father would never commit suicide!"

"Nevertheless, it is true." Claudius watched sympathetically as Flavius strode around the room, obviously distressed by this news. He said carefully "I know this was out of character for your father, but he was left with no choice."

Flavius spun round and said angrily "No choice? Why?"

"The day he died, your mother came to me, begging me to help them. She said that Praetorian Guards, led by Prefect Naevius Sutorius Macro, had visited them at the family villa that morning telling your father that the Emperor had asked after his health... you know what that means, Flavius?" He saw a shocked Flavius nod. "Your father knew what it meant too. Your mother said that when your father asked Macro what he was supposed to have done, Macro replied, 'You are reported to be the leader of a revolt against our beloved Emperor.' She said your father nearly choked laughing at that accusation, but Macro did not find it funny. He issued a stark warning: 'Sort out your affairs, Senator. We will be back later tonight!' Realising his last hours had come, your father sent your mother here for me to take care of. He also sent his slaves." He sighed. "I wanted to help your father, but how could I fight against Tiberius' command?"

He took another drink, then said, "Your father was a proud man and knew Tiberius would inflict the most degrading punishment upon him, thus tarnishing the family name forever, so he took the honourable way out." He drained his wine cup. "Later that night I went to your villa and saw that the place had been ransacked of its treasures." He swallowed. "I found your father lying dead in his bath. He had cut his wrists. I didn't know what to do. Were the Praetorians coming back? I left things as they were until the next day, then, making sure all was clear, with the help of Atticus, my strongest slave, we removed your father's body and buried it under a fig tree in your garden."

He saw the horrified look on Flavius' face and held up his hands in a placating gesture. "It was all we could do at that time, Flavius."

"I thank you for all you have done and I understand why you had to quickly bury my father's body in secret," Flavius said. "What I do not understand is why anyone would be so vile as to accuse my father of such treachery. Did he speak against anyone in a Senate speech?"

Claudius grimaced. "Not that I ever heard. As for who spread lies about your father, I have my suspicions, but I will not voice them until I have proof. These days it is too dangerous to own a loose tongue. Macro is as callous and cruel as his predecessor, Sejanus. He enjoys issuing death threats and carrying out murders ordered by the Emperor, or more likely by the orders of the Emperor's chief spy, Calpurnius Aquila."

Calpurnius Aquila! That name again! The man who was at Pilate's Saturnalia party. The man who had corrupted Prefect Alae Antonius and ensnared the foolish, greedy scribe, Adolfo. Why would Aquila want his father's death?

"What about my mother?" he said through tight lips.

Claudius replied, "I had the unpleasant duty of telling her about your father's death. It nearly broke her."

"My poor mother," Flavius said sadly. "Where is she now? Can I see her?"

"She stayed here for two nights. It was obvious she could not go to your own family's country estate as the Praetorians would be waiting there, so, dressed as a slave, she travelled with my daughter, Claudia, and other slaves, including Atticus, to my villa and farm in Latium." He took a breath. "Your mother is there now. I ordered one of her own female slaves, together with Atticus, to stay at the villa and take care of her. Claudia, accompanied by two slaves, returned here the next day. If we were being watched and the change in slave numbers was noticed, Claudia was to say that the other slaves stayed at the farm in order to ready it for the family's summer visit. Fortunately that problem did not arise. Nobody knows where your mother is."

"And my brother, Marius, where is he?" Flavius queried, wondering why he had not been mentioned.

"I don't know," came Claudius' simple reply. "He was not there when your father died. He has not been home for some time. I am not sure he even knows about these tragic events." He saw Flavius' questioning look and said "That's all I can tell you, Flavius."

He looked at Flavius' sunken, dark-shadowed eyes, the tension lines around his mouth and his travel-stained garments. "I know this has come as a great shock to you, Flavius," he said. "You dare not return to your villa, so I think it best you stay here with us." He smiled as Flavius nodded and murmured his thanks. "Now, it is almost time for dinner. I don't think you are ready to be questioned by the rest of the family, so I will have a slave accompany you to the bathhouse, unpack your clean clothes, and then take you to your room. Dinner and wine will be brought to you there."

Claudius clapped his hands and a slave appeared. He issued his instructions adding, "You will then escort Tribune Flavius to the room overlooking the garden it is quiet there." Before the slave led a grateful Flavius away, Claudius added "I wish you a peaceful night, Flavius"

Claudius watched dolefully as the young man, shoulders hunched with weariness and worry, followed the slave out of the room.

Flavius had bathed and fed well and was now lying on his soft bed, but his tortured mind would not let him rest peacefully. He turned Claudius' words over and over in his head. How long would it be before he could see his mother? Where was Marius? When he'd learned of his father's death, Pilate had said he could take as long as he liked to help his mother. He determined that however long it did take, he would never give up trying to find the answers to his questions.

CHAPTER TWO

The next morning, weary after a fretful night, Flavius entered the empty dining room. The doorway leading to the garden was open and the perfume of aromatic thyme, mixed with the powerful smell of rosemary and various shrubs, drifted into the room through the peristyle, the columned walkway leading to the garden.

He looked around, impressed by what he saw. There were the usual three couches – the head couch, with a right-hand and a left-hand couch joined to it – and each had comfortable seat cushions piled high on them. A beautifully-carved wooden and bronze table stood between them. The walls to the right and left of the room were exquisitely painted in vivid reds, bordered by ochres and yellows; the wall facing the table depicted a colourful scene from Homer's Odyssey, showing Odysseus and the beautiful witch, and, as if watching over the diners, a magnificent painting on the wall behind the table depicted the god Mars surrounded by armoured warriors.

Claudio came into the room. He greeted Flavius warmly, saying, "Flavius, old friend." Then, his voice tinged with sadness, he said, "I am so sorry for your loss."

"Thank you." Flavius looked at Claudio and saw that his face still held a boyish look but that frown lines had begun to appear, probably through his hours of concentration on his studies. If Claudio was surprised by the changes in him, his expression did not show it. He sat down on the right-hand couch and pointed to the empty space next to him. "Come, Flavius, sit by me," he said.

Flavius sat down beside him, not knowing what to say. This was not the time to reminisce about their boyhood and the mischievous things they had got up to back then.

After a long moment of awkward silence, Claudio suddenly said, "What's it like in the Legions?" Flavius wanted to say 'Worse than you could ever imagine' but instead he said "It's a hard life and sometimes dangerous. I..." He stopped, his attention turning to Claudius as he entered the room. He was followed by Claudia.

Flavius blinked at the change in the girl he had known only as an irritating nuisance. Now, her brown hair was ornately arranged, her body was slim but shapely and her facial features, although not beautiful, were pleasant. He stood up to greet Claudius and his daughter. Claudius reclined on the head couch, and Claudio and Flavius followed his lead. Claudia smiled shyly at Flavius as she reclined on the couch opposite.

The slaves brought in their breakfast. Flavius looked at the platters laid out on the table before them, which contained salted bread, eggs, cheese and fruit, together with bowls of honey and milk. He had no appetite, but he knew he had to eat something or be thought of as rude. He took a small selection of each but the only thing he enjoyed was drinking a bowl of honeyed milk. Flavius was thankful that his father's death was not mentioned.

After the remains of breakfast had been cleared away, Flavius walked through the peristyle and out into the garden. It was a warm day. He wandered over to the large fountain set in the middle of the path flanked by tall cypress trees and ornate flowers. The water pouring out from the mouth of the large bronze Triton set on top of the fountain, splashed him, cooling him. He heard a noise behind him and turned round to see Claudia approaching him. He smiled at her and said, "Look at you, all grown up."

She laughed. "Well, it has been a long time since we last saw you."

"You are not married?"

She shook her head. "I have not met the right man, and my father will never contemplate an arranged marriage for me with someone I do not love. Besides, since my mother's death two years ago, I am happy to stay here and look after my father and brother." She looked at him and said, "How are you, Flavius?" She saw a shadow cross his face. "You must have experienced bad times in the Legions and now, to come home to this..." she stopped, seeing the sadness in his eyes. "I am sorry," she said gently.

Flavius gripped the edge of the fountain bowl, remembering those bad times. Without looking at her he said, "All I want now is to see my mother."

"Please be patient, Flavius. You must take care, your life is in danger." She looked away briefly, then turned her face to his and said, "I will speak to my father, I am sure he will find a way for you to see her."

Claudius did find a way, the same way he had saved Flavius' mother. Dressed as a slave, Flavius travelled with other slaves to the villa and farm in Latium. He was looking forward to being reunited with his mother, his only regret being that he had to leave Saturn in the care of Claudius' groom.

After an uneventful journey, they reached Latium. Flavius looked around at the extensive farmlands owned by Claudius. One large field contained a herd of sheep happily grazing on rich grass, while further on, many slaves were busy tending vast corn and vegetable fields; others were working in the olive groves or overseeing neat rows of grape-heavy vines growing in the vineyards. Flavius could see that the farm yielded much-needed food and wine and would command a high price in Rome, making Claudius a very wealthy man.

The wagon stopped outside the villa. Flavius jumped

down onto the stony path. The wagon then took the slaves to their quarters. He hesitated briefly before approaching the villa, then taking a deep breath, he knocked on the door. The doorkeeper pulled back the grille and Flavius announced himself. The doorkeeper looked at him warily. He went away, returning a few moments later, satisfied the man standing outside answered Lydia Flavia's description. He unbolted the door and let Flavius in.

His mother was standing in the atrium. She opened her arms and he ran to her. She held him close, weeping with relief that he was safe, then led him to a stone seat in the garden where, gazing lovingly at him, she took his hands into her own and said through her tears, "Flavius, I am so glad you are here."

"How could I stay away?" He studied her face. She had aged whilst he had been away. Streaks of grey now ran through her dark hair, her eyes were shadowed by grief and worry lines had etched themselves around her mouth.

She started to tell Flavius what had happened, but seeing her distress, he gently placed a finger over her lips, saying, "Claudius has told me everything, mother."

"He has been so very kind to me, I do not know what would have happened if he had not given me sanctuary." She looked out into the garden, then back at Flavius. "Flavius, who could have done this to us?"

Flavius heard the fear in her voice and felt anger rising in him against whoever had caused the death of his father and the near-destruction of his family. Through gritted teeth he said, "I don't know, but I promise you I will find out." He swallowed. "Do you know where Marius is?"

"Truly, Flavius, I do not know where he is." She wrung her hands nervously. "He has changed since last you saw him. He has given up on his studies and has become a pleasure-seeker. I fear he has fallen in with a bad crowd, whose leader is the Emperor's great-nephew, Caligula, the son of the noble Germanicus." Afraid to be overheard, she said quietly, "Never was a son less like his heroic father!"

His brother's friend was Tiberius' great-nephew? "Why would Caligula befriend Marius?" Flavius asked, bemused.

"Your father took Marius to the Palace with him to attend a reception. Caligula was apparently impressed by your brother's knowledge of history; they became friends, much to your father's disgust."

Flavius frowned. Mixing with the Emperor's family carried great risks. The Julio-Claudians were notoriously fickle. One day they would count you as a friend, the next...? It seemed he would now also have to discover the whereabouts of Marius.

Flavius reassured his mother that he would do everything he could to resolve both problems.

CHAPTER THREE

Sheikh Ibrahim's caravan safely reached the Kingdom of Nabatea. Ruth was hot and uncomfortable after spending hours travelling in the silk-lined carriage. She looked at baby Mary-Farrah, who lay sleeping peacefully, and smiled. The journey had not disturbed her at all; rather the movement of the carriage had seemed to soothe her.

Ruth opened the curtain of the carriage and looked out. She was staggered by what she saw. They were travelling through a ravine, with high mountains surrounding them on both sides. The occasional bellow of the camels and sharp voices of the drovers echoed in the still, arid air. The ravine suddenly opened up and before her lay a vast area dominated by tall, rose-coloured buildings cut into the sandstone rocks. Ibrahim pulled his horse up by the side of the carriage and said, smiling, "We are here."

Dismounting, Ibrahim ordered the chief drover to take the caravan to the unloading area, and then helped Ruth, holding Mary-Farrah closely to her, out of the carriage. He told Drubaal to take the cedar wood casket containing the ashes of his niece, Princess Farrah, to his house, then followed on with Ruth at his side.

The house was cut into the red rock. She entered though the intricately-carved wooden and bronze door, amazed to see the luxury inside. Soft carpets were scattered across the multi-coloured tiled floor, silk couches were spread around the large room with small carved tables embellished with gold standing nearby; silver filigree lanterns hung from the high ceiling and the walls were adorned with costly silk hangings. Ruth thought she had stepped into a palace.

Ibrahim went to the window and opened up the wooden shutter. As the daylight streamed through, he said, "That is better." Turning to Ruth, he said, "The journey has been arduous. Rest now while I go and report to King Aretas, I have much to tell him."

She nodded, then watched him go. Drubaal came in and smiled at her, then retired to his own quarters built into the side of the house.

After a while, a solemn-faced Sheikh returned. Ruth asked him how the King had received the news.

Ibrahim shook his head. "At first he was very angry at the loss of a distant relative, but when I told him that her murderer, ben-Ezra, had been caught and executed, it seemed to pacify him. He said, 'At last justice has been served on the man who killed your brother, my faithful Hassan, and his family. We will give Princess Farrah a royal funeral.' Then he looked at me and said, 'It is for you alone, Sheikh Ibrahim, to continue the Al-Khareem family name.' When I asked him if I could make you my officially adopted daughter, he readily gave his consent. He was pleased when I told him that your child is named after Princess Farrah."

He looked at Ruth. "Ruth, would you do me the honour of accepting my family name of Al-Khareem as your own? Would you agree to become my formally adopted daughter, with Mary-Farrah as my granddaughter?"

Lost for words, Ruth stared at him. Ruth bint Ibrahim Al-Khareem? Yes, it would give her child a family name and some standing in the world. For herself, it would be a privilege and a joy to honour him as her father. She said, "Yes. I thank you with all my heart."

Ibrahim was overjoyed. He took her hand and said gravely, "I must arrange for my niece's funeral rights to be performed. In two days' time, she will be buried in her family tomb. In the meantime, propriety demands that you cannot stay in this house with me." He thought for a moment, then said, "There is a small empty house just a few doors away. I will buy it for you." He went out. Not long afterwards he returned smiling and said, "The house is yours."

He was delighted to see her grateful response. "I have also employed the widow of the brother of Abdullah. She will live in the house and take care of you and Mary-Farrah."

Later that day, Ruth moved into her house, her very own home. Hagru, the widow, was waiting there for her. Hagru bowed her head in deference and made it plain that she was more than willing and very able to take care of such an important man's adopted daughter and granddaughter. Ruth immediately liked the affable woman. She thanked Ibrahim, marvelling at how the tables had turned from her being a servant to becoming the mistress of the house.

Early in the morning, before the sun reached its zenith, King Aretas, dressed in a white robe threaded with gold and with a golden diadem on his head, led his Queen, Shuqilat, Princess Phasaelis and the rest of the Royal Family along the Processional Way leading to the Temple of Winged Lions, set on the mountainside overlooking Petra. They were closely followed by Ibrahim, who was holding the cedar wood box covered in silk containing Farrah's ashes, with Drubaal and Ruth walking behind, holding a quantity of wine and an incense container.

As they walked, Ruth looked around, amazed by the monuments, sculptures of gods and sacred animals and blocks of stone representing the Nabatean gods. The procession passed by the Lion Fountain, the Garden Tomb, the Quarry and two standing obelisks, finally reaching the great rock-hewn staircase leading up to the Temple dedicated to the powerful goddess Al-Uzza.

They entered the magnificent entrance flanked by enormous columns. A priest stood inside, ready to take them to the inner sanctum of the Temple. Ruth stood open-mouthed as she saw the walls and columns colourfully painted with floral and figure designs. There was a podium with an altar in their midst. Surrounding the podium were niches containing offerings and idols of the Nabatean gods.

The focus of the temple was a large standing stone with a carved face, which she guessed represented the goddess. Knowing that Jewish Holy Law, laid down by the Most High God to the Prophet Moses centuries before, did not permit idols of any kind, she looked away. Sensing Ibrahim looking at her, she turned her face back again and stared straight ahead so as not to upset him, but carefully avoiding looking directly at the graven images.

At a signal from the King, the offerings were handed to the priest, who, intoning solemn prayers, poured out a libation of wine and waved the incense holder over and around the stone. He then laid the remainder of the offerings in front of the stone. The sweet smell of the wine mixed with the pungent scent of frankincense filled the air. A specially chosen young camel was brought forward by one of Ibrahim's caravan drovers.

A second priest joined the first. He held a bowl beneath the camel's neck. Ruth closed her eyes as the first priest took his sacrificial knife and with one deft movement, cut the animal's throat. The second priest caught the camel's blood in the bowl. After the dead animal had been dragged away, Ibrahim stepped towards the altar and held up the cedar wood casket, intoning prayers to the gods. The second priest poured the camel's blood over the altar.

Ruth had never visited the Temple in Jerusalem, but John Mark had told her about the animals that were sacrificed to God there on certain religious occasions. It seemed that many religions did the same thing. But he also said that the Nazarenes no longer sacrificed animals, as the Lord Jesus had been the ultimate sacrifice for mankind. At first she had been confused. Only later had she begun to understand.

The ceremony ended with more prayers, then King Aretas led the procession back outside. The King spoke briefly to Ibrahim, then he and the Royal Family returned to the palace, leaving Ibrahim to carry out the private burial ceremony.

Ibrahim, followed by Ruth and Drubaal, walked along the pathway to the Al-Khareem family tomb. Ruth was astounded when she saw that it was surrounded by a garden with an eating hall for feasting. She remembered the Sheikh once telling her that the Nabateans, like the Egyptians, believed in an afterlife and that the deceased's comforts had to be maintained by offering them food and wine. She had thought it strange at the time, but now she herself drew comfort from the fact the Princess and her family would never be forgotten.

Standing outside the door of the tomb, she looked up and saw the shape of an eagle carved into the lintel. Ibrahim saw her puzzled look and said quietly, "The eagle is the symbol of Dushara, our great god. He guards my family in their tomb for all time."

He asked Drubaal to open the solid door to the tomb. Drubaal did so, then stood back as Ibrahim entered in. The sunlight cast shadows on the walls of the dimly-lit tomb as he reverently placed the casket next to the wrapped bodies of her parents, brother Kadeem and tiny new-born sister. With tears streaming down his face and voice choked with emotion, he intoned prayers to the gods that Farrah and her family would find everlasting joy and contentment in their afterlife.

Ibrahim came back out into the daylight and Drubaal closed the tomb door firmly behind him. Ruth could see distress etched onto her adopted father's face and went to him, taking his hand in her own. He looked at her and smiled a thin smile. Ruth and Mary-Farrah would be a great comfort to him.

The next day, Ruth, who had been wondering how there was a continuous supply of fresh water in such an arid place, asked Ibrahim to explain. He smiled and said, "Come, let me show you."

Leaving Mary-Farrah with Hagru, she followed him to the base of a mountain and gasped as she saw terraces of shaped rock ledges fashioned along the bottom. "If you look up," Ibrahim pointed to the mountain, "you will see channels cut into the sides. When it rains, the rainwater flows into the ledges and along a pipeline system into reservoirs, underground cisterns and dams. We also collect floodwater and groundwater, and there are some natural springs."

He saw her quizzical look. "You are wondering how we stop the water from evaporating." He smiled. "Our ancestors invented a waterproof cement to line the cisterns to stop that from happening."

Ruth was amazed, but she had one last query, "How does the water stay fresh?"

"Stone walls and pillars shade the collected water, keeping it cool. There are also settling basins able to purify the water."

Ruth shook her head. "If you had not shown me, I would never have known the rock terrace ledges were there. And I cannot see the underground reservoirs and cisterns at all,"

"Exactly, Ruth. We hide our water system structures away from the prying eyes of passers-by and would-be invaders. It is why, even though the rainy season is only for a short time, we have a constant supply of water for our own purposes and to sustain the crops we grow."

Ruth was impressed. "I think your people are very clever to have thought of this.

He beamed. "I agree."

They walked away from the mountain and made their way back to their homes.

CHAPTER FOUR

Holding Mary-Farrah in her arms, Ruth looked up at the beautiful Treasure House. She had been in Petra, the Nabatean Capital, for a month now, but she never tired of looking at the magnificent building built into the sandstone rock.

A voice said, "The Treasure House is truly a work of art, isn't it?"

Startled, Ruth turned round to see a richly-dressed woman smiling at her. Ruth stared at the woman. She was statuesque, with lightly-tanned skin and raven black hair, half-hidden under a golden silk veil.

Seeing Ruth's expression, the woman introduced herself. "Please, do not be afraid. I am Princess Phasaelis, daughter of King Aretas." She smiled as she saw a shocked Ruth bow her head in deference. Phasaelis gently lifted

Ruth's chin and looked at her. "You are Sheikh Ibrahim's adopted daughter, and this is your child?" She pointed to Mary-Farrah, who looked up at the Princess with large dark eyes, fringed by thick eyelashes.

"She is beautiful," Phasaelis said wistfully. "I know you are from Jerusalem."

Ruth nodded. Was it her imagination, or did she see a look of sadness cross the Princess' beautiful dark brown eyes?

"Tell me, what is the baby's name?" Phasaelis tickled the baby under her little chin, bringing forth gurgles of pleasure.

"Her name is Mary-Farrah, Your Highness," Ruth said proudly.

The Princess was puzzled. "Your daughter has a Jewish and a Nabatean name? How curious." She smiled. "I must go now, but I should very much like to hear how you became a member of the Sheikh's family."

Ruth returned the Princess' smile. "And I would very much like to tell you Your Highness."

Phasaelis nodded. "I would also like to know what is happening in Jerusalem now. I wonder if anything has changed there."

Phasaelis walked away, leaving Ruth pondering how the Princess knew about Jerusalem. When she saw the Sheikh she would ask him.

Later that day, when Ibrahim returned to the house, Ruth did ask him. She was staggered by his reply.

"Princess Phasaelis was married to Herod Antipas for a number of years. Their time together was spent travelling between his palace in Jerusalem and his desert fortress of Machaerus. It seemed a perfect love-match, not just a marriage of state forged between Antipas and Aretas, and I believe Phasaelis truly loved him." He took a deep breath. "Until Antipas visited Rome."

"What happened in Rome?" Ruth asked excitedly.

Ibrahim cleared his throat. "It was on that visit that he first set eyes on his half-brother Philip's wife, Herodias." He shook his head. "From that moment on, he wanted no other woman except that harlot. He divorced our beautiful Phasaelis and, breaking Jewish Law and alienating his people and ours, he married Herodias. Protected by Aretas' guards, our Princess duly returned to her father. Needless to say, King Aretas was angry and pledged to one day take revenge on that minor potentate."

Ruth was wide-eyed with curiosity. "And did he?"

"Yes. They have argued over the boundaries of Gilead for a long time." Seeing her puzzled look, he went on to explain. "You see, Gilead lies south of Herod's Peraea and borders our King's territories ..." he hesitated for a moment. "I can tell you now it is over. When I left Bethany on the King's business it was not all about seeking new trade routes." He forestalled Ruth's questions by saying, "During that time, the King made war on Antipas, I was with his army in Gamala, in the tetrarchy of Iturea, ruled by Antipas' brother Philip."

Ruth stared at him. She said breathlessly, "What happened?"

Ibrahim smiled. "King Aretas won the battle. As you saw, I returned to Jerusalem unharmed."

"You did not say anything about this when you returned," she said, shocked by his revelation.

"I could not. You see, the King feared Rome's retribution. They favour Antipas, not he, nor our kingdom." Deep creases furrowed his forehead. "Aretas still thinks that one day Rome will retaliate. We must hope he is wrong."

Ruth suppressed a shudder at the prospect of war with Rome.

Ibrahim changed the subject. "But let us not dwell on these unpleasant things, come and see what I have for you." He led Ruth to a table where a closed wooden box sat. He pointed to it and said, "Open it."

Excited, Ruth opened the lid. She gasped as she saw the beautiful silver bracelet, adorned with sapphires, nestling in the silken folds lining the box. She carefully picked up the bracelet and slipped it onto her wrist. She turned her arm and the sapphires sparkled as they caught the sunlight shining through the latticed window. "It is so beautiful," she breathed.

Ibrahim beamed. "It is my gift to you for consenting to be my daughter." Tears filled his eyes as Ruth stood on tip-toe and kissed him on the cheek. "Thank you, my child, it has been a long time since I received such affection."

Ruth looked at his careworn face and haunted eyes, the

result of the constant anxiety and grief he had suffered over the past few years. Overcome with emotion, she made a silent vow that she would do all she could to bring happiness into his life.

Ruth was surprised when she received an invitation from Princess Phasaelis to visit her in her private apartment, with the instruction to bring Mary-Farrah with her.

Holding the child in her arms, she walked through the columned portico of the palace. One of the King's Royal Guards escorted her to the Princess' private apartment, where Phasaelis sat waiting for her. Ruth marvelled at the opulence of the room, which was filled with costly silk wall hangings, ornate furniture and luxurious carpets.

Phasaelis' beauty was enhanced by a large Egyptian-style collar studded with emeralds with matching emerald drop earrings which brought out the colour of her dark brown eyes. The Princess gestured to Ruth to sit down on a silken couch opposite her. She smiled at Ruth and said "Please, may I hold the baby for a few moments?"

Surprised, Ruth immediately rose up from her couch, walked across to the Princess and gently placed Mary-Farrah into the Princess' outstretched arms. She smiled as Phasaelis cooed and tickled the baby under her chin, bringing forth gurgles of joy. The look of longing in Phasaelis' eyes made Ruth feel sad for her.

Without taking her eyes off Mary-Farrah, Phasaelis said sadly, "Antipas and I were not fortunate enough to have any children."

Ruth thought that Phasaelis would not be amused to think she had been gossiped about, so she did not say that Ibrahim had already told her about the fated marriage.

"You did know I was married to Herod Antipas?" Seeing Ruth shake her head, Phasaelis said, "I see. Of course, when all of that took place you would have been but a child." She went on to briefly explain what had caused the divorce, being careful not to insult too greatly her ex-husband and his new wife, Herodias. She was too well mannered to give vent to her hidden anger and humiliation. Then she changed the subject. "Tell me, Ruth, by what strange fortune are you here in Nabatea with Sheikh Ibrahim? It is a long way from Jerusalem."

"I am here by even stranger fortune than you could ever imagine, your Highness."

Phasaelis was filled with curiosity. "Please, tell me your story."

Ruth did not really want to remember the terrible things she and Princess Farrah had suffered, but knew she had to answer Phasaelis' request. She started at the very beginning, when Sheikh Ibrahim had first chosen her to be a servant for his niece, Princess Farrah, then went on to tell how they had been kidnapped by Eleazar ben-Ezra and his gang of cutthroats, of their ordeal in the caves of the Judaean hills and of her repeated abuse by ben-Ezra's second-in-command, Abraham bar Saraf. She ended with the battle at Beth-Horon, the death of Farrah and her rescue by Drubaal and the Romans, but decided not to tell the Princess about how she and Mary-Farrah had been miraculously brought back from the dead by the Lord Jesus through Peter, His Disciple. She would wait until she knew Phasaelis better and was sure she could trust her.

When Ruth had finished, Phasaelis looked intently at her and said, "So Abraham bar Saraf fathered your daughter, yet you seem to love her."

"I did not at first," Ruth said, embarrassed, "but the child was an innocent victim, it was not her fault I was brought so low."

Phasaelis shook her head sadly as Ruth wiped away her tears. "So much has happened to you in your young life. I am sorry I have evoked memories of that terrible time. I cannot imagine what it was like for you and Farrah. My father showed me the letter Governor Pilate sent to him explaining the events surrounding that terrible time and of the execution of the man responsible for Farrah's death. I am glad that foul criminal ben-Ezra received his just punishment."

She stood up, handed Mary-Farrah back to her mother and said, "I hope that now you are here and part of Sheikh Ibrahim's family, you will find some peace and joy in the raising of your beautiful daughter. Now I must go to my stepmother, the Queen."

"Stepmother?" Ruth said, surprised, "but I thought…"

Phasaelis shook her head. "Queen Shuqilat is my father's second wife. My mother's name was Queen Chuldu Huldu, sadly no longer with us." She saw Ruth's embarrassment and smiled. "My stepmother wants me to be with her as she receives a very important merchant who wishes to show her some new dress-making fabrics. She values my opinion on these things."

Phasaelis called for the guard to escort Ruth from the palace, but before he arrived, she said, "There is another Jewish visitor from Damascus here in Petra just now. He was brought here by one of our caravan chiefs, Abdullah. At present the visitor lives in a cave on the outskirts of the city. He is a tentmaker and repairer by trade and helps Hussain, our master tent-maker, whenever he is too busy. Perhaps you can go and see him."

Ruth wondered who the man was and why he was here in Petra living alone in a cave. She nodded, curtsied and said, "I will. Thank you, your Highness." The guard appeared, Ruth curtsied again and then, escorted by the guard, she left the palace.

Calpurnius Aquila, his face twisted in hatred, sat in his office set deep in the Palatine Palace. He pulled a scroll out of his desk drawer and began reading, for the fourth time, the message sent to him by Lucius Vitellius, the Legate in Syria, reporting that Pilate had discovered and named Prefect Alae, Antonius, as one of his spies and had stripped him of his rank and condemned him to the Libyan mines.

He slammed the scroll down onto his desk and swore out loud. "Damn you, Pilate!" Now he had lost one of his best spies. And yet, Antonius knew too much about him and the way he worked. It would be better for him if Antonius stayed in Libya. "Let him rot!" Calpurnius growled. He had more important things to worry about.

Irritating as Vitellius' message had been, his more immediate goal was to find Flavius Silvanus. He knew he had landed at Ostia, the Port Commander had told him so, but that had been weeks ago. Where had he gone? He needed to find out –and quickly. He had urgent things to discuss with him. He swore again. "Body of Bacchus! Where are you, Flavius Silvanus?"

CHAPTER FIVE

During the weeks Flavius had spent at Claudius' farm in Latium, he had made sure he had kept his mind alert and his body fit and toned. The farm's slaves, some of whom he recognised from his own family estate, were curious when they discovered he had willingly taken instructions from the farm managers on how to help in the general running of the farm. With Atticus accompanying him, he had worked in the vineyards, in the fields growing cereal crops and vegetables and in the gardens surrounding the farmhouse. He had even acted as a shepherd's assistant to the farm's large flock, and herdsman to the many cows grazing in the fields. The one thing he did not do was go near the vast array of beehives. He knew they were best left to the experienced beekeepers as, having been stung as a child, he was anxious to avoid that pain again.

He was fascinated by the olive groves on the estate. Up until recent times, olives and their oil had always been imported from Israel, Iberia, Greece and North Africa, but as the population in Rome and surrounding areas had grown and the Legions had demanded more and more, some wealthy landowners, such as Claudius, found the growing of olive trees to be a very lucrative business. The sale of olives as a whole fruit, or by being pressed by vertical grindstones into tubs forming a paste from which the oil was extracted, added enormous amounts to his coffers.

At first, the slaves had been suspicious of his motives. Why would a patrician, an important man, wish to dirty his hands doing the work of slaves? Was he checking up on them on behalf of their master in Rome, to make sure they were working to full capacity and not slacking? They took their complaints to the head farm manager, who passed them on to Atticus. Atticus reassured them that the young master was not a spy and as time went by, the slaves realised that he seemed to actually be enjoying the hard work.

Flavius was happy to know that his mother, Lydia Flavia, who had never entered a kitchen in her life before now, was happily watching the cooks of the villa go about their work. Much to her maidservant's horror, Lydia Flavia asked the head cook to show her how to put together a simple meal. She relished the chance to see how bread was fashioned and baked. But the most fascinating new adventure for her was watching the seamstresses make and repair clothes for the men and women who worked and lived on the estate. She found this novelty deeply satisfying; it brought her contentment and helped to stem her grief. Seeing the diligence with which they went about their work and their pride and good humour in accomplishing their tasks, she made a vow that she would never look with disdain upon slaves again.

As the weeks passed by, Flavius let his hair grow long and developed a fine beard and moustache. His once smooth hands had now become roughened and calloused from his labours. He had purposely done this to carry out a plan that had been formulating in his mind. When the time was right, he would test that plan out.

That time came a few days later when Flavius asked Atticus, "When is the next consignment of goods being taken to Rome?"

Atticus looked at him quizzically, then replied, "In two days' time."

Flavius nodded and said firmly "Good. I am going with it." As Atticus began to protest that he would be placing his life in danger, Flavius said that with his long hair and beard along with his guise as a country slave, he would not be recognised as the young Tribune the authorities were looking for.

Atticus reluctantly agreed. "As you wish, master, but I am going with you," he said.

Two days later, just after sunrise, the ox-drawn cart, loaded with tightly-lidded amphorae of olive oil pressed from the farm's own olive groves, began its journey to Rome. On the second evening, the cart reached Rome's gates, where it joined the queue waiting to enter the city.

Once inside the city, they drove to the main market area and went to Claudius' usual olive-oil trader. After agreeing the price, the trader took out a wax tablet and wrote out an invoice for the sum with a stylus. Closing the tablet by placing another on top and tying it with a ribbon, he gave it to Atticus, ensuring him that the money owed to Claudius for the goods received would be handed over to the argentarii, a guild of highly respected bankers, who handled the financial business of very wealthy people. Satisfied, Atticus and Flavius unloaded the amphorae ready for the trader to sell.

When all of the amphorae had been unloaded, Flavius said to Atticus, "I have to go and see someone, but I'll be back before dawn. Stay here and wait for me." He pulled his floppy hat down over the top half of his face and walked off into the city.

He wanted to call at two of his old drinking haunts in the city, hoping to find the man he was desperately searching for, but he was not there. His last hope was to visit a notorious wine bar built in the most unsavoury part of the city: the Subura. He set off walking in that direction.

The noxious smell of urine hit him as soon as he entered the grimy alleyway, conjuring up a host of past memories.

Before he had left the farm, knowing he might have to visit that area, he had secured a knife down his boot as protection from the villains who, he knew, lurked there waiting to rob unsuspecting people.

He stayed alert as he walked down the narrow, dark alleyway, constantly looking over his shoulder in case he was being followed. Eventually he found the wine shop he was looking for. He entered the Poseidon tavern and looked around the busy place. It had not changed and was still filled with Rome's undesirables. Relieved, he saw the man he had so hoped to find sitting at a small table in the corner. He walked over to it and said "I see you're still drinking in this god-forsaken dump."

He was answered by a deep growl but went on regardless. "Hello, Decimus, remember me?"

The man looked up at him and said gruffly, "No, I don't. Now go away!"

Flavius sat down next to him and said quietly, "It's me, Flavius Silvanus."

Decimus almost choked on his wine. "Flavius Silvanus? What in Hades are you doing here?" he said loudly. Flavius gestured to him to lower his voice. Decimus immediately did so, guessing that all was not well with his old friend and comrade.

"The last time I saw you, you were about to go to Judaea," he said, bemused. He cast an eye over Flavius' unkempt look, his country-style clothes and floppy hat and grimaced. "Look at the state of you. Are you going to tell me why you look such a mess?"

Flavius was pleased his disguise was working. "It's a long story," he replied. "I hoped I might find you here."

"Why?" Decimus looked at him. His mouth gaped open as Flavius quickly and quietly told him why he had returned from Judaea and Samaria, briefly giving the details of his father's suicide. He knew he could trust Decimus. They had both served in the Legion 1 Italica, the first Legion Flavius had served in, based on the outskirts of Rome. During that time, they had become good friends, often gambling, womanising and getting drunk together as well as being involved in many fights with the locals at various taverns and wine shops throughout the city, especially this one.

Decimus Cotta was a year or two older than Flavius. He was tall and wiry, but strong. During their time serving together, he had told Flavius on several occasions that it was his ambition to transfer from the 1 Italica to join the Praetorian Guards, something Flavius was now hoping had materialised. He asked tentatively "Did you join the Praetorians, Decimus?"

Decimus puffed out his chest and said proudly, "Yes, I'm in the Guards. Getting my transfer request approved by the Praetorian Guard hierarchy was the best thing that ever happened to me."

This was what Flavius wanted to hear. Perhaps Decimus would help him. He took a chance and asked, "Could you find out some information for me?"

Decimus looked at him with narrowed eyes. "It depends on what it is you want me to find out."

Flavius came straight out with it. "I need to know who gave the Emperor the false information accusing my father of being a traitor. And why Praetorians are guarding the Silvanus family villa. Can you find out for me?"

Decimus whistled through his teeth. "Now look, Flavius, we may be old comrades, but what you are asking me to do is a very dangerous thing."

Flavius wondered how Decimus would act when he told him what the other thing was that he wanted. "There is something else I need you to do," he said. "I have been told that Caligula has befriended my brother, Marius. I must speak urgently with my brother but I don't know where to find him. Do you know where Caligula and his friends go for entertainment?"

Decimus raised his eyebrows, astounded. "By the testes of Bacchus! Have you become a madman? Now you really are wading into deep waters, Flavius. Be careful you don't drown, and take me down with you."

Seeing Flavius' downcast look he scratched his head, pulled a face and said "Look, I'll do what I can, but I won't promise anything. If it gets too risky, I'm walking away." He shuddered. "I would prefer to keep my head on my shoulders."

He looked around to make sure no one was listening, then dropped his voice even lower so Flavius had to lean forward to hear him. "Prefect Macro is a nasty bastard," he said. "He is cruel and unforgiving. If he should find out..."

"I understand, Decimus, but I would be very grateful

if you could do this for me." He got up, went to the tavern keeper and ordered two cups of watered wine for himself and Decimus and some bread and cheese for himself. Decimus drained his cup and started immediately on the cup of wine Flavius had just set down before him. Flavius hungrily ate his bread and cheese and winced as he drank the rough, inferior wine. To relieve the tension that had grown between them, they spoke about old times and the mischief they had got up to.

"Whatever happened to that Marcia Virilis you used to tumble with?" said Decimus with a grin.

"I don't know," Flavius replied, remembering all the times he had bedded her in the past. "To be blunt, I don't care either. She means nothing to me." How could she after the deep love he had felt for Farrah.

Decimus saw Flavius' expression change for a brief moment. "What happened in Judaea, Flavius? You seem different somehow. It is as though you carry a great weight on your shoulders." He saw the haunted look in Flavius' eyes. "I have heard stories about that place, none of them pleasant. If you want to talk about it some time, I will be listening."

"Thank you," was all Flavius said. He drained his cup and got up from the table. Clasping arms with his old friend, he said "I will be back in Rome next month. Will you be here?

Decimus nodded. "I am usually free at this time of night, unless I'm on night duty, or there's an emergency."

As Flavius turned to go, he said, "I will try and find out as much as I can for you. Hopefully I will have some news for you the next time you come to Rome."

Flavius smiled, then walked out of the door and hurried along the alleyways leading back to the market, where Atticus was sitting on the wagon waiting impatiently for him. Seeing the slave's annoyed look, Flavius apologised to him, saying, "I'm sorry, I did not mean to be so long but I had some urgent business to attend to." He quickly climbed up onto the wagon and sat beside Atticus.

Atticus wondered what business was so urgent that it could have put the young master's life at risk, but said nothing. As a simple slave, no matter how much he was valued by the family, it was not his place to query what his betters did. He waved his whip across the oxen's backs and the wagon moved off.

As the cart manoeuvred its way through the bustling city, Flavius' thoughts returned to the time when he and Decimus had swaggered, drunk and mourning their gambling losses, through these streets wearing the impressive uniforms of officers of the Legion 1 Italica. Was it only a year ago? So much had happened during that time. His hand went instinctively to the golden amulet hidden beneath his rough tunic: the talisman given to him by his lost love, Princess Farrah. He forced himself to concentrate on the here and now and the threat of discovery. He slumped on his seat and pulled his hat down over his eyes, pretending to be asleep as they travelled through the city in case any of the guards should recognise him. If the gods were with them, they would be back at Claudius' villa before the dawn curfew began.

CHAPTER SIX

Dawn was breaking as the cart drew near to the Caelian Hill. Flavius was pleased when Atticus told him they would be staying at Claudius' villa for the night, as he desperately wanted to see Saturn.

When they reached the villa, a slave told Atticus that Claudius had risen from his bed and was in his office. Atticus went straight to him to give him the wax tablet invoice and to report the successful sale of the olive oil.

Flavius was making his way to Claudius when he suddenly heard a stern voice say, "What are you doing here, slave?"

Flavius turned and saw Claudio standing there. "It's me, Flavius," he said.

Claudio was astonished to see his friend looking so unkempt and dirty. "I see you have quickly become adjusted to country life, Flavius," he said with a grin.

Flavius looked down at his poor-quality clothes, scratched his beard and grinned. "It's only temporary. I have not become a country yokel yet."

Claudio grew serious. "Why are you here, Flavius?"

Flavius shrugged. He did not wish to tell Claudio about his little adventure. "I have come to see your father and hopefully, Saturn," he said. Then he changed the subject quickly before Claudio had the chance to ask him how he had got there. He smiled at Claudio then walked off in the direction of Claudius' office.

Claudius had completed his business with Atticus, and now sat alone at his desk. He was putting the invoice in a drawer when Flavius walked in. Shocked by Flavius' appearance he said, "Why are you dressed like that?"

Flavius was ready with his answer. "This outfit and my unkempt appearance suit my purpose, for now."

Claudius was curious to know why. "What purpose?" he asked. He was startled when Flavius told him about his meeting with a friend who had offered to help him in his investigations, leaving out Decimus' name and the fact that he was a Praetorian Guard.

"By the gods, Flavius, you took a chance," Claudius said, shaking his head.

"I know, but my friend may be able to give me the answers I need. How else will I discover the truth about my father's death?"

"I beg you to be careful, you obviously have enemies in Rome," Claudius said gravely. "You are sure you can trust this man?"

"I would trust him with my life," Flavius answered decidedly.

"I hope you're right."

"Can you send a communication to Pilate for me please?" said Flavius, changing the subject. "I daren't do it. I just want him to know that I will need more time away from Caesarea. It is going to be more difficult to get to the truth than I could ever have imagined."

"I will gladly see to that for you," Claudius replied.

"Thank you." Flavius smiled in return. "However, before we return to Latium, I would very much like to see Saturn."

Claudius nodded. "Of course. Don't worry, Flavius. Your horse has been well looked after." He moved towards the door. "You are welcome to breakfast with us Flavius, but I am sure you will agree with me that you cannot sit at table dressed like that, so I suggest that first you visit the bath house. I will arrange for some clean clothes to be brought to you there."

Flavius thanked him. "I must keep my long hair and beard for a little longer, it's the best disguise I have."

Claudius reluctantly agreed. "I will tell my slave that he must not throw away the garments you are wearing now as you will need them for your journey later." He escorted Flavius out of the room.

Flavius relished his time in the bath house. Clean and refreshed, he dressed in the tunic the slave had brought him, then made his way to the dining room. When he entered the room, Claudia and her brother were already seated there. Claudio had warned his sister that Flavius looked very different from the last time she had seen him. She stifled a giggle as she saw him standing in the doorway.

All through the meal, Flavius was conscious of Claudia looking at him. He looked up once and met her eyes, seeing the amusement there. Once the meal was over and the general chat had finished, Flavius gave his apologies, saying he needed to see his horse. Thanking Claudius for his hospitality, he made his way to the stables.

Saturn whinnied and tossed his thick mane in pleasure at seeing his master again. Flavius threw his arms around the black stallion's silky neck in delight. Claudius was right: Saturn looked superb: his coat was sleek, his eyes were bright and he looked the picture of health.

One of the stable grooms came from out of another stall. Startled to see a stranger stroking the young Tribune's prized possession, he shouted, "You there! Move away from that horse!"

Flavius turned to see the furious man, pitchfork in hand, bearing down on him. He held his hands up and said in a placatory voice, "I am Tribune Flavius Silvanus".

The groom recognised Flavius' voice. Lowering his pitchfork, he dipped his head.

"I'm sorry, Tribune, sir," he said apologetically, "I didn't recognise you, I thought you were doing harm to Saturn there." He pointed to the horse.

Flavius smiled. "I'm glad to see that you are alert and

ready to tackle anyone wishing to hurt Saturn. Tell me, are you the groom responsible for taking care of my horse?" The groom nodded. Flavius touched him on the shoulder, "You have done very well. Thank you. I will certainly tell Senator Claudius that he has a good and conscientious groom working in his stables."

The groom dipped his head again and said, "Thank you, Tribune. It is an honour to serve you." He turned and walked away, leaving Flavius alone with Saturn.

Flavius stroked Saturn's neck and whispered, "How I miss you, old friend. I hope it will not be too long before we are reunited." As Flavius walked away, Saturn let out a loud whinny as if in reply.

Well-fed and rested, Flavius and Atticus continued their journey back to Latium.

The days passed by quickly, and soon it was time for Flavius and Atticus to travel back to the market place to sell corn from the farm. He left Atticus to haggle with the corn merchant over the price and went off to the Poseidon in search of Decimus Cotta. He found him sitting at a table in the corner of the room. When Decimus saw Flavius, he beckoned him over. As soon as Flavius had sat down, Decimus told him he had some news concerning his brother.

"I made some enquiries about why your family's villa is under guard, but got nowhere. I gave up when an officer asked me why I was so interested in the place. I made up an excuse, saying that it was just idle curiosity. Fortunately he took my word."

He gulped down his wine. "However, I had better luck in tracing your brother's whereabouts."

Flavius leaned in towards Decimus, eager to hear his findings.

"I was on duty with another guard. We were patrolling the streets around the Circus Maximus area when I saw him with a group of men. At first I didn't recognise Caligula as he was wearing a wig, but when he turned around his features were clear. Your brother, Caligula and his cronies, were coming out from one of the brothels situated under the Circus arches."

"What's wrong about that? Prostitution is legal in Rome," Flavius said.

Decimus took another drink. "Nothing, unless you come out laughing and bragging loudly about killing one of the girls." Decimus saw Flavius' shocked expression. "Keeping to the shadows, we followed them, until they came to a house known for all kinds of debauchery available to 'special' customers." He sneered. "Things even the worst kind of deviant would frown at."

Flavius had heard rumours about such places, where men and women were used for all kinds of indecent activities. It was not his style. Besides, he had never had to pay a woman for her favours.

Decimus continued, "Apparently, Caligula and his friends are regular visitors." He took another drink,

"They went inside. We hung around for a while, until it was almost time for us to finish our duty, but they didn't come out again. We had to leave, but we made a pact that we would not report this to Macro for fear of retaliation. Fortunately we didn't have to."

Decimus drained his wine cup, wiped his mouth with the back of his hand and said gravely, "The next morning, when I arrived at the guardhouse, the brothel-keeper was already there, complaining loudly that one of his girls had been brutally raped and killed and moaning that her death would cost him a lot of money. The Guard Commander said to him, "Why are you bothering me with this? Surely this is a job for the Vigiles?" When the brothel keeper told him who her last customers had been, the Guard Commander went white. He handed the brothel keeper a bag of money for his inconvenience, reassuring him that he would do his utmost to bring the perpetrators to justice. That seemed to satisfy the man and he left. The Commander went straight to Macro and reported the incident to him."

"What happened?" asked Flavius.

"Nothing!" Decimus swore under his breath. "It will be the usual thing. Macro will send guards to threaten the brothel keeper to make sure he keeps quiet about the crime. That's the way it works when the high-ups are involved in scandal."

Flavius felt sick. What had his brother got himself into? He must have stood by and watched the girl suffer, or worse, have had a hand in raping and killing her. What had happened to the boring, studious young man he had last seen the day he left for Judaea? Even at his most hedonistic, he had never behaved in such a way.

He looked straight at Decimus and said, "Can we go and see this house?"

Decimus stared back at him. "Now?"

"Why not?" replied Flavius. "If we are lucky we may see my brother arrive there with his new friends."

"And do what?" Decimus said cautiously.

"Maybe I can get him on his own and talk to him," said a hopeful Flavius.

"Now I know you are mad!"

"Surely it's worth a chance?" pleaded Flavius.

Decimus gave a deep sigh "All right. But make sure we are not seen."

Flavius and Decimus watched the house for an hour. They were about to give up when the door opened and out spilled Caligula and Marius, along with some other men. One was built like a gladiator. Flavius wondered if he was Caligula's bodyguard.

Disgusted, Flavius saw that Marius was so drunk he could hardly stand. His clothes were dishevelled and stained with wine.

Keeping a safe distance, Flavius and Decimus followed the group as they lurched along the road until they came to a block of expensive-looking apartments. Marius called out goodnight to the others and went through the doorway leading to the apartments. Flavius and Decimus stopped where they were and watched as Caligula and the rest of the bawdy men carried on down the street.

Decimus stopped Flavius from going to his brother, warning him that it would reveal his identity and put his life in danger. There was nothing Flavius could do except stand by and hope the gods would protect his foolish brother. He thanked Decimus for the information he had given him and for coming with him to the house of ill repute, then hurried back to Atticus.

Flavius spent a fretful night wondering how Marius had got into such dangerous company. He had never really got on with Marius, who had often behaved spitefully towards him. He remembered the day he had left Rome for Judaea, how Marius had looked at him with his mocking eyes and a sneer on his lips. Flavius had always known that his younger brother was jealous of him, of his looks, his popularity with women and, most importantly, that it was Flavius, as the elder son and heir, who would inherit their father's fortune and property. But they were tied by blood and Flavius hoped there was something he could do to rescue him from Caligula.

When Flavius and Atticus arrived at the farm in Latium, Flavius went straight to his mother, who was sitting in the garden. Her face lit up when Flavius told her he had seen Marius and that he was well and happy, but when she tried to question him some more, Flavius said that he was tired from his journey and needed to rest. He could not tell her the truth about what he had seen, knowing she had already suffered enough.

The heat of summer was beginning to pass when Flavius and Atticus journeyed to Rome again. Flavius sought out Decimus at the Poseidon, but there was still no news of who had betrayed his father. He and Decimus followed Marius as he caroused around Rome with his new friends, visiting many taverns and brothels. Flavius was becoming increasingly worried by his brother's actions.

Flavius and Decimus met again, some days later. Decimus' expression was serious. "Flavius, for your sake and mine, leave it alone," he said. "There is nothing more I can do. Some people are becoming suspicious, however carefully I ask my questions." He took a deep breath. "The order must have come from the Emperor, possibly through Aquila, because nobody I have tried to gain information from knows anything about it, or if they do, they are too scared to talk."

Reluctantly, Flavius thanked him for trying and assured him that he understood his reasons for giving up on the case. Disappointed, he decided he would continue alone.

CHAPTER SEVEN

Ruth had pondered the idea of going to see the stranger from Jerusalem for some time. The thought of entering a cave brought back so many terrible memories that she had baulked at the idea. Today, she decided that she would put away those dreadful thoughts and go to see the mysterious man. Sheikh Ibrahim gave his permission, but insisted that Drubaal go with her.

As they neared the entrance to the cave, Ruth stopped and began to tremble. Drubaal assured her that as long as he was with her, no harm would come to her. His words soothed her, and she agreed to enter the cave.

Drubaal went in first with Ruth following closely behind. Fortunately the cave was not very deep and was lit up by the sun shining through an aperture in the rock. They saw a man sitting cross-legged on the floor. He was concentrating on a tent he was repairing. Ruth looked on fascinated as he sewed together strips of cloth woven from camel hair ready to be joined to other larger pieces.

Conscious of being watched, the man stopped sewing and looked up. He stared at them for a brief moment, then said, "Who are you?"

Ruth replied warily, "I was told you are a Jew recently come from Damascus." She stopped as she saw sudden fear fill his eyes.

"What do you want?" The man dropped the cloth and shuffled away from her.

"I mean you no harm. It is just that I too am Jewish. I originate from Jerusalem and I would like to speak to you." She saw his confusion.

He replied sharply, "I have not been there for some time," then turned his face away from her.

Ruth had seen his expression change from one of wariness to abject grief, and wondered what had happened in Jerusalem to upset him. She told the man her name and introduced Drubaal, but when she asked the man his name, he was reluctant to tell her.

After gentle prompting, he said, "My name is Saul. Saul of Tarsus."

Saul of Tarsus! Ruth's mouth fell open with shock. She shrank back from him. How many times had she heard John Mark, Peter and the other Disciples speak of the man who had mercilessly persecuted them and the new converts and had caused the death of John Mark's best friend, Stephen of Alexandria? Fear overwhelmed her. She turned and ran out of the cave, a bemused Drubaal following closely behind.

Outside the cave, Ruth began to weep. She had been standing so close to the man who had terrified half of Jerusalem with his relentless cruelty and had inflicted terrible punishments on the followers of the Lord. Seeing her distress, Drubaal escorted her back to her house. Concerned, he asked her why she had reacted so badly to the man's name. When she explained who he was, Drubaal grew angry. Why should such a man be given sanctuary in Nabatea? He wondered if his master knew. He and the Sheikh had become friends of the Disciples and believers in Jesus and had heard the terrible stories about Saul.

"I will go back to the cave and kill him," he said.

Ruth begged him not to go. "You cannot go against the wishes of King Aretas. If he has given Saul sanctuary, you have to respect that sacred law."

"You're right Ruth," Drubaal said reluctantly, "but I will stay on guard outside your house. I do not trust the man in the cave."

In the cave, Saul picked up the cloth he had been working on, sighed deeply and began to sew. He wondered if it would always be like this. When would he be able to wipe away the terrible stain of the crimes he had committed before his conversion?

Several days passed by, but Ruth could not forget the man in the cave. The Princess had said that he had been brought there by a caravan from Damascus. She was puzzled. Surely Saul had gone to Damascus to arrest the converts of the new religion there, so what was he doing in Petra? And living alone in a cave? Curiosity got the better of her and she decided she would be brave and discover the truth. She sought out Drubaal, and the pair returned to the cave.

Seeing the fear in Ruth's face, Drubaal instinctively placed himself between her and the stranger, his hand flying to the hilt of his great, curved sword, ready to protect her if the man should threaten her.

Saul shuddered when he saw the huge man standing menacingly before him with the young girl cowering behind him. He said disconsolately, "You know who I am". When Ruth nodded, he went on, "You have nothing to fear. I am no longer that man." He saw the look of confusion on Ruth's face and pre-empted her by saying, "You are wondering why I am here in Nabatea living in this cave."

Ruth said nothing. She saw the ghost of a smile cross Saul's thin face and the gesture of his hand inviting them to sit on the hard ground. Keeping their distance, Ruth and Drubaal sat down. Ruth urged him to begin his story.

Saul began by telling them about his life-changing journey to Damascus to arrest all Nazarene converts there and bring them back to the High Priests in Jerusalem for imprisonment. He smiled as he spoke of his conversion by Jesus; of his blindness; his visit by Ananias and the subsequent return of his sight, and of his baptism, adding, "The Lord Jesus forgave my many sins. Since that day, I have tried to atone for my past."

Ruth was shocked to the core. The Lord Jesus had forgiven him for all the terrible things he had done. What miracle had been wrought on this man to bring about such a change in him?

Ruth grew ever more astounded when he told them about his time spent in Damascus and of the new friends he had made there, but she frowned when he told her of the cruelty of the Governor of Damascus. She gasped when Saul told her how he had escaped from Damascus, thanks to his convert friends there who had arranged for him to be let down over the city walls in a basket to join a caravan outside the city journeying to Petra. His face shone as he told her, "It is my dream to travel the known world to tell people about the Lord Jesus."

Ruth smiled inwardly. A dream so much like her own.

The next day, Ruth wanted to see Saul by herself, but Drubaal was still not sure about him and insisted that he accompany her. This time Ruth told Saul her own story, including her time with Peter and the other Disciples.

Saul looked at her wide eyed and said, "You know Jesus' Disciples?" She replied that they were her friends, and he said, "You are truly blessed." She left out the part where the Sheikh and Drubaal had met with Peter and had begun to believe in the Lord Jesus. That would be for them to reveal when they were ready. She also left out how she and her daughter had been brought back from the dead by the Lord, through Peter. Instead she said, "Sheikh Ibrahim brought me and my child here to Petra, where he was given permission by King Aretas to adopt me as his daughter." She looked down briefly. "We have also placed the ashes of Princess Farrah in her family tomb."

"Will you stay here in Petra?" Saul asked.

She smiled, "For now, but you see, I too long to tell people about God's love and mercy, but for the moment I don't know where I have to go to do that."

Saul nodded and said, "I too share that mystery. For now, I am content to stay here, but I know He will choose the right time for me to leave and carry out His work. When that time comes, I will be ready."

Ruth left the cave with renewed hope. Perhaps, one day soon, the Lord would reveal His purpose to her too.

Princess Phasaelis clapped her hands with delight as she watched Mary-Farrah toddle unsteadily along the pathway of her private garden, smiling when her tiny legs gave way and with a cry, sat down on the ground. Laughing, Ruth gathered her daughter up into her arms and sat down with her on a nearby bench. She looked around and sighed. How beautiful the Princess' private garden was with its shady fig trees and tinkling fountain.

Mary-Farrah settled down in her mother's arms and fell asleep. With the child peacefully sleeping, Ruth said, "May

I ask you a question, your Highness?"

"What is it you wish to know, Ruth?"

Ruth swallowed, then finding her courage, she asked, "Have you spoken to the man in the cave?"

Phasaelis shook her head.

"May I suggest Highness, that one day soon you invite him to come and tell you his story? It is a most remarkable one."

"Then why don't you bring him here to me now?"

Ruth handed Mary-Farrah to Phasaelis, bowed and went off to find Saul.

At first, Saul made an excuse. "I once trained as a Pharisee. Judaic Law forbids me to enter a Gentile's house."

Ruth replied, "The Princess is aware of that. She will see you in her private garden outside her apartments. Who knows, your story might convert her into the faith."

Saul smiled. He got up and followed Ruth to the palace.

Standing before Phasaelis, Saul bowed his head, then, at her behest, he sat down on the bench next to Ruth. At first he was nervous and hesitant, but urged on by Ruth, he began.

Phasaelis gasped as he relayed his tale. When he had finished, she shook her head and said, "Your story is exceptional." She leaned forward. "This Jesus of Nazareth, the one you now call the Son of God, He seems to be a very forgiving deity, especially after you persecuted His followers and were instrumental in the death of one of them. Why choose you, of all men, to do His work on earth?"

Saul shrugged. "It is a question I ask myself every day, your Highness. When Jesus is ready, I am sure He will reveal the answer to me."

Phasaelis nodded. "I would learn more about this Jesus. You must come and speak to me again."

Saul bowed his head. "Thank you, Princess."

Phasaelis stood up, handed a still-sleeping Mary-Farrah back to her mother and left the garden, with Ruth and Saul staring after her.

CHAPTER EIGHT

It was time for the annual harvest, and Flavius helped the slaves to bring in the crops. It was hard work, but it helped to ease the worry of his brother from his mind. The wheat was taken to the storehouse, where Flavius tried his hand at beating it to separate the chaff from the kernels, then helped spread the wheat on the drying floor, under which was a hypocaust. Later, he watched as the donkey-driven mill ground large amounts of the grain ready to be put in the grain store until needed.

Much to Atticus' unspoken disapproval, Flavius took off his boots, climbed into a large tub and pressed the grapes by treading on them. For the first time in weeks he was beginning to relax. As he did so, he saw several of the female slaves looking at him. How easy it would be for him to take any of these girls to his bed, but he resisted the temptation, knowing they belonged to Claudius.

As he climbed out of the tub, he heard laughter coming from the garden. Cleaning his feet and replacing his boots, he went to see what had caused such merriment. He smiled as he saw some female slaves trying to teach his mother how to fashion ready-washed sheep wool into yarn. A laughing Lydia Flavia was struggling to rub the clump of wool over a card with prongs on one side to make the wool stick to it. Taking a second card, she attempted to pull it back and forth over the wool on the first card, trying and failing to turn the wool into individual fibres ready for spinning. Her fingers were not used to such work, and she could not synchronise the action to accomplish the task. She gave up and handed the cards back to a slave, who quickly finished the job.

Flavius was relieved to see the worry lines begin to smooth on his mother's face, although he had noticed that when she sat alone, her eyes were haunted by the memory of her husband's death.

When the harvest had been gathered in, the celebrations in honour of Ceres, the goddess of corn, began. Offerings of the first fruits and pigs of the harvest were made to Ceres by the farm manager. Afterwards, games and various sports were played, followed by music and dancing.

Flavius clapped his hands as the slaves played their home-made reed instruments whilst others danced. He was invited to join in with the dancing but declined, feeling that this merriment should be purely for those who had toiled to bring the harvest to fruition.

Later that night, a thanksgiving feast was held. Finally, filled with good food and copious amounts of wine, Flavius staggered, tired but happy, to his bed, all thoughts of worry for the future temporarily put to one side.

It was time for the farm goods to be transported for sale in Rome. On Flavius' last visit there, Decimus had warned him to stop following Marius. At first he had been angry, but eventually he realised that his own life would be in danger if his presence in Rome was discovered, especially with Decimus no longer willing to help him. This time his visit would be just to sell the goods, return to Claudius' villa, then go back to Latium.

The next celebration was for the Saturnalia festival. Flavius and his mother spent a quiet time at the farm villa, not taking part in any sacrifices or entertainments; the only ritual they observed was the pouring of a libation over the statue of Saturn and offering prayers to the deity in the privacy of their rooms.

A year ago, Flavius had harnessed high hopes that Farrah would be found alive and well. His hopes had been tragically dashed. Now he worried about the future, about the trouble his brother was getting into, the loss of the family estate, the possibility that Claudius would tire of them and their problems and turn them out of the farm to fend for themselves, but mostly about his mother's health. Outwardly, she put on a brave face, but he knew that inwardly, she was in turmoil. There was nothing he could do except hope that the gods would look kindly on them.

The New Year festival honouring the god Janus came and went, but life continued in the same way. Flavius was bored. It was the wrong time of the year to work outside on the farm, but he did not dare to return to Rome. There was no news about what was happening to the Silvanus villa and estate. The villa and its extensive grounds must surely be deteriorating with no one to care for them. He would just have to hope that when spring came their luck would change, something he prayed fervently for every day.

Pontius Pilate sat in his office in the Governor's Palace in Caesarea. Livid with anger, he glared at Senior Tribune Paullus, who stood at attention before him, and growled, "What do you mean?"

Paullus was not cowed by the Procurator's anger and repeated his message calmly. "I have been informed by some of our troops patrolling in that area that in the village of Tirathana, many Samaritans are beginning to gather together." He swallowed. "When they were asked what they were doing there, the Samaritan leader said he knew where the treasure buried by their Prophet Moses was hidden. It was on their Holy Mountain, Gerizim, and they were going to search for it."

"And we gullible Romans are supposed to believe that?" Pilate said sarcastically.

Paullus gave no reply; he just said, "What are your orders concerning this, Governor?"

Pilate shuddered at the thought of another insurrection unfolding so soon after the battle at Beth-Horon, where he and his troops had come under attack from the forces of the notorious criminal Eleazar ben-Ezra. If the Commander of the Jerusalem Garrison, Quintus Maximus, had not been forewarned of the attack by a member of ben-Ezra's gang, they might easily all have been killed. This time he would act first. Any plan by the Samaritans to overthrow their masters would be stopped.

He got up from his desk, walked around it to face Paullus and snarled, "I want you to lead two cohorts of legionaries to stop these would-be insurrectionists from climbing that mountain. Try to disperse them peaceably, but if there is any sign of resistance, you have my authority to stop them forcibly." He sat down again, looked up at a surprised Paullus and growled, "Are you still here?"

Paullus straightened up, saluted and made his way to the door. He stiffened as he heard Pilate's clipped voice say, "Find my staff officer Marcus Tullio and send him here to me. Quickly man!" He nodded and went out.

Marcus entered Pilate's office, saluted and stood waiting for Pilate's instructions. He was surprised when Pilate said, "I have ordered Senior Tribune Paullus to take two cohorts to Mount Gerizim to stop a possible rebellion. I want you to take a squadron of cavalry and follow him, to make sure he obeys my orders."

Marcus wondered why two cohorts had been deployed to the Samaritan Holy Mountain, but he did not question Pilate.

"If it looks like the mob is growing angry, Paullus must try to disperse them peacefully, before it gets out of hand," Paulus continued. "But if an insurrection begins and he does not act swiftly, you will take command and make sure my instructions are carried out. Is that understood?"

Marcus felt uneasy about his orders, but he replied, "Perfectly understood, Governor Pilate."

Pilate waved him away, saying curtly, "You had best be on your way. There is no time to lose. If a rebellion is planned, it could begin at any moment."

Marcus thought that since Beth-Horon, Pilate had become increasingly paranoid at the prospect of another uprising, but he knew he had to obey the Governor's orders. He saluted and went to mobilise his cavalry squadron.

Pilate did not trust Paullus; he was too unpredictable. It had not taken him long to grow to detest the officious upstart. There was not a soldier in the Caesarea garrison, be it legionary or officer, who liked the man. He was known to be harsh and good at throwing his weight around with the rank and file, and this attitude had quickly alienated them. He wondered why Roman officials had thought he was the right man for the job in this part of the Empire. It would have been better if they had sent him to a more remote area with fewer problems.

He sighed. He had not realised how much he missed Flavius until a few days before, when he had received a communication from Senator Claudius Marcellus in Rome. He had read the Senator's letter concerning Flavius' continued search for answers to his father's death and asking for more time to discover them. What was going on there to cause this delay in his favourite Tribune's return? Whatever it was, it must be more serious than just arranging a funeral and sorting out the family estate.

Frustrated, he picked up one of the scrolls splayed out on his desk. He hoped that soon, Flavius would return to him.

CHAPTER NINE

Tribune Paullus relayed Pilate's orders to the officers of the two chosen cohorts of the Tenth Fretensis Legion, then prepared himself to carry out Pilate's instructions, dangerous as they were to his mind.

Marcus and his squadron kept a discreet distance behind the marching legionaries led by Paullus. What was he supposed to do with Paullus if the man decided to disobey Pilate's instructions? Kill him? Arrest him and drag him back to the garrison? He would have to decide quickly if and when that time came.

Paullus and the legionaries came to the foot of the Samaritans' Holy Mountain. He swallowed hard as he saw the vast group of would-be treasure-hunters drawing nearer. Sizing up the situation, he ordered the legionaries to stop their advance. The Samaritans saw the Romans blocking their route, but continued to march until they were confronted by the heavily-armoured troops. Incensed by this Roman intrusion, some of the more hot-headed Samaritans began to protest loudly and try to force their way through. Paullus decided to obey Pilate's instructions. He immediately ordered the legionaries to move forward and cut down any protesters.

Marcus watched, horrified, as an unnecessary slaughter began. Anger engulfed him. Paullus had not even tried to disperse the mob. He shouted to his cavalrymen to ride into the fray and drive a wedge between the legionaries and the Samaritans. Most of the legionaries stopped when they saw the cavalry riding towards them, but some chased after the frantically retreating Samaritans, killing many more and capturing others.

As Marcus manoeuvred his horse between the legionaries and frantic Samaritans, he suddenly felt a sharp pain. He looked down and saw a dagger protruding from his right thigh. He grimaced with pain, turned his head and saw a laughing Samaritan glaring up at him. A cavalryman immediately brought his sword down, the blade slicing into the Samaritan's neck. The man fell to the ground. The cavalryman plunged his sword into the dying man's side, finishing him off.

Soon the ground around the base of Mount Gerizim was slippery with blood. Satisfied that the day had been won in Rome's favour, Paullus recalled his troops and triumphantly led his cohorts and their prisoners back to the

Caesarea garrison. Wincing in pain with each movement of his horse, Marcus followed on with the cavalry.

Marcus was taken to the garrison hospital, where the medical orderlies carefully removed the dagger from his thigh, cleaned the wound, smeared it with ointment and wrapped the area in bandages. He spent a restless night, the pain of his wound preventing him from getting the sleep he so desperately needed. He felt hot and waves of nausea swept over him. He cursed Paullus. If only that damned fool had tried to disperse the crowd peacefully, none of this mess would have happened.

Pilate was pleased at the outcome, and glad that the possible rebellion had been stopped. But what to do with the captured ringleaders of the rebellious Samaritans? He decided he had no choice but to put them to death.

Lucius Vitellius, the Legate of Syria, stared blandly at the Samaritan spokesmen as they complained to him about the massacre at Mount Gerizim. He offered insincere apologies to the dignitaries, making sure he showed no sign of weakness. But deep down, Vitellius was angered by this news. He had had just about enough of Pilate's dangerous incompetence. After the dignitaries had left, Vitellius sat for a while contemplating how Pilate should be punished. He came to a decision. He called for his scribe and dictated a letter to Pilate ordering that he return to Rome to explain his actions before the Emperor.

Pilate angrily threw Vitellius' communication onto his

office floor and cursed out loud. If he was to be disgraced, then he would make sure Paullus went down with him.

He wondered if it had anything to do with his arrest of Prefect Alae Antonius and his subsequent punishment. He had sent Antonius to the salt mines in Libya without consulting the Legate first. The Prefect Alae and his cavalrymen had been sent to Jerusalem by Vitellius to swell the ranks in the search for the missing Princess Farrah and the criminal, Eleazar ben-Ezra, both now dead, but Antonius had proved to be more of a hindrance than a help. He had dealt badly with those troops stationed at the Fortress Antonia and had turned out to be a traitor. In his mind Antonius had been given a fitting punishment for his many crimes; perhaps Vitellius thought differently.

He sent for his scribe then dictated a letter to be sent back to Vitellius saying he would obey his order. He went to see Claudia Procula, anxious about how he would break the news to her.

Claudia was shocked and worried by the news. What would happen to her husband? She knew he had made some bad mistakes during his time in Judaea, but this massacre had to be the worst of them all. Nevertheless, she still loved him. She took his hand and said, "Whatever the outcome and consequences, I will stand by you."

Pilate took her in his arms and said "For that I thank you, my beautiful wife, but I do not know what will happen to me. You have many influential friends in Rome. I urge you to go to them."

She stepped back from him, tears beginning to sting her eyes. "No, I will not leave you!" she gasped.

Pilate smiled. "You can and you must. I cannot let anything happen to you because of my misguided judgement. You are too precious to me." He kissed her, then called for his body-servant to help ready him for the journey to Rome.

Later that day, one of the orderlies came to check on Marcus. He was disturbed to see his pallor, restlessness and sweat-soaked bedding. He called for a second orderly to check and verify his suspicions. The second orderly agreed that the wound should be looked at again. Marcus moaned as they unwrapped the bandages and studied the wound, then turned to each other and slowly shook their heads. The wound was red, and foul-smelling pus was collecting between the jagged edges.

The first orderly grimaced and said, "The point of the blade must have been dirty, or had poison smeared on the tip. My guess is the second."

The second orderly nodded in agreement and went to fetch a bottle of mithridatum, a concoction made from many different herbs and plants mixed with honey and castor, a supposed good antidote against poisoning. The first orderly held up Marcus' head, while the second opened his mouth and poured the contents down his throat.

Marcus lay back on the bed, exhausted and in pain, murmuring "Julia" over and over again. "Who is Julia?" the first orderly queried.

The second orderly replied in a sad voice, "Julia is his wife. They have only been married a short time. Unfortunately, there is nothing more we can do for now, except give the antidote time to work." They moved on to another patient lying in the bed opposite.

Despite the orderlies' repeating doses of the antidote, it did not work. During the early hours of the next morning, Marcus' suffering came to an end.

When Centurion Cornelius was told the news about his son-in-law, he asked if he could be the one to tell his daughter about the death of her husband. Pilate readily agreed.

With a heavy heart, Cornelius made his way to the house Julia and Marcus had shared for such a short time. He remembered the joy of his beloved daughter's wedding day only a few months before. Now that joy would be replaced by sorrow.

He knocked on the door. The doorkeeper recognised Cornelius immediately, opened the door and let him in. Julia's maidservant came out of a side room. "Where is my daughter?" Claudius asked her.

She led him into a room overlooking the small garden, where Julia was sewing a new garment for Marcus. She smiled, overjoyed at seeing her father, but when she saw the look on his face, she knew something was wrong. She dropped her sewing onto her chair, stood up and went to him, asking in a soft voice, "Has something happened, father?"

Cornelius struggled to find the words. "I am afraid it is Marcus…"

"Is he unwell? Has he had an accident at the Garrison?" she asked, bemused.

He took her hand and said softly, "He has been killed."

Julia screamed "No!" and collapsed into her father's arms, weeping uncontrollably.

Tears streaming down his face, Cornelius held her trembling body in his arms, wishing that his wife, Helena, was alive to comfort her at this tragic moment.

Distraught, Julia ran to her bedroom and collapsed onto the bed. Cornelius sat on the edge of the bed and explained what had happened to Marcus. He stayed with her until, worn out by grief, she fell into a troubled sleep. Before he left, Cornelius instructed the maidservant to keep a close eye on her mistress, saying he would come back in the morning to see her.

Because of the health risk to the legionaries, Marcus' funeral rites were arranged quickly. He had set aside enough of his army pay in the Legionaries' funeral club to cover the expense of the ritual meal, his cremation and commemoration, with enough left over to pay for a fitting memorial stone.

The whole of the Cavalry based at the Caesarea Garrison, as well as some of Pilate's personal staff, turned out for the ceremony. With the soldiers surrounding her, Julia stood near to the prepared funeral pyre. Her drawn face was set in a grim expression. Although heartbroken, she had vowed not to cry in front of her husband's comrades. She was an officer's wife and needed to show courage and pride for the sake of his memory.

Standing next to her was the Commander of the Garrison, who stood ramrod straight, trying to hide his anger at the needless waste of a good officer. Cornelius stood amongst the legionaries. From time to time he glanced at Julia, anxious for her but very proud of the way she was bravely conducting herself before the men.

Julia became aware that some of the officers were staring at her. She recognised Marcus' friends who had attended their wedding, the men who had shocked her servant Martha by singing ribald songs on the procession to the house Marcus had bought, and had bawdily wished Marcus and herself a happy wedding night.

One of those friends was a Cavalry Officer named Linus. Linus had always envied Marcus for having the unswerving love of such a beautiful girl. This was not the day to think of how he might make Julia his own, but the thought that one day she might love him as she had Marcus ignited a fire in his heart.

Julia trembled uncontrollably as the pyre containing Marcus' body was lit. She closed her eyes, not wishing to see what was happening to her beloved husband. Feeling suddenly faint, she began to sway. Realising her distress, the Commander held her arm, steadying her. At that moment, it took all of Cornelius' strength and discipline not to go to her side and comfort her.

When the ordeal was over, Julia watched as Marcus' ashes were collected and placed in an elaborate urn, either to be returned to his wealthy family in Rome or to be interred in one of the military cemeteries along the roads that led out of the camp. She hoped her husband's remains would stay in Caesarea so she could visit him to commemorate his life and give offerings for his spirit, but that would be for his family to decide.

Marcus had been popular both in Pilate's service at the Governor's palace and amongst the soldiers at the garrison. As Marcus' house was too small to hold all the mourners for the ritual feast, the Commander had given permission for it to be held at the Garrison. All through the meal, Julia sat silent, not having the appetite to eat the feast laid out before her.

When the feast was over, Cornelius approached her, took her hand and said, "I don't like the idea of you staying in your house while you are mourning. Please come home with me. I know Martha is longing to take care of you."

Julia shook her head, saying wistfully, "Thank you, father, but I wish to stay in the house I shared with Marcus."

Cornelius nodded. "I understand, but promise me you will not stay locked away in your misery for too long."

"I promise," came her mournful reply.

Several days later, a grim-faced Cornelius came to Julia bearing bad news. Asking her to sit down he said, "I have received a communication from Marcus' father in Rome." He knew his next words would add to his daughter's anxiety, but they had to be said. "He instructs me to tell you that Marcus had borrowed money from him to buy this house. Now that his son is dead, the loan cannot be repaid, so it legally belongs to him. He intends to sell it to recoup his losses."

Julia cried out, "But what of me? Where am I to go?"

Cornelius sat down by his daughter's side and took her hand. "He has agreed to return your dowry, so you will not be left penniless. However, he will not be swayed by argument. If you have slaves of your own you may do with them as you will, but the doorkeeper must stay on to keep the empty property safe until a new buyer is found."

He took a deep breath, knowing that the next order from Marcus' father would cause Julia even more heartbreak. "He also insists that Marcus' ashes be sent to Rome to be interred in the Tullio family tomb there. He does not wish his son to be interred in a foreign, hostile land."

This final revelation was too much for Julia to bear. Cornelius held her as she sobbed her heart out.

He said, consolingly, "You will not be homeless, for I want you to come back to your family home. Martha, I know is longing to see you again. Will you come home?"

Too upset to speak, Julia nodded.

Cornelius stood up. "I will write to Marcus' father and say that you will be moving out of the house immediately and returning to my house. He can do what he wants with his property," he added curtly. He was wondering how Marcus' family could be so cruel.

Julia's heart was heavy with sorrow as the next day, she gathered together her personal things, including the beautiful marble statuette of Venus and the winged god Eros her father had bought as a wedding present. She was determined that Marcus' family would not have it. She said goodbye to the handmaid who had served her since her wedding day. She had sold her to one of her bridesmaids who was about to be married to one of Marcus' friends whom she had met at the wedding.

Later that day, Cornelius came to collect her and her few personal possessions and took her back to her childhood home. When they arrived, Martha rushed out to greet her, tears rolling down her cheeks. Without a word, Martha encompassed Julia in her arms, then led her to her old bedroom, where she threw herself down onto her bed. Martha offered what comfort she could, then left the room, closing the door behind her. She knew it would take a long time for her young mistress to recover from this terrible tragedy.

Sitting alone in his garden, Cornelius was wondering where Flavius was now. He knew he was no longer in Caesarea. He would surely want to know of Marcus' death, but without knowledge of his address, Cornelius could do nothing. He sighed deeply. How could such happiness turn so quickly to disaster? First the loss of his beloved wife, now the loss of his daughter's husband. Life could be so cruel.

Later that night, he took out a scroll from his desk containing some Jewish Psalms and read it. He found one, a psalm from David, the one-time King of Israel, who had triumphed through many afflictions. He thought it was meaningful for the family's present troubles. It began: 'Lord, I cry unto thee: make haste unto me; give ear unto my voice when I cry unto thee...' As he read on, he decided to try to find Philip to speak some more with him about the man called Jesus. His own gods had not looked kindly on him, or his daughter. Perhaps the Jewish God would.

CHAPTER TEN

Vitellius frowned and let out a deep sigh as he read the Imperial order sent from Emperor Tiberius. The business of Pilate's disgrace had been difficult enough, but now he was faced with Tiberius' instructions to mobilise two legions to make war on King Aretas of Nabatea.

So Tiberius had come down on the side of Herod Antipas in the conflict between him and Aretas over the Gilead boundaries. The gods alone knew why the master of the known world should bother himself with these petty, insignificant rulers. As far as he was concerned, they could wipe each other out.

Vitellius had a special hatred for Antipas, who he considered to be no more than an irritating flea he wanted to crush with his fingers. He knew there was no love lost between the two protagonists because of Antipas' shameful treatment of the King's daughter, Princess Phasaelis, as well as the territorial dispute, but why must the legions be dragged into it? Despite the Roman army being more professional and disciplined, legionaries would still be injured and killed, and for what? So that Aretas' ambitions would be curtailed stopping him from becoming too powerful.

He threw the scroll across his desk in frustration and anger, knowing he had no choice but to obey the order. Calling for his senior officers, he sat back in his chair and concentrated on how best to proceed. After hours of discussions and poring over maps, the decision on which route to take and the best area in which to wage this war was agreed. Vitellius dismissed his officers with their instructions, breathed a deep sigh and began to prepare for the long journey to Nabatea.

Phasaelis, Ruth and Mary-Farrah were sitting in the Princess' private apartment. Ruth looked on, smiling at her daughter's reaction to being tickled by Phasaelis. Aretas strode into the room. When Phasaelis saw the serious look on her father's face, she handed Mary-Farrah back to Ruth. Ruth curtsied and made a tactical exit.

Aretas handed a scroll to Phasaelis. His heart sank as he saw his daughter's face change into a mask of fear as she read the contents. The Roman Legate was on his way to Petra with two legions to fight her father, all because Antipas felt that Rome should protect him after losing the battle for Gilead.

She handed the scroll back to her father and said, "How could Antipas do this? His army was fairly beaten. I know he can be spiteful if he doesn't get his own way, but to do this…"

Aretas shrugged and said "I have consulted my diviners, who tell me that it is impossible for Vitellius' army to enter Petra, for one of the rulers will die. Either the one who gave the orders for war, meaning Tiberius, Vitellius, who is carrying out the orders of Tiberius – or myself?"

"Oh father!" Phasaelis went to her father and took his hand. "Please don't say such things. You are frightening me."

He held her close and said sagely," We are in the hands of Manawat, decider of our destiny and fate."

Ruth was telling Mary-Farrah a story as Hagru prepared their evening meal. She looked up and saw Ibrahim standing in the doorway of her house. His face was clouded with anxiety. He said, "I have just left the King. It seems we will soon be at war." He saw Ruth's shocked look and explained. "Tiberius has ordered the Roman Legate in Syria to make retribution on the King because of his victory over Antipas. When the time comes, you and Mary-Farrah must go with Hagru to our secret location in the desert." He saw Hagru turn from her work at the mention of the secret location. He looked intently at her and issued a command to the older woman. "Hagru, you know where that secret place is. I place my daughter in your care. See to it that she and her child arrive there safely."

Hagru nodded in agreement, but a horrified Ruth looked at Ibrahim and said anxiously, "What about you and Drubaal? Will you come with us?"

Ibrahim shook his head. "No. It is my duty to fight for my King. Drubaal will be with me."

Ruth burst into tears. Ibrahim tried to comfort her, saying, "It has not come to war yet. I pray to God that something will happen to stop this madness."

When Vitellius and his legions reached Judaea, important leaders of the Jews came to him and complained that because his troops were marching through Judaean territory, they and their people were being forced to look upon the graven images on the Roman military standards, something forbidden by their Holy Law. Not wishing to cause any further trouble, Vitellius grudgingly ordered the army to travel along the Great Plain, thus skirting Judaea. He did not travel with them but went to Jerusalem, where he was welcomed by Antipas, who invited him to stay in his palace, an invitation he accepted.

Antipas arranged a feast to be held in the Great Hall of his palace, in honour of his important guest. Antipas and Herodias sat side by side on their ornate thrones. Antipas was dressed in a multi-coloured silk robe. His hair and beard had been oiled and curled while Herodias sat resplendent in an emerald green gown. Her throat, wrists and hands were bedecked with jewels and her dark brown hair was curled and held in place with large emerald clips. Both wore golden diadems.

The couple greeted Vitellius with an oily smile. Antipas gestured to him to sit on an ornate chair next to him.

Vitellius sat down stiffly, trying to hide his anger. These two vain upstarts had the audacity to sit on their thrones as if they were a king and queen. Who did they imagine they were? To think that Tiberius had ordered the elite legionaries of Rome to fight a war on this arrogant pair's behalf.

The feast having been eaten, there followed a succession of entertainments, including scantily-clad dancing girls who whirled around the floor in front of Antipas, Herodias and Vitellius. Vitellius glanced at Antipas with an undisguised look of disgust. The potentate was sitting forward licking his lips lasciviously as he looked at their beautiful faces and svelte bodies.

Herodias saw Vitellius' look and pressed her long fingernails hard onto Antipas' hand, giving him a warning hiss. Antipas turned and saw the Legate's hostile stare, hurriedly composed himself, and sat up straight on his throne. Trying to hide his anger at the interference of his pleasure, he picked up his wine cup and drank deeply from it.

Vitellius drank sparingly, needing to keep his wits about him before two people he neither liked nor trusted. To ease his tension, he enquired about Herodias' daughter, the fabled Salome.

Herodias replied, "My daughter married her cousin, Aristobulus of Chalcis," adding proudly, "she is now Queen of Chalcis and Armenia Minor."

Vitellius swallowed hard. So this upstart family had gained a throne, thereby increasing their power. He smiled to himself, thinking that one day, their ambition might lead to their downfall. To him, that day could not come soon enough.

When the acrobats began their display he made a show of clapping enthusiastically at their athleticism, but by the time two sets of wrestlers began their bouts, he was already wishing the night would come to an end. After a farewell and thanks to Antipas for his hospitality and a cursory nod to Herodias, it was with great relief that Vitellius returned to his room.

He was awakened the next morning by the insistent knocking on the door of his room. Annoyed, he barked, "What is it?" He was surprised when Tribune Commodus of the Fortress Antonia entered the room.

Saluting, Commodus said, "I am sorry to awaken you, Legate, but an Imperial Courier is waiting outside. He says he has an important communication for you."

Vitellius sat up in bed and said irritably, "Give me a moment and I will receive him." Not waiting for his slave, Vitellius hurriedly got up and dressed himself. An Imperial Courier? What now? "Send him in," he ordered. The Courier saluted Vitellius, then took the communication out of his dispatch bag and handed it to him.

Shocked, Vitellius took in its contents: the Emperor Tiberius was dead. He swore out loud "Body of Mars!" The late Emperor had named as his successors his grandson,

Tiberius Gemellus, and his great-nephew, Gaius Julius Caesar, more commonly known as Caligula, or 'little boots', a name given to him by the legionaries commanded by his father, Germanicus, for, as a child, Caligula had spent some time with them, always dressed in a smaller version of the legion military uniform. Vitellius remembered that Germanicus' legions had annihilated the Germanic tribes who, almost thirty years before, had massacred the Seventeenth, Eighteenth and Nineteenth Legions, commanded by General Varus, in the Teutoburg Forest. He smiled at the memory of the great celebrations that had followed when Germanicus had brought those lost legions' Eagles and Standards back to Rome. He wondered if the army and the people would rather have Caligula, the son of that great hero, as their sole Emperor. He did not think that Gemellus was popular with them as he was the son of Tiberius' daughter-in-law, Livilla, the notorious adulteress, possible poisoner of her husband and family – and most damning of all, the one-time lover of Sejanus.

He made a quick calculation and worked out in his head that Caligula must be approaching his twenty-fifth year, whereas, Gemellus was about eighteen, with no political or army experience. He scratched his chin. It was just a wild guess, but he could not see Caligula sharing the role of Emperor with this spindly adolescent for too long. Time would tell.

Vitellius put down the communication and sat deep in thought for a moment. He hoped that these two young men had very different personalities from Tiberius and would conduct themselves in a more temperate fashion. Over many months, rumours of Tiberius' perverted behaviour on his island of Capri had filtered through communications he had received from different sources. However, Vitellius knew all too well that absolute power could corrupt even the most humble of men.

He wrote an answering communication, gave it to the courier then dismissed him. When he had gathered his thoughts together, he sent for Quintus, the Commander of the Antonia fortress.

Quintus stood with a ramrod straight back as Vitellius relayed the message about the deceased Tiberius to him. After saying how sorry he was to hear the news, Quintus was then told by Vitellius that he had decided that, due to his outstanding courage and unwavering dedication to duty at the battle of Beth-Horon, Chief Centurion Sextus was to be promoted to the rank of Centurion Princeps prior and transferred to the Headquarters of the Tenth Fretensis, based in Syria.

The final shock came when the Legate told him that Pilate was returning to Rome to answer charges that had been brought against him, adding that a new Governor was on his way and as soon as he arrived, Pilate would sail to Rome. He told him to pass on the message of the Emperor's death to the troops based at the Fortress Antonia.

Quintus was relieved when Vitellius dismissed him.

Sitting at his desk in his office at the Antonia, Quintus

thought long and hard. He had been in this accursed land for far too long. He had no idea if Pilate would one day return to Judaea, and knew how much he would miss Sextus, a brilliant Centurion, and one who was much admired by himself and the legionaries who served with him. Who knew what a new Emperor might do? Especially two of them vying for supreme power. New masters were unpredictable and had a habit of changing everything, not always to the army's advantage.

He had been thinking for some time that now the criminal elements that had plagued Judaea had been dealt with, it might be the right time for him to retire. After all, he had served more than his allotted time, and there was a nice parcel of land waiting for him in Philippi. Who knew, there might even be a woman there he could finally make a life with?

CHAPTER ELEVEN

That evening, before Sextus' departure, Quintus invited him to dinner. After a hearty meal, Quintus raised his wine cup and saluted Sextus for his much-deserved promotion, saying "Old comrade, we have served together for a long time. I offer you my sincere congratulations and wish you good luck in your future career."

Sextus smiled. "Thank you Commander. It has been a pleasure to serve under your command."

They laughed together, remembering some of the funny situations they had been caught up in. Then Quintus grew sombre. "We have been through some tough times together, old friend."

"Yes, sir, it was a bad business about the loss of Princess Farrah." Sextus grimaced. "At least we destroyed ben-Ezra and his rag-tag army. I will always remember that..." – he just stopped himself from swearing in front of his superior – "that vile brigand. In my opinion he deserved his barbaric death."

Quintus smiled thinly. "I made a promise that when he was caught, his execution would be one people would not forget in a hurry."

"No, they will not, sir," Sextus replied grimly.

They reminisced some more. At the end of the evening, Quintus congratulated Sextus again, wished him well and with a heavy heart, watched as his old friend left the room.

The next morning, Quintus was filled with a deep pride, tinged with sadness, as he led officers and legionaries onto the parade ground. The men stood proudly in line to honour their much-loved Centurion on his departure from the Antonia. Quintus swallowed hard. He had worked with both Sextus and Pilate for many years knowing the mutual trust between them. Who would take their place? He saw Sextus look back once, then walk straight-backed through the fortress gate. Quintus sighed. It was the end of an era. He dismissed the men and returned to his office.

Sitting at his desk, he made his decision: he would retire while he was still young and strong enough to enjoy it. He picked up a wax tablet and stylus and wrote a letter to Vitellius requesting that he be allowed to retire from the Legions, sealed it with another clean wax tablet on top, then bound them together, fixing the ribbon ends with wax and his ring seal. He called for a legionary. "Deliver this communication to the Legate now, before he leaves Jerusalem." The legionary took the tablets, saluted and hurried out of the room. Quintus sat back in his chair, hoping the Legate would agree to his request.

Antipas was suffering from a hangover. He put a hand on his head, trying to still the hammering in his skull. He winced as Vitellius slammed the communication from the Imperial Courier onto the breakfast table and said, "What is it?"

Vitellius barked out, "Read it."

Antipas sat shocked and bemused as he read the news. "Tiberius, dead?" He looked at Vitellius. "What happens now? What about the war against Aretas?"

Vitellius got up from his couch and began to pace. "I have struggled all night to find a solution to that problem, he said. He turned to face Antipas and said, "We cannot continue with it."

Antipas stiffened. "Why not? Your army must be almost at the meeting point."

"I know that!" Vitellius answered irritably. "But the new Emperors have given me no remit to fight with the Nabateans. That was Tiberius' order, not theirs." He sat down heavily. "I have no choice but to recall the army."

"But you cannot!" replied an irate Antipas.

"I can and I will," replied Vitellius defiantly. "Unless the joint Emperors give me express orders to continue, and I don't think they will, the army will return here and go with me to Antioch." He cut short Antipas' continued protests by saying "I will send someone from the Antonia to my Commanders giving them my orders. That is an end of it! I will brook no argument!"

Whilst he was still speaking, the legionary carrying Quintus' request arrived. His frown deepened as he read the contents of the wax tablet, but then he smiled. Perhaps it was for the best that Quintus Maximus should retire now. As Legate, he had written such a damning report to the late Emperor about Pilate, one he knew would also displease the new rulers, that he doubted he would ever see the Governor again. He smiled. With Pilate, Quintus and Sextus out of Judaea, that would enable him to make a clean sweep.

He had already communicated with his friend Marcellus, inviting him to replace Pilate as Governor. Marcellus had readily agreed. Vitellius was pleased, knowing that Marcellus would be easy to manipulate to his will. Now he would also have to find an accommodating new Commander for the Antonia and a Centurion who was hungry for promotion to replace Sextus. It seemed the gods were smiling on him.

He called for his personal slave, who stood nearby awaiting his instructions. He ordered him to bring writing materials and a pot of wax to the table, then wrote to his generals commanding his army, instructing them to return immediately to Antioch. Then he wrote another letter to Quintus, commanding him to send a cavalryman to ride to his army with that message. He also gave his permission for

Quintus to retire honourably from the Legions, finishing by expressing thanks to him for his unswerving duty to Rome. Sealing the communications with his official ring, he gave both communications to the legionary, saying, "Take these to Commander Quintus Maximus." The legionary saluted and smartly marched away.

Picking up his wine cup, Vitellius gave Antipas a contemptuous look as he saw tears rolling down the Tetrarch's flabby face. He silently thanked the gods that he would soon be leaving this puffed-up nonentity, his shrew of a wife, and this accursed city.

When news reached Aretas of the death of the Emperor Tiberius and the return of Vitellius and his army to Antioch, he gave a deep sigh of relief. So, his diviners had been right: one of the three men involved in the conflict had died, and it was not him. He immediately ordered a ceremony of thanksgiving to be held in the Temple of Winged Lions.

The Royal Family led the procession to the Temple, where Ruth, accompanied by Ibrahim and Drubaal, joined the relieved people as they poured out their thanks and praise to Al-Qaum, the god of war, and to the whole Pantheon of the Nabatean deities. Ruth offered a silent prayer to the Lord, grateful that war with Rome had not come.

When the ceremony was completed, the King invited his people to a great feast. The people ate and drank heartily, their joy and merriment replacing their fear and imagined suffering at the hands of the Romans.

The new Governor, Marcellus, arrived in Caesarea. The next day, Pilate, Claudia and Paullus boarded a military trireme and began their journey to Rome.

CHAPTER TWELVE

Vitellius' guess proved to be correct, for the Legions, Consuls and Senate ignored Tiberius' will and made Caligula the sole Emperor. Gemellus was too young and lacked experience both politically and militarily. To appease Gemellus, Caligula adopted him as his son.

It was not until their trireme docked in Ostia, that Pilate, Claudia Procula and Paullus heard the news of the death of Tiberius and learned that the new Emperor was Caligula. Pilate hoped that Caligula, who did not know much about his past history, would be lenient.

When they arrived in Rome, Pilate kissed Claudia, then watched as a litter set off, carrying her to the villa of her family's friends. Then Pilate and Paullus went to the Palatine, where, guarded by four Praetorian Guards, they were taken to the Imperial Palace. They entered the Audience Chamber, where Caligula, seated on his throne and surrounded by Praetorian Guards, was waiting for them.

Caligula ran his hand through his wispy, fair hair and threw a haughty look in Pilate's direction. After a moment of silence, Caligula got up from his throne, stepped down off the dais and walked around a nervous Pilate, a look of contempt on his face. "So, you are the troublesome Governor of Judaea?" he asked. "What shall I do with you?"

Pilate stood silent, his eyes not daring to meet those of the most powerful man in the known world.

Caligula smoothed a crease from his toga. "Shall I have you executed for the trouble you have caused?" He saw Pilate begin to tremble. "Or shall I banish you from Rome forever?" Caligula grinned as he saw Pilate grow pale and said matter-of-factly, "No. I think I shall have you thrown into the Mamertine Prison and leave you there to rot."

Without raising his eyes from the exquisitely tessellated floor, Pilate mumbled his answer. "Throughout my career I have always served Rome and my Emperor. You are now my Emperor, you have the power over life and death. My life is in your hands to do with as you will."

Caligula gave Pilate an imperious look, saying smoothly, "Yes, it is, isn't it?" His voice took on a threatening note, "Never forget that!" He returned to his throne.

Pilate dared to look up. He said imploringly "I was not alone in carrying out the massacre in Samaria, mighty Caesar."

Caligula sat forward. "Who else is involved in this sorry mess?"

"My Senior Tribune, Gnaeus Aeneas Paullus."

"Where is he?" Caligula demanded.

"He is outside waiting under guard, Caesar," Pilate replied.

Caligula called out to one of the Praetorian Guards standing by the door. "Bring me the Tribune!" The guard saluted and went off to fetch Paullus.

Paullus stood rigidly at attention before his Emperor. Caligula sniffed loudly, not liking the Tribune's arrogant look. He questioned Paullus closely. Paullus began to protest by saying he had only carried out the Governor's orders. Caligula held up an elegant, be-ringed hand to silence him. "I have heard enough!" he snarled. "Guards!" Instantly two of the Praetorians standing by his throne stepped forward awaiting instructions. "Take this snivelling coward to the Mamertine Prison." Caligula watched, laughing, as the Guards took hold of Paullus' arms and led him away.

He turned his attention back to Pilate. "You are to be held under house arrest in a house of my choice in the city while I decide what to do with you. Your future will depend on what mood I will be in on that day." He summoned a guard. "You know where you have to take him?" The guard nodded. "Then take him there now!"

Pilate bowed, grateful for a respite from punishment, however briefly that might be. The guard led Pilate out of the room. Outside, further Guards escorted Pilate to the chosen house in the Aventine District, where he was to stay with two guards policing his movements. How could he let his wife know where he was?

Calpurnius Aquila's spies informed him of Pilate's arrival at the Palace. It was only later that those same spies told him that Pilate had been placed under house arrest until the new Emperor decided what to do with him. He smiled. Now was his chance to get revenge on the man he detested, by a whisper here, an innuendo there, dropped into conversations he knew would get back to Caligula. He sat back in his chair and began to plot Pilate's downfall.

In the beginning, Caligula enjoyed immense popularity amongst his subjects and most of the Senators, including Gnaeus Claudius Marcellus. He often visited the Senate House, where he overturned some of the harsh laws decreed by Tiberius and ordered new laws to be drawn up in their place.

On this particular visit, having torn up Tiberius' law concerning prisoners who had committed treason and certain other crimes, he ordered that a new law freeing them be enacted immediately. This was met with gasps from the Senators, most of whom applauded the act, while some, knowing the Emperor would punish them for disagreeing with his will, tried hard to hide their misgivings at what might happen once the freed prisoners were back out in the city and outlying districts, especially when it had been these same Senators who had condemned them in the first place.

Caligula leaned forward in his chair and solemnly announced, "Concerning my new order, I send greetings to the son of the late Senator, Gaius Quinctilius Silvanus. If he is in Rome, or living somewhere in her outlying areas, I make this offer to him: that he should come to me as I wish to speak with him. Let it be known publicly that I will not have him arrested, but also let it be known that it will be in his best interests to accept my offer. I order the Orators to announce this news in the Forum for the next five days." He sat back in his chair.

Senator Silvanus had been popular with most of the other Senators, and they had been shocked and saddened by his death. They had been bewildered by the charges that had been brought against him, believing those charges to be false, but had done nothing to speak up in his defence, too afraid of Tiberius. Now they wondered what the new Emperor was going to do to Silvanus' son and heir.

Claudius in particular was dismayed. What did this mean? In view of the Emperor's statement that treason prisoners would be freed, should he take it that, as the son and widow of the condemned man, no harm would come to Flavius and his mother? Could Caligula be trusted to keep his word? As soon as he returned home, he would send a warning message to Flavius.

The messenger reached the farm in Latium early the next day. Flavius read Claudius' letter with mixed feelings. What should he do? He went in search of his mother and showed her the letter. Shocked, Lydia Flavia looked at her son and said imploringly, "What are you going to do?"

Flavius thought for a long moment, then came to a decision. He took his mother's hand and looked deep into her worried eyes. "We cannot stay like this forever, mother. Something has to happen. I will go to Rome and see the Emperor. Let us hope he will allow us to return to our family estate."

Tears stung Lydia Flavia's eyes. "When will you go?" she asked.

"Tomorrow."

She shivered. "I know I cannot stop you from doing this, my brave son, I can only pray to our family goddess, Fortuna, to keep you safe from harm and return you to me."

Flavius kissed her hand, then went off to find Atticus, who he knew was going to Rome the next day. He would travel with him, stopping off at Claudius' villa first to bathe and most importantly, to have his face shaved and his long, unruly hair cut by Claudius' personal bath-house slave and barber. His Tribune's uniform was at the villa. He would wear it to meet the Emperor.

CHAPTER THIRTEEN

When Flavius arrived at the villa, Claudius greeted him warmly and invited him into his office.

"My mother and I cannot thank you enough for your protection these last few months," Flavius said, "but I am going to see Caligula tomorrow. This situation has to be resolved, one way or another."

Claudius frowned. "You are a brave man. I hope the Emperor will keep his word and not have you arrested."

"It is a chance I will have to take."

Claudius nodded. "Well, if your mind is made up, I suggest you go to the bath-house, get your hair cut and your face shaved, and then have a relaxing bath." He smiled. "I look forward to seeing you at dinner later."

As he left Claudius' office, Flavius saw Claudio walking towards him. He was holding a scroll.

"Flavius, I am so glad to see you." He waved the scroll. "I have just received my orders to join the Sixth Victrix Legion, the victorious legion formed by the Emperor Augustus himself," he said proudly.

Flavius was happy for him. "When do you leave?"

"I travel to Ostia tomorrow, then take ship to Hispania. I am looking forward to it."

Flavius did not want to disillusion him about how hard legion life was, so he congratulated him and said they would speak later. He watched as Claudio went in to tell his father the news.

Before going to the baths, Flavius went to the stables. Upon seeing his master, Saturn whinnied excitedly. Flavius stroked his horse's muzzle and said softly, "My beautiful stallion, how I have missed you. We will ride out together soon." He put the thought of his possible death at the hands of the Emperor to the back of his mind and tried to think positive thoughts. As if understanding his master's troubled mind, Saturn tossed his head. "Easy boy, easy," Flavius said softly. "I must leave you now, but I hope we will be together again very soon." Saturn flared his nostrils and stamped the ground as he watched his master walk away.

Much later, with his hair cut short, his face clean-shaven and his tense body more relaxed, Flavius made his way to the dining room for the evening meal. When Claudius saw him he gave a nod of approval, saying, "It is good to see you looking more like your true self, Flavius."

He pointed to a couch and gestured to Flavius to sit down. Soon after, Claudio and Claudia walked in. When Claudia saw Flavius, her face lit up in a smile. Claudio went to his old friend and greeted him warmly.

The meal was delicious, the wine excellent. Flavius felt comfortably full as the conversation flowed back and forth. No one mentioned Flavius' meeting with the Emperor. After Claudius and Claudia had left the room, Claudio drew Flavius to one side. His voice was grave as he said, "I urge you to be wary of Caligula. He is not to be trusted."

Flavius looked at him. "I thank you for your warning, Claudio, but my mother and I cannot go on hiding ourselves away. This matter must be settled once and for all."

"But if Caligula has you killed, what then will happen to your mother?"

Flavius shrugged. "I have to put my trust in the gods and hope that they will take pity on us."

"You know that given the choice, I would come with you and stand by your side before Caligula," Claudio said stoically.

Flavius smiled. "I know that, Claudio, you have always been a good friend to me, but duty to your legion must come first."

Claudio looked Flavius squarely in the face. "I am not a good friend if I leave you to face the Emperor alone."

"Please, Claudio, do as I ask. If things go badly for me, I do not want you or your father involved in my downfall."

Claudio knew that Flavius would not be swayed. "Then I shall be with you in thought and pray that the gods, especially your family goddess, Fortuna, will be by your side." He clasped arms with Flavius, then watched sadly as he left the room.

That night, sleep eluded Flavius. He tossed and turned in his bed, wondering what the next day would bring.

Early the next morning, too strung out with nerves to eat, Flavius let himself be dressed by the slave Claudius had loaned him. During his time in Latium, his Tribune's uniform had been looked after by this slave. He thanked the slave when he saw that his tunic was clean and fresh, his armour and helmet had been polished to perfection and his leather military boots had been cleaned and repaired with new hobnails in their soles. Once dressed, he presented himself to Claudius.

"My dear boy," Claudius said approvingly, "You look very smart and perfectly presentable to meet the Emperor." He tried to keep his voice light and calm, but deep inside he was worried. "Will you ride to the palace on your horse?"

"No," came Flavius' quick reply. "If I may, sir, I should like Saturn to stay here until this is all over. If I do not return here, will you keep him safe?"

Claudius replied soberly, "Of course. But let us not look on the dark side. You have right on your side, for you have done nothing wrong. Let the Goddess of Justice prevail."

Flavius hoped that she would.

Claudia watched with a heavy heart as Flavius stepped into his hired litter. She whispered a prayer to Juno, Mother of the Gods. *"Please let him live."*

CHAPTER FOURTEEN

Flavius stepped out of the hired litter and looked up at the magnificent building looming over him. He climbed the imposing staircase leading to the palace entrance, where two Praetorians stood on guard. Decimus was one of them. For their own safety, Flavius ignored him. He looked at the second guard and said, "I am Tribune Flavius Quinctilius Silvanus. The Emperor has asked me to attend him."

Hearing Flavius' name, the guard went to fetch a senior officer. When Flavius told the officer his name, the officer said stiffly, "Follow me, Tribune."

Flavius followed the guard down a long, columned corridor. The sun shone through the latticed windows set high above, highlighting the colours of the marble floor below. As they strode along, Flavius cast quick glances at the painted walls. Some had different coloured marble panels with vibrantly-coloured friezes on them, whilst others depicted various Bacchic rites. A line of imposing, beautifully-carved statues stretched down the corridor, amongst them life-sized statues of Greek Artemis and her Roman counterpart, Diana, goddess of the hunt. On beautifully-carved pedestals were also set smaller busts of the Emperors Augustus and Tiberius.

Flavius had never visited the Palatine, but his father had on several occasions. His father had given him glowing descriptions of the palace, but none had done justice to the beauty and artistry of the things Flavius was now seeing with his own eyes. As he came to the Imperial Audience Chamber, he wondered if this would be the last time he would see such beauty.

The guard told Flavius to wait outside the door while he entered the Chamber, saluted Caligula and waited.

Caligula was seated on his throne, dictating a letter to a scribe. He became aware of the guard and without looking up, said irritably, "What do you want? Can't you see I am busy?"

The guard saluted and said, "Forgive the interruption, Caesar, but the Tribune Flavius Quinctilius Silvanus is here."

Caligula sat up, surprise written on his features. "Here? Now?"

"Yes, Caesar. He is waiting outside. Shall I bring him in?"

"Let him wait!" Caligula snapped. "I will see him when

I am ready." He called the guard closer and gave him an order. The guard said, "Yes, Caesar, I will have him found and brought to you."

Caligula barked out, "Bring him through the side door."

The guard saluted and hurried away.

Caligula continued dictating to the scribe, then suddenly dismissed him. The scribe gathered up his writing implements, bowed and beat a hasty retreat. Sitting alone, Caligula pondered the situation. He had not expected to see the Tribune quite so soon. He smiled to himself, wondering how the son of the traitorous Senator would take the news he was about to give him.

Flavius paced up and down the corridor. He had been waiting for what seemed like an eternity. He wondered if this was part of the Emperor's plan to keep him on edge worrying what his punishment would be. He was about to turn around and leave the Palace when the huge bronze door opened and the guard came out.

"The Emperor will see you now Tribune. Follow me," he said tersely.

Flavius took a deep breath and followed the guard into the Imperial Audience Chamber. He looked at the new Emperor seated on his throne and was disappointed by what he saw. He knew the Emperor was the son of a great hero, and thought he would emulate his father. But this was no athletically-built, handsome man. Caligula had a pale face with sunken eyes set beneath a broad and furrowed forehead, topped by fair, wispy hair; his neck was long, his body and legs were long and thin. His expression was one of bored arrogance.

Caligula stared at Flavius. "Flavius Quinctilius Silvanus. Here you are at last. Where have you been these past few months?" When Flavius stayed silent, Caligula gave him a penetrating look and said, "No matter, you are here now." He leaned forward. "What shall I do with the son and wife of a traitorous Senator? I take it your mother has not yet joined her husband?" He saw Flavius bristle at the mention of his mother. "Ah, I can see by your action that she is still alive. Good. Good." He sighed theatrically and said, "And what of your dear brother? Do you think he is alive and well?"

Flavius was tempted to say that the Emperor knew he was, as he was one of his partners in crime, but such an outburst would surely cost him his life and ruin his mother's future.

Caligula gestured to the guard, who went immediately to a side door and opened it. In strode Macro, who took up his position close to the throne. He was followed by Marius. Caligula beamed. "Flavius, here is your brother. As you see, he is indeed alive and well."

Marius walked over to Caligula, who greeted him affectionately. Flavius looked on, disgusted by the seeming closeness between his brother and Caligula, but forced himself to concentrate on his own predicament.

Marius looked at Flavius. "Hello, brother," he said.

After a brief silence, Flavius narrowed his eyes and said testily, "You have not asked about our mother."

Marius gave an oily smile. "No, I haven't have I? Well, how is she? Still alive?"

It amused Caligula to see Flavius trying to control his anger. He said, "Stop it, Marius. Let us get on with the task in hand, I have a banquet to attend later and I need time to prepare for it." He looked down at the huge ruby ring he wore on his index finger and smiled. "I love rubies, they are the colour of blood." He licked his lips at the thought, then looked up at Marius and said, "Do you like rubies, Marius?"

"If my Emperor likes them, then so too do I."

Caligula smiled at Marius, then turned an icy look on Flavius and said abruptly, "Enough of this procrastination. Flavius, you are the rightful heir, by law, to your father's estate, is that not so?" Seeing Flavius nod in agreement, he continued, "Well I am the law now and I decree that you shall not have it!"

Flavius almost wavered at the news and fought to keep himself calm.

"Moreover, you were one of the Staff Officers of the ex-Governor of Judaea." He saw Flavius' shocked features and said sarcastically, "Of course, you would not know about Pilate's fall from grace. How could you? After all, you have been hiding yourself away from us for a long time."

Flavius wondered what Pilate had done to warrant his dismissal from a post he had served for so many years. He forced himself to concentrate on Caligula, who was still speaking.

"Because of your association with Pilate, your remaining time as a Tribune will end with immediate effect and any back-dated Army pay due to you will come to me. I also decree that you will forfeit your rights to the Silvanus Estate, which will now be given to my dear friend, your brother Marius." He turned to look at Marius, who had triumph written all over his face.

"Oh, Caesar," Marius said obsequiously, "Thank you for this great gift!"

It took all of Flavius' self-control to stop himself lashing out at Marius, who seeing the murderous look on his brother's face, quickly retreated behind the throne.

"What about our mother?" Flavius said through tight lips.

Caligula gave him a haughty look. "I gather she is a cousin of Pilate. She is lucky that I do not have her banished, but, after all," he gave a sly grin, "one cannot help one's family connections. It is up to you if you wish to look after her, or let her fend for herself. I really do not care either way."

"But she is innocent of all this. Why..."

"Do not question my decisions!" Caligula shouted angrily. "Let it be enough that I have granted you and your mother your lives. Go back to wherever you came from and stay away from your brother and his estate. Guards!" Instantly two Praetorians appeared. "Escort this person out of here."

Too shocked by the outcome of the meeting to protest, Flavius let himself be forcibly removed from the Audience Chamber. He walked unsteadily down the long corridor, wondering how he would break the news to his mother.

Calpurnius Aquila came out of his office and walked straight into Flavius. Seeing him, he said, "Well, well. Young Silvanus. I have been searching everywhere for you, and here you are in the middle of the lion's den. What are you doing here?"

Flavius frowned at the Chief Spy. "You know why I am here. You make it your business to know everything."

Aquila narrowed his eyes. "It is my *business* to know everything. Looking at your face, I think this present meeting with the Emperor did not go well." He drew Flavius to one side and said sternly, "Look, I cannot and will not help you, why should I? I am no friend to you, but I offer you this advice: if you do not wish to end up like Pilate and your father, you must look over your shoulder every waking moment and most of all, trust no one!"

Flavius was on the point of asking what had happened to Pilate when a loud voice filled the corridor. He turned and saw Macro coming towards them.

"The Emperor needs you, Aquila." Macro said in a gruff voice. Aquila hurried off in the direction of the Audience Chamber. Macro turned on Flavius and said threateningly, "The Emperor dismissed you." He placed his hand on the hilt of his sword. "Get out! Now!"

Flavius needed no second telling and walked away, his

thoughts in disarray. After the shock of the Emperor's edict concerning himself, he wondered what Aquila meant when he warned him not to end up like his father. And what had Pilate done? He would make it his business to find out.

Decimus was still on duty at the entrance to the Palace. During their time together in the Legion, the two friends had used secret signs, dreamed up by Decimus. Each sign had a meaning that only the two of them recognised. As he passed Decimus, Flavius gave the sign for meeting up at their favourite tavern. Decimus gave an imperceptible shake of his head.

Flavius knew the answers to his questions would have to wait.

Whilst Flavius was with Caligula, Claudio was walking proudly into his father's office. He was dressed as a Tribune Laticlavius, the wide purple band hemming his tunic displaying his rank as an aristocrat who would use the legions as a stepping stone to a political career.

He grasped his father's hand. "I must leave now, father." He looked intently at Claudius. "I pray that while I am gone, the gods will be with you."

Claudius smiled. "And I will pray every day that the gods will be with you, Claudio."

Claudio walked out into the atrium, where Claudia stood waiting for him. She held him closely and said tearfully, "I will miss you so much, Claudio."

"And I you," he replied. "Do not cry, little sister. I will

only be away for two years. The time will pass quickly." He kissed her forehead.

Their farewell was interrupted by a slave who had come to tell him that his luggage had been put in the carriage and that all was ready for his journey to Ostia. With one last kiss on her cheek, Claudio went outside.

He entered the carriage. Claudio's personal body slave climbed up and settled himself next to the driver, as two armed bodyguards positioned their horses behind the carriage.

Claudius and Claudia walked out from the atrium and gave Claudio a wistful wave as the carriage moved off. Claudia's tear-filled eyes followed the carriage until it was out of sight.

Inside the carriage, Claudio was filled with excitement. This was going to be the adventure of a lifetime. He settled back in the carriage, eager to reach Ostia to take ship to Hispania and join the famed Sixth Victrix Legion.

CHAPTER FIFTEEN

When Flavius arrived back at Claudius' villa, Claudia was walking through the atrium. Her eyes lit up when she saw him. "Thank the gods," she whispered.

"Where is your father?" he asked.

"He is working in his office. I'll tell him you are here." Claudia went to tell her father the good news. Soon after, Claudius came out. He went straight to Flavius and said in a voice filled with relief, "You have returned to us safe and well." He led Flavius into his office. Claudia left them alone. Seeing Flavius' pale face, Claudius told him to sit down, then poured wine into two cups and gave one to Flavius. When Flavius was ready, Claudius said, "Tell me what happened."

Claudius narrowed his eyes as Flavius told him. "So, you have been cheated out of your inheritance, and by your own brother too," he said angrily. "What about your mother?"

Flavius shrugged. "My brother is not in the least bit concerned about his own mother's welfare." The full impact of Caligula's verdict was overwhelming him. He shook his head and said forlornly, "How can I tell her she has lost her home, her status and her wealth through the greed of her own son?" He grimaced. "Where will she live? I have no army pay to help her or myself."

Claudius raised his eyebrows. "What do you mean, no army pay?"

"Caligula is taking it for himself. I am no longer a Tribune. My army life has been cut short now that Caligula has taken away the Governorship of Judaea from Pontius Pilate." Flavius saw Claudius' quizzical look and said, "I have no idea what Pilate has done to warrant this dismissal, nor do I know where he is at present, or if he is still alive, but I have been dismissed from the Legion because I was his Staff Officer."

Claudius shook his head in disgust, thought for a moment then said, "I have a high regard for you and your mother. You are both welcome to stay at the farm, or now that you are free to walk the streets of Rome, you may wish to stay here. I hope you will choose here. Now that Claudio has left for Hispania, I would welcome the company of another man."

Flavius was overcome by Claudius' generosity. He stood up, went to Claudius and said humbly," You would let us stay here?"

"Why not? You have lost your home and possessions through no fault of your own. I would be insulting your father's memory if I turned my back on you and your mother."

Flavius thanked him again and again. "Tomorrow I will ride to Latium to tell my mother the news," he said.

"On Saturn?" He smiled when Flavius grinned in reply. "I suggest that after dinner, you get some rest. You have a long day ahead of you tomorrow."

Flavius smiled and thanked his saviour again. Then, feeling a great weight had been lifted off his shoulders, he went to his room. He threw his Tribune armour and tunic onto the floor. What need did he have for them now? Would he keep them, or have a slave dispose of them? He would make up his mind in the morning. He went to the bathhouse, then prepared himself for dinner.

When morning came, Flavius decided he would keep the uniform after all. He had been wearing it when he and Farrah had first declared their love for each other. It was too precious to throw away. He ordered his slave to put it away somewhere safe and take care of it.

After an early breakfast, Flavius rode to Latium. It felt so good to be reunited with Saturn. Claudius had kept his word. Saturn looked magnificent; his coat gleamed and his muscles rippled as he thundered along with head held high and luxurious mane flowing in the breeze. It seemed Saturn too was glad to bear the weight of his master once more.

All the way to Latium, Flavius thought of various ways to tell his mother the bad news. In the end, he decided he would just tell her the truth.

Later that day, Flavius arrived at the farm. He left Saturn with a trusted slave and went to his mother's room. When Lydia Flavia saw him, she rushed to him and clung to him. Overcome with relief, she said, "Oh Flavius, I thought I might never see you again. But here you are, safe and well."

"I have something to tell you, mother." He saw her worried expression. Taking a deep breath, he said, "As you see I am safe, but the news is not good." He told her what had taken place at the Palace.

His mother was deeply shocked. "My own son, your brother, would do this to us? Why?"

Flavius knelt by her side and took her hand. "He has somehow wormed his way into the new Emperor's affections." He would not tell her about what he and Decimus had witnessed when they saw Marius with Caligula and his cronies carrying out their drunken escapades. He knew that would destroy her. He went on, "You know he has always been jealous of me as the heir to the estate and spiteful to you because he thinks you favoured me over him, and now that our father has gone…" He did not finish the sentence.

Lydia Flavia wiped away her tears and said, "You have always been my favourite son, even when your behaviour was not as it should have been." She saw Flavius' face redden at the memory of his waywardness before he had been sent to Judaea. She continued, "Marius was undoubtedly your father's favourite, but I never treated him differently. I do not understand. Why is he being so cruel now?"

Flavius stood up. "Because his jealousy and misguided feelings have made him become power mad and hungry for retribution. Having Caligula as a friend has helped him to obtain his goals." He wondered why Caligula should be bothered with his brother. Perhaps it was because they both delighted in cruel acts and debauchery. That was evident from Decimus' revelation concerning the murdered prostitute.

He saw his mother shake her head sadly and knew that now was the time to tell her the good news. He smiled as he said, "We may have lost the estate, but we will not be homeless. Claudius Marcellus has offered us a home. We can stay here, or share his villa in Rome. What do you think?"

Lydia Flavia was shocked. "He would let us share his home?"

"Yes," Flavius replied. "Personally, I would like to be in Rome. While I'm stuck here, I can't easily discover the reason for my father's suicide." He saw his mother's hesitancy and said, "We are both free by the Emperor's decree, no one will touch me, or you. We will be safe in Rome."

His mother thought for a moment. "Although I enjoy the beauty and peace of the countryside, I do miss Rome and my friends, if I still have any," she said wistfully. "Yes, let us return to Rome."

Flavius ordered the slaves to pack their few belongings, and Atticus gladly volunteered to drive the cart. Soon, led by Flavius riding on Saturn, the cart carrying Lydia Flavia and her maidservant were travelling along the road to Rome.

CHAPTER SIXTEEN

When the new Commander of the Antonia arrived, Quintus Maximus greeted him, then accompanied him around the fortress. Sallow-faced and thin-lipped, the new Commander watched as the legionaries were put through their paces by their officers. He grimaced. "Not bad, but I can see there is room for a great deal of improvement," he said. Walking off with his hands behind his back, the new man said harshly, "Now, show me the workshops and your cavalry blocks."

Quintus gritted his teeth. Who did this jumped-up Commander think he was? He pitied his officers, who would have to deal with this character. He had spent years building up their trust. Under this man he knew it would quickly disappear.

After the inspection, Quintus handed over his quarters to the new Commander. He was to spend his last night at the Antonia in an empty officer's house. He ordered Gebhard to make sure his personal belongings were packed safely for that night, and for the long journey eastwards to reach the farmland he had been allocated.

Gebhard, relieved and delighted to be staying with his long-term master, set about his tasks joyfully. He had served Quintus Maximus for many years. Captured in Germany, he had been taken to the slave market. He had caught Quintus' eye because of his strong physique and proud bearing, and Quintus had bought him to be his personal slave. As he packed his master's belongings, he wondered why the young Tribune, Flavius, had not returned to Jerusalem. The Passover Festival had come and gone and still there was no news. He hoped nothing bad had happened to him.

Early the next morning, Quintus forcibly held back his tears as he entered the parade ground and saw that the whole fort had turned out to say goodbye to him. Senior Tribunes, Centurions, Cavalrymen and legionaries, as well as armourers and equine experts, including Zeno, who had been in charge of Saturn during Flavius' time at the fortress, stood straight backed as they saluted their much-loved Commander.

Quintus returned their salute, then made a short speech.

"For the past ten years I have commanded this fortress. I have seen many legionaries come and go; some through transfer, like our much-admired Senior Centurion Sextus, and some lost through battle. I will never forget your bravery and resilience, especially during the recent battles at Beth Horon and here at the Antonia. It has been a privilege and an honour to serve with you." He extended his arm. "Gentlemen, I salute you!"

His speech was answered with a roar from every man.

Quintus mounted his horse. Gebhard mounted his own steed and took hold of the reins of the pack mule carrying Quintus' and his possessions. As they rode towards the main gate, the legionaries began to bang their shields with their swords to honour the man they had been proud to serve with. Quintus could no longer hold back his tears.

Julius sighed with regret as he watched the departure of the man he had come to admire greatly. He had got off to a bad start with the new Commander, who, upon his visit to the cavalry block, had found fault with everything. How he wished Tribune Flavius was here. He was worried. Where was Flavius? Why had he not returned to Jerusalem?

After an overnight stop, Quintus and Gebhard reached Caesarea, where they boarded a merchant ship for their journey to the Roman port of Brundisium. From there, they would board a ship taking them across the Adriatic Sea to Dyrrhachium, where they would disembark and continue their journey overland to Philippi, east of Macedonia.

Quintus knew it would be a long journey overland to reach their destination, but he was not worried. He was retired now and had plenty of time and money to explore that part of the Roman world. He had never visited that area and was anxious to see it before he journeyed to his farmland to begin a new, and very different, adventure in his life.

The officer commanding the salt mines in Libya frowned as he read the latest communication from Rome. At first he thought it was a joke, but on seeing the Emperor's seal at the bottom, he realised the command was deadly serious. Antonius was to be released as, in the Emperor's opinion, he had been working for the State when he had been arrested by the now disgraced Pontius Pilate. Incredulous at the new Emperor's decision, he barked at the guard standing before him, "Bring Antonius to me!" The guard saluted and hurried away.

Antonius, the one-time Prefect Alae who had been under the command of Quintus at the Antonia, was working two shafts down in the salt mines. Sweating with the unbearable heat, he brought his whip down hard across the back of one of the slaves working the mine and yelled, "Work harder, you useless dog!"

Antonius never lost an opportunity to take out his frustration and anger on the slaves. His superior officer had warned him many times that a dead slave was of no use to Rome. He had nodded and cursed under his breath at the warning, knowing that none of the other guards would speak up for him, rather, they all kept their distance from him, knowing why he was there. He knew that they

123

spat in his food, 'accidentally' spilt his foul-tasting wine or dropped something heavy or hot onto his feet, but he could do nothing to stop it for fear of retaliation.

He had been arrested and sent to Pilate by Quintus Maximus, Commander of the Antonia. Pilate had demoted him for acting as a spy for Calpurnius Aquila, gross dereliction of duty at the battle of Beth-Horon, and for the attempted murder of Drubaal, the Carthaginian bodyguard of Sheikh Ibrahim of Nabatea. As punishment, Pilate had sentenced him to serve in the Libyan salt mines. Now, after several months here, his hatred against his superiors had grown.

After all the years he had faithfully served Calpurnius Aquila, he could not understand why the Chief Spy had abandoned him to his fate. He swore to himself that if ever, by some miracle of the gods, he was able to leave this accursed place, he would have his revenge on Quintus, Pilate and Aquila.

The guard appeared as he continued to whip the slave. The guard looked at him with contempt and said sharply, "The Commanding Officer wants to see you."

Wondering what he had done wrong now, Antonius nodded, then followed the guard to the Commander's office, which was set on the highest level of the mine.

He stood before the officer, wondering what his punishment was going to be this time. He gasped in surprise when the officer looked straight at him and said, "Antonius, you have been reprieved from duty at this mine by order of the new Emperor's edict to free certain criminals." Antonius frowned at the word 'criminals'. In his mind he had only been obeying Aquila's orders. The officer did not go into detail but said, "You will be taken back to the fortress in Libya tomorrow, and from there you will be placed on the next galley returning to Caesarea, or Ashdod. The choice is yours. Get your personal things together."

Free? It took a moment for this news to sink into Antonius' brain. He gave a thin smile, then asked the officer, "What month is it? I have lost track of time." He grinned when the officer said "It is early April."

"Then I will take the ship to Ashdod." That worked perfectly for him. By the time he reached the Jewish port and travelled on to Jerusalem it would be time for the Jewish Feast of Pentecost, meaning Pilate would be in Jerusalem. Once there he would avenge himself on both Pilate and Quintus Maximus, the architects of his downfall. Then, he would make his way to Rome, where he would at last have the chance to carry out his revenge on Calpurnius Aquila, the man who had done nothing to help him.

Giving a half-hearted salute, he thanked the officer, went back to his small room and began gathering together his sparse belongings. For a brief moment he thought of ways he could get back at those mine guards who had tried to make his life a misery, but decided it was not worth it as it could interfere with his freedom. Freedom!

CHAPTER SEVENTEEN

When Antonius reached Ashdod, he offered an animal dealer the ring he wore on his little finger. The ring was of no sentimental value to him; he had won it from a fellow officer in a game of dice when he was stationed in Syria. The ring was made of silver with a raised cornelian centrepiece carved with the likeness of the god Mars. The animal dealer could see that it was of fine quality and gave him a good price for it. Using some of the money, Antonius bought a donkey from the dealer.

After a few overnight stops, he reached Jerusalem, where the Feast of Pentecost was being celebrated. Not wishing to show his face near the Antonia Fortress, he asked around in the local taverns if Pilate was still in charge. He was bitterly disappointed to learn that Pilate had been recalled to Rome and had not returned. A new

Governor had been installed in his place. His second choice, Quintus Maximus, had also gone, along with the fearsome Centurion Sextus. No one knew where they had gone.

Antonius grimaced. His well thought-out plans had been thwarted. What was he to do? There was one plan left now: to go to Rome and seek out Aquila.

After turning various ideas over in his mind, he thought of a way to raise the funds needed for his trip. Back in Picenum, his father had been a builder by trade and had employed two other builders. Throughout his youth, Antonius had helped his father by fetching and carrying various tools and small blocks of stone. All of that time he had watched as his father worked, learning the trade until he had been skilled enough to help with the building himself. But his temperament was not cut out for such painstaking work. If he damaged a block of stone with his cutting tool, or mistakenly hacked off a piece of marble, he would curse and throw the implements around, sometimes narrowly missing his father or another builder working close by.

On one particularly annoying day when nothing had seemed to go right, he had angrily flung his cutting tool away. It had caught the leg of another worker, badly cutting it. Antonius' father had seen this and heard him swearing in frustration. Seeing the damage done to the unfortunate man's leg, his father had instantly dismissed him and told him he would never work with him again.

Much aggrieved by his father's reaction, Antonius had

left Picenum and travelled around for a while. When his money ran low, he joined the Tenth Fretensis Legion, eventually being sent to Judaea, where he had first met Aquila.

When Aquila had visited Pilate in Jerusalem, he had seen him on duty at Herod's Palace. Later, when he was off-duty, Aquila had approached him, telling him that he had heard he was a hard, ruthless man. Knowing that the other legionaries detested him, Aquila had flattered him by offering him the chance to work for him as a spy. If he agreed, Aquila had told him, he would see to it personally that he rose higher in the legion than he could ever have imagined, earning a great deal of money in the process.

When he had asked how much money, he had been staggered, even more so when Aquila had said that he would be working for him alone and that it had nothing to do with the State. Antonius had wondered where the money would come from. He doubted it would be out of Aquila's own pocket, but he did not care. He only knew that if he accepted the job, he would receive wealth and, most of all, power, giving him a chance to get even with those who had treated him badly. Aquila had warned him that secrecy was everything and that if he broke that rule, he would have him killed. Despite that threat, he had accepted the job. It was only later that he found out Aquila wanted him to spy on Pilate.

Putting those memories aside, he knew there was no need for him to stay in Jerusalem now, so he travelled to the city of Sepphoris in the area of Galilee, where he knew buildings were always being constructed or in need of repair. When he arrived there, he trudged around the city trying to find work. He had almost given up hope when, at the last builder's workshop he visited, the builder told him that he had become very busy and was looking for someone to help him. Antonius told the builder he was experienced in the trade and, after negotiating a wage suitable to both employer and employee, he was taken on.

The builder asked Antonius, "Do you have a place to stay?"

Antonius shook his head. "I have just arrived in Sepphoris and have not had time to look."

The builder nodded. "There's a spare sleeping mat in the back room of the workshop, you can stay there if you like. There have been a number of burglaries recently and a lot of expensive tools have been stolen. I'll feel more secure knowing that after I've gone home, someone will be here looking after the place."

Antonius jumped at the chance.

"Make yourself at home and be ready to start work bright and early tomorrow." The builder returned to his task.

Antonius knew that if he wanted to earn the money he needed to pay for his journey to Rome, as well as his accommodation there, he would need to control his temper. He would make sure he did so.

The weeks flew by. He worked hard, trying his best not to damage any of the building materials he was working with, and bit his tongue to stop his bad temper if something did go wrong. Soon, he would have enough money to pay for his passage to Rome

Another month went by. After a hard day's work, he came back to his temporary home at the back of the workshop and added the money he had earned that day to the bag of coins hidden in an old amphora. He smiled as he counted it out. He had more than enough to pay for his journey to Rome.

He did not want to have to explain to the builder why he was suddenly leaving, so just after dawn the next morning, he gathered his few belongings together, placed the money in a spare tunic, rolled it up and stuffed it into his bag. He fixed the bag to his donkey, and without a backward glance, began his journey to the northern port of Akko. When he reached Akko he found a ship travelling to Ostia. Having no further use for the donkey, he sold it to a merchant. As the ship pulled out of the harbour, a wide grin spread across Antonius' face. He was on his way to Rome. And Calpurnius Aquila.

CHAPTER EIGHTEEN

When Antonius reached Rome, he soon found a place to stay. He guessed that Aquila's office would be situated in the heart of the Imperial Palace, so he spent the next few hours planning how he could get into the palace without being seen by the Praetorian Guards. He decided to try out an idea. Under the cover of darkness, he went to the Palatine. He waited close to the Palace all night, patiently waiting to see if any of the Palace servants would come out of the building so he could speak to them.

Early in the morning a workman carrying a bag of tools sauntered out from a building in the Palace grounds. He stopped and began to inspect a crack in an outer wall. Antonius grinned. He was in luck. The workman was obviously a builder.

Antonius approached the man and said, "I have noticed

the walls need a lot of repair. Could you do with some assistance?"

The builder, whose name was Mario, looked him up and down. "Yes, I could, but it's not up to me, I'm only a worker. You need to speak with the Master Builder."

"Is he here?"

"Yes. I'll go and see if he's available." He was soon back with a tall, imperious-looking man.

"I am the Emperor's Master Builder," the man said haughtily, looking down his large nose at Antonius. "I understand you are looking for work." Seeing Antonius' strong build and bulging muscles, he added, "There's a lot of work to be done in and around the various buildings, and I've just lost a skilled man in an unfortunate accident involving a large piece of granite." He looked intently at Antonius. "I hope you're not a runaway slave, for if you are..."

"No, sir. I am a Roman citizen," Antonius replied quickly.

The Master Builder nodded. "I take it you have experience in the building trade?"

"I've just come from Sepphoris, where I helped to repair a number of very important buildings," Antonius said matter-of-factly, hoping the name would impress the man. It did.

"Sepphoris, eh?" It's well known that Herod used the best skilled workmen and craftsmen money could buy in the construction of that place."

"In Picenum, my hometown, I trained alongside my father, a very experienced builder," Antonius said proudly. He was glad that his father had died years ago, so he could not be questioned about that statement.

The Master Builder thought for a moment, then said, "Show me what you can do."

He instructed Mario to hand Antonius his tool bag, then said, "Pick out the right tools for the job." He watched closely to see if Antonius knew which ones were needed for the repair work and nodded when Antonius chose correctly. "Do you know how to mix cement and concrete?" Antonius said he did. "Come with me. You," he snapped at Mario, "get on with your work." Mario immediately continued with his task, afraid to upset his powerful master.

The Master Builder took Antonius to the workshops. "Now, prove to me that you do know how to make cement. Find the correct ingredients and mix them in there." He pointed to a large bowl. Antonius looked into various sacks and carefully chose the ingredients required: aggregates, volcanic ash, lime and water. He mixed the items together until the cement reached the right consistency.

The Master Builder was satisfied. "You're hired. Start work right away." The two men went outside. The Master Builder called Mario over and said to him, "Take our new employee to the servants' quarters. He can have the room vacated by our previous builder. Show him where other cracks in the wall need repairing, then carry on with your own work." Then he turned and walked away.

Relieved that he had the job, Antonius followed Mario to the servants' quarters. This would be his opportunity to get closer to Aquila. He knew his chances of getting close enough to kill him were remote, but he had another way to destroy him.

When Aquila heard that the Master Builder had taken on a new worker he was not worried. If the man had found him to be suitable, then that was fine as far as he was concerned. He had no need to check.

It was a decision he would come to bitterly regret.

When Antonius had been working at the Palace for two months, he had still had no chance to get closer to the well-guarded Aquila. The Master Builder had been pleased with his work, but some of the other servants were not so happy. They had watched and listened as Antonius had flattered the Master Builder, complementing him on his expertise, and the Master Builder delighted in this. The servants also saw the other side of the stranger: the way he constantly picked on and bullied the young apprentice worker, who was scared of the much larger man. They did not like it. They were afraid to report Antonius to the Master Builder, knowing he would not have a word said against his favourite. Their anger grew worse when the Master Builder upgraded Antonius to do more specialised work, including work in the palace itself.

Antonius was in the Emperor's garden repairing a column that had been damaged in a recent storm. He was busy working when he became conscious of a presence behind him. He felt a hand stroking and squeezing his bare, hard-muscled biceps. The hand was soft and feminine. He hoped that it was the buxom female slave who worked in the kitchen. He had often caught her looking at him as he sat eating. The last time she had smiled at him - an open invitation. It was one he would readily accept.

He turned and saw that it was the Emperor who was stroking his arm. He was shocked, not knowing how to react. Then Caligula began to stroke his bulging thigh. He was repulsed by the look on the Emperor's face and wanted to recoil from his touch, but he knew that he did not dare. Instead, he stood perfectly still, hoping that the Emperor would move away from him.

Caligula's voice was smooth. "What is your name?"

Antonius replied, "It is Leon, great Caesar." That was the name he had called himself upon his arrival at the Palace, not wanting Aquila to know that he was here in Rome.

"Leon." Caligula nodded. "A lion. Yes, it suits you. You have strong arms and thighs." He walked around Antonius, appraising him. "Your physique is magnificent. I need someone like you."

Antonius was feeling distinctly uncomfortable, but he kept a bland expression. He had heard tales from some of the other servants about Caligula's illicit activities and liaisons. Was he to be added to the Emperor's list of conquests?

Caligula laughed. "I see the anxious look on your face. Do not worry, all I require from you is that you attend me as my bodyguard." He briefly looked away. "I have many enemies. I can trust no one." He looked back at Antonius. "With you close by me, with your size and bulk, I will feel safe, especially when I go on my nocturnal sojourns. I will tell the Master Builder that from now on, you will work exclusively for me. I know he will not argue."

Caligula grimaced as he looked at Antonius' sweat-stained, cement-covered tunic.

"Go to the baths, a servant will be waiting for you there. After you are clean, fresh clothes will be provided. Clothes more suitable for your new appointment."

Trying not to shout for joy, Antonius forced himself to concentrate. Caligula said in an impatient voice, "Go on! What are you waiting for?"

Antonius watched as Caligula walked away, relishing in the fact that he, Antonius, was now an Imperial Bodyguard. He walked, straight-backed, to the baths, filled with pride at this unexpected advancement.

CHAPTER NINETEEN

Claudius returned to his villa from the Senate House. Flavius had just come in from the garden and was about to greet him, but when he saw Claudius' grim expression, he knew something was wrong. Claudius called his daughter, Flavius and Lydia Flavia into his office.

"I have some bad news," Claudius began. "The Emperor is gravely ill. He may not live." He grimaced as surprised gasps filled the air. "He has been struck down by a sudden, mysterious illness. The doctors attending him agree that he has not been poisoned."

Flavius knew that this was indeed bad news. If Caligula should succumb to this illness, the whole Empire, Rome in particular, would be in turmoil, for who would succeed him? It could easily lead to another civil war where would-be contenders for the throne would battle for supremacy.

"The people are in uproar," Claudius went on. "I witnessed some lying prostrate on the ground praying earnestly to the gods to restore their Emperor to them, promising loudly that they would willingly offer their own lives in place of his." He ran his hand through his hair. "Some were injuring themselves with knives, whilst others tore at their hair and faces. All to no avail I fear, for the gods will have their way."

He sat down heavily on his chair.

"What can we do, father?" Claudia went to him and placed a delicate hand on his shoulder. She shuddered as he replied coldly, "There is nothing anyone can do, except pray to the gods to be merciful."

All through the Emperor's illness, Rome was under a cloud of gloom. The Consuls, Senators and most of the people wondered who would rule them if he died. No one wished to be embroiled in yet another civil war. Some older members of the community remembered the stories told to them by their fathers and grandfathers about the carnage war had brought, and they had no desire to live through a repeat of those terrible days.

There was great relief when the news was announced that Caligula had recovered. People danced in the streets, praising the gods for his safe delivery and thanking them for their mercy.

The mood changed when Caligula put out an edict thanking those who had offered their lives to the gods to save his. As their prayers had been granted, they would now be required to carry out their offers to appease those same gods. Men and women began to die cruelly. As time went on, rumours began to circulate that Caligula was conducting orgies in the palace and that he was responsible for having important people murdered, amongst them Gemellus and the father of Caligula's dead first wife, Julia Claudilla. It was no secret that the Emperor was seducing the wives of Senators, even his own sisters. The people stayed tight-lipped for their own safety, but they could not help but wonder what had happened to their once magnanimous Emperor, at first so popular after the reign of terror of Tiberius. Why had he become so cruel and licentious? Was it his illness that had left him like this? No one could be sure.

But Flavius knew that Caligula had always been cruel. He and his mother were testament to that. Since he and Lydia Flavia had moved into Claudius' villa, he had passed by the Silvanus estate only once. He had hoped to reclaim his father's body for proper burial, but that had been impossible, for the estate had been filled with soldiers overseeing workmen who were clearing the overgrown gardens and renovating the villa and its outbuildings, no doubt on Caligula's orders. Anger had threatened to consume him, but he had forced it to the back of his mind, knowing that it would change nothing.

One night after dinner, Claudius drew Flavius aside and

said, "I think it is time you took your father's place in the Senate."

Flavius was taken aback. "But I don't know how to."

Claudius smiled and said, "I can instruct you, if you wish."

Flavius turned this out-of-the-blue offer over and over in his mind. In the past, he had never wanted to become embroiled in politics, but that was before his rightful position as heir had been taken away from him. If he accepted Claudius' offer, it could be the answer to his prayer for justice. He forced himself to concentrate on what Claudius was saying.

"How old are you?"

"Twenty-five," Flavius replied.

Claudius nodded. "Good. You have military experience, but you are lacking in administrative skills. That will cause a delay in your advancement to the Senate." He saw Flavius' look of concern and said reassuringly, "We have plenty of time for you to reach your goal, that is, if you will accept my offer."

Flavius wondered what that offer might be and was surprised by Claudius' next words.

"I would like to place you in charge of my commercial dealings. You have already taken my commodities to the marketplace."

Flavius nodded, wishing he had paid more attention to the way Atticus had dealt with the merchants instead of going to the Subura to meet Decimus to find out news about his brother.

"I know it's a daunting task, but I will instruct Atticus to help you," Claudius went on. "Besides, you may not have to go to the market too many times, as I am more interested in you helping me with the bookwork and daily running of the operation involved – it will take a load off my shoulders. I take it your literacy and numeracy levels are up to standard?"

Flavius felt a pang of guilt, remembering that when he had been growing up, his father had spent a fortune on hiring a Greek scholar to take care of his education. And how had he repaid his father? By behaving in a reckless and immoral way during his youth. Now it was too late to thank his father and say sorry for his wild behaviour.

He put those uncomfortable remembrances to one side and said, "Yes they are, but forgive me, what about Claudio? As your heir surely he should be the one to carry out this task."

Claudius shook his head. "I asked him once if he wanted to learn the business, but he refused. He said he was more interested in a life of adventure. That's why he joined the Legions." He looked down for a brief moment and said dolefully, "After what you told me about life in the Legions I worry about him, but his mind could not be changed." He looked at Flavius. "Now, do you accept my offer?"

"Yes please," Flavius gratefully replied.

Claudius smiled. "Good." He placed a hand on Flavius' shoulder and said warningly, "It will take time to achieve your goal, but if you are successful in this administrative role and get the traders and the common people on your side, as well as some of those Senators who remember your father with affection, then you can gradually work your way through the process of becoming a Senator."

Claudius went to his desk, pulled out a fresh scroll and began to write on it.

"I will have an account opened in your name at my bank and give you an allowance for the administrative work you do. This should help you to rebuild the fortune that was so cruelly taken from you."

Flavius was overwhelmed by Claudius' more than generous offer.

Claudius looked at the expensive marble water clock, sitting in a place of honour on a nearby table. "It's getting late now. We'll begin your training first thing after breakfast tomorrow."

Flavius spent the next few weeks taking instruction from Claudius. He had always been a quick learner and soon got to grips with the complex bookwork and day-to-day mathematical accounts recording the incomings and outgoings of Claudius' business dealings.

Claudius had been delighted that his protégé had so quickly learnt the tasks set before him. He decided that Flavius should go with Atticus on the next visit to the marketplace and deal directly with the merchants, some of whom he had dealt with for years; he knew they would receive Flavius with patience and kindness.

A consignment of olive oil arrived from the farm in Latium, and it was time for Flavius to meet the olive oil merchant. Flavius was nervous as the loaded cart, driven by Atticus, drew up close to the market stalls. Atticus and Flavius climbed down from the wagon as the merchant stallholder stepped forward. Atticus introduced Flavius and told the merchant that from now on, Flavius would be in charge of the business side of Senator Claudius' estate. The proprietor could see immediately that Flavius was of the patrician class and greeted him with due respect.

Flavius tried hard to overcome his nervousness. Atticus stood back, only interfering when asked to by his young master to clarify a point during the negotiations. A sum of money was agreed and the merchant called on his helpers to unload the amphorae containing the oil. Flavius and Atticus moved out of their way. The merchant prepared an invoice to be given to the Senator and handed it to Flavius, stating that the money for the goods would be transferred to the bank in the usual way.

Flavius and Atticus got back up onto the cart and moved off. With his head held high, the merchant looked around at the other merchants watching jealously nearby, knowing that they had seen him dealing directly with a member of the upper class. Surely, when word spread, as he knew it would, it could only enhance his business.

Several nights later, as Flavius was dealing with the merchant again, he saw two men hurrying along nearby. One he recognised as Marius, while the other was a heavily-cloaked man whose face was hidden by a voluminous hood. Both were being protected by a bodyguard. The light of the torch carried by the slave accompanying them, briefly illuminated the bodyguard's face, who, on seeing Flavius looking at him, quickly turned his face away.

Flavius watched as the men disappeared into the crowd. He thought the bodyguard looked like the disgraced Prefect Alae, Antonius, but that was impossible; Pilate had sentenced him to work in the Libyan mines months before. Nevertheless, he felt distinctly uncomfortable and was glad when his business was completed.

CHAPTER TWENTY

It was early November. Although chill winds blew off the Tiber, the unpleasant smell of human sweat, animal dung and accumulated piles of household waste dumped down alleyways permeated the air.

On one particular visit to the marketplace, Flavius, having completed his business with the olive-oil merchant, decided he needed to wash the rancid smell and taste of the city out of his parched mouth. He told Atticus to take the now-empty cart, together with the invoice, back to the villa, saying that he would stay behind to visit a friend. Then he made his way to the Poseidon tavern, hoping to see Decimus there. He wanted to find out if there was any news of Pilate.

He was disappointed to find Decimus was not there, but he decided to stay anyway to have that much-needed drink. He sat down at a table, pondering what he had witnessed. Who was the bodyguard who had reminded him of Antonius? Was the hooded man Caligula? It was definitely Marius walking with them. They had probably been making their way to some illicit bawdy house. He and Decimus knew their preference for brothels and wild parties in unsavoury places.

As he drank the last of his wine, Decimus arrived, saw Flavius sitting there and wearily sat down beside him. "I've been trying to see you for the past few weeks," said a relieved Flavius. He ordered a jug of wine and another goblet to be brought to their table.

"I have hardly had time to breathe, let alone have time for leisure," Decimus replied. "Macro has had us running around all over the place keeping watch on people he thinks want to bring down the Emperor." He shook his head. "All thanks to his Chief Spy, Aquila. That man sees assassins everywhere."

Decimus drank deeply, wiped his mouth with the back of his hand and changed the subject. "Have you been to any of the Plebeian Games, Flavius?"

Flavius shook his head. "No, I have not had the time. Have you?"

"I was given some time off yesterday, the first day of the chariot races. I even won a bet on the Green Racing Team. They were magnificent. I'll have to miss the last two races though."

"What about the plays and the athletic entertainments held on the previous days?"

"No, I was too busy keeping an eye on one of Macro's suspects. I was sorry to miss the athletic contests, but I wasn't bothered at all about missing out on the plays." He laughed. "You've known me long enough. When have I ever been interested in all that boring theatrical stuff? Not exciting enough for me." He took a sip of his wine. "I was on duty at the ritual Feast to Jupiter on the first day of the Games. A fat, pompous Senator sat at table on the Capitoline Hill gorging himself with plate after plate of food, all courtesy of public funds, of course, while the common plebs made do with smaller portions down in the Forum." He took another drink. "Makes my blood boil. Still, the plebs seem to put up with it. In any case, they get more than we Praetorians do when we're on duty."

Flavius felt uncomfortable at that statement. He remembered when it had been his father sitting at that table on the Capitoline Hill and at that time, he had been proud to see him there. Now, after his own recent unfortunate experiences, he was beginning to understand the vast differences between the patrician and plebeian lifestyles. He said matter-of-factly, "Do you have any information about Pilate, or his wife, the Lady Claudia Procula?"

"I was on duty the day Pilate came to the Imperial Palace. I saw Pilate and another Tribune go in to see the Emperor." He shook his head. "But there was no woman with them, so I don't know what happened to her."

Flavius silently prayed that Lady Claudia was somewhere safe, preferably away from Rome. He did not know that she had been spirited away from the city by her friends soon after her husband's arrest.

"All I know about Pilate is that he was taken to a house in the Aventine District and placed under house arrest there." Decimus finished his wine, placed his goblet on the table ready for a refill then continued, "But there are several rumours running around..."

Flavius sat forward. "What rumours?"

"One says that Pilate was killed by the Praetorians guarding him in the house, another that he committed suicide, yet another that the Emperor relented and set him free in lieu of his long service. The choice is yours. Only the Emperor and Macro know the truth. I doubt we ever will."

Flavius frowned. "What happened to the Tribune that was with him?"

"Tribune Paullus, I think his name was. He was taken to the Mamertine Prison and was apparently murdered in his cell by his guards."

Paullus – Flavius was familiar with that name. He had disliked the Tribune on sight, but thought he did not deserve to die like that.

Decimus gestured to a boy serving wine at a table close by. "Bring us another jar of wine." He held out the empty jar. The boy was soon back with the refilled jar and laid it on the table. Decimus poured it into their goblets. "Speaking of Macro, it is my belief that he is falling out of favour with the Emperor."

"What makes you say that?" Flavius asked, surprised.

"I was on duty outside the Audience Chamber when I heard Caligula threatening Macro with execution if he did not address him as Divinity."

Flavius frowned. "When did Caligula make himself a god?"

Decimus leaned forward, lowering his voice, "It was just after he had recovered from his illness. He suddenly announced that he was the living version of our most revered god, Jupiter. It seems our 'divine' Caesar," Decimus said, with a hint of sarcasm in his voice, "wants a temple built in his honour, with his own chosen priests, and with a golden statue of himself placed inside it so he can be worshipped by everyone in Rome." He shook his head. "Even the great Augustus Caesar was not made a god until after he was dead."

Decimus shook his head. "I have seen some indescribable things going on in that palace, things that have turned my blood to ice, even as a seasoned soldier. Sometimes it is like being in the worst kind of whore house. At other times we have been ordered to inflict the most brutal tortures on those who have supposedly upset Caligula, but who I think are innocent victims chosen just to satisfy his bloodlust."

Decimus gulped down his wine as though he wished to wash away the memories of what he had witnessed and had been ordered to carry out. He wiped his mouth with the back of his hand and said, "I tell you Flavius, I don't know what horror is coming next. I think we're being ruled by someone on the brink of madness."

Unsettled by his friend's words, Flavius drank down the last of his wine. "It's getting late. I think I had best go home. I will see you again soon, Decimus. In the meantime, take care of yourself."

"You too, Flavius."

All the way home, Flavius anxiously pondered what Decimus had told him. He decided he would speak to Claudius about it in the morning.

When he was told, Claudius shook his head. "The Senate too is aware of these rumours surrounding the Emperor," he said. "We Senators are worried, but what can we do? Caligula gets to hear about every word that is spoken in the Senate. No one dares to speak out against him." He sat at his desk and looked up at a grim-faced Flavius standing before him. "All we can do, Flavius, is pray to the gods and hope that they intervene and stop this madness before Caligula brings this city, and the Empire, to its knees."

Claudius forced a smile. "Let us speak of more pleasant things. It will soon be time for the Saturnalia Festival." He picked up a stylus and took a series of scrolls from out of his desk drawer. "I will miss Claudio's presence, but I intend to make a merry time of it. After all, we need all the fun we can get these days and I think you and your dear mother need a little happiness in your life too. It's been a hard time for you both."

He opened one of the scrolls. "Now, if you will excuse me Flavius, I need to start writing out the invitations for the feast. I think a personal note from me and not something dictated to and copied by a scribe will be very well received by my guests. Besides, I need to ask a special favour of my would-be business associates." He saw Flavius' quizzical look and added, "I am going to ask them to serve the food and wine to my Senator guests and their wives at the feast."

Shocked at this idea, Flavius blurted out, "What if they say no?"

Claudius smiled. "If they wish to continue to have my patronage, they will obey. These people with whom I act as Patron know that they can come to me and I will support them in a number of ways, including financially, if so required. On the other hand, I benefit by getting their votes in return for these favours, so everybody wins."

Flavius thought this bordered on blackmail, but he stayed silent. He thanked Claudius again and went to find his mother to tell her the good news.

CHAPTER TWENTY-ONE

Claudius told his slaves they could rest on the Saturnalia Feast Day, so they worked late into the night preparing the villa for the forthcoming festivities. He was determined to lay on a magnificent celebration for the god Saturn to impress those guests who had accepted his personal invitation.

The next morning, Flavius and Lydia Flavia accompanied Claudius and Claudia to the Temple of Saturn to take part in the rituals and sacrifices associated with the ancient custom honouring that god. They watched as the hollow statue of the god was filled with olive oil, a symbol of his agricultural functions, and his feet, bound with woollen strips, were ceremoniously unbound. When the rituals had been completed, the Senators, including Claudius, cried out 'Io Saturnalia!' Hearing that, the excited crowd outside quickly dispersed and returned to their homes, eager to begin their own celebrations.

When they returned to Claudius' villa, they were delighted by the sight that greeted them. Overseen by Atticus, Claudius' slaves had transformed the villa and its gardens into a magical place. Silver stars were fixed to the trees and shrubs in the gardens; a huge green wreath had been placed over the villa door, and swathes of greenery hung from the roof. The atrium walls were hung with garlands with silver stars adorning them and a row of green branches surrounded the rainwater pool. A garland had been hung around the neck of a statue of Saturn standing nearby.

Flavius thought the decorations here were even more luxurious than those used at the Caesarea Palace. Although it had been two years ago, he remembered that Pilate had disregarded the ancient custom and had not changed places with a servant to conduct the evening celebrations and feast. He wondered if a powerful man like Claudius would do so.

As the household gathered around the statue of Saturn, Claudius intoned the appropriate prayers to the god and then poured a libation of olive oil over the statue's marble head. Following the ritual, a suckling pig was sacrificed to the god. Then Claudius suggested that they might like to rest before they began readying themselves for the night's festivities.

Back in his room, Flavius looked at the presents he

had bought for his mother, Claudius and Claudia. He had managed to accumulate some savings from the allowance he received from Claudius, but the presents had cost less than those he had purchased for Pilate and Lady Claudia. He examined the gift he had bought for his mother, a silver brooch designed as a cornucopia, the symbol of abundance and plenty, in homage to Saturn's sister/wife, the goddess Ops. His gift to Claudius was a silver wine cup with Saturn, holding his customary sickle, engraved on it. Finally, the dainty star-shaped silver earrings were for Claudia. He was satisfied that they were presentable and would be well received.

Later that evening the guests began to arrive. All were dressed in clothing suitable for the Festival: tunics with gaudy patterns or in different shades of green for the men and gowns of green with either silver or gold edging for the women, whose elaborate hairstyles were held in place by beautiful hair decorations. Flute-players entertained the gathering guests, creating a happy atmosphere filled with greetings and laughter.

Flavius escorted his mother into the room. She looked resplendent in a new emerald green gown edged with silver, a Saturnalia present given to her by Claudius. Flavius wore a new tunic in deep bronze with a dark green leather belt fixed around his waist – both presents from Claudius.

The chattering stopped, replaced by applause as Claudius and his daughter made their entrance, her hand resting lightly on his arm. Flavius smiled as Claudius acknowledged him and Lydia Flavia. Claudius was dressed modestly, and Flavius assumed that he would be acting the servant that evening. He wondered who would be the master of ceremonies in his place. He returned Claudia's smile. She looked elegant in her silver dress edged with gold. This was not the tomboy he remembered from his youth, but a girl who had grown into a gracious lady.

A loud clash of cymbals sounded from the atrium, announcing the arrival of the 'Master of Ceremonies'. A burst of applause resounded around the room as, with his head held high, Atticus walked into the room. He was dressed in a splendid robe with silver slippers on his large feet. Cries of 'Bravo!' came from the assembled gathering as he took his seat. Claudius stepped forward and gave him a cursory bow. As was the custom, Claudius had supplied his slaves with food and wine to enable them to celebrate in their quarters. He would be in charge of serving his guests.

He clapped his hands and several of his wealthy business associates came in carrying silver jugs and proceeded to pour their contents of expensive wine into eagerly held-out silver wine cups. They then stood back ready to refill them when they were empty. Soon after, more of Claudius' associates carried in platters containing piles of fresh oysters surrounded by other shellfish. Cheers went up when the next course of suckling pigs was served up. For the final savoury course four men carried in, on a huge platter, an enormous wild boar, surrounded by spicy sausages. It was met with applause.

After the savoury courses had been eaten, a huge cake shaped like a swan was brought in, its head topped by a silver crown. The ladies sighed with delight when they saw it, and some of the male guests stood up, unsteady on their feet through the copious amounts of wine they had drunk, and voiced their approval of the magnificent, artistic skills of the baker.

The evening wore on with much merriment and delight at the feast their host had provided. Everyone had eaten and drunk well, but not to the extent of them having to visit the vomitorium Claudius had set up in an outer room. The feast finished, Atticus was unceremoniously carried in to another room where he would preside over the entertainment Claudius had arranged.

Gambling tables had been set up, some with dice or knucklebones. Various board games were also available, including a game called 'a game of twelve lines' where each player had three dice and fifteen small counters to move around the board, and a game of strategy called the 'game of brigands', which had pieces of glass in different colours as counters, the winner being the one who had 'captured' the most pieces of glass. Upon seeing these, the male guests eagerly went to the tables and began to lay down bets against each other.

Their wives did not usually participate in such entertainments, so they sat down on couches in another room and gossiped amongst themselves.

Flavius played at the tables, and smiled to himself as

one of the guests shouted an expletive when the dice did not roll in his favour. After a while he became bored. It was hot in the room and he had drunk far too much wine than was usual for him. He needed some fresh air to clear his head, so he wandered out into the garden. The silver stars affixed to the trees and bushes gleamed in the bright moonlight. He leaned on the edge of the fountain and held out his hands, letting the water pouring out from the Triton's mouth splash over them, cooling him down.

This had been a fun evening, so unlike the Saturnalia party Pilate had thrown at the palace in Caesarea. Here there were no young junior officers chasing after pretty girls, and no tension caused by the unexpected arrival of Calpurnius Aquila, who had clearly had a big impact on Pilate's mood that night.

He remembered the pretty young girl he had encountered weeping in the palace gardens who had been abandoned by her young escort, Marcus. That girl had turned out to be Julia Cornelia, the sister of Decurion Julius, a young Decurion he had befriended at the Fortress Antonia in Jerusalem, and the daughter of Centurion Cornelius stationed at the fortress in Caesarea. He and Cornelius had become good friends.

It had taken him a while to get to like Marcus because of his bad behaviour towards Julia, but after the battle of Beth-Horon, the young man had matured and calmed down. He wondered, now that they were married, how life was for him and Julia. They probably had a young family now.

He frowned. What had brought back those memories? That had happened two years ago. He had a sudden thought. He had not had time to see Cornelius to tell him of his unexpected return to Rome. He must have thought him rude to leave without a word of apology at missing Julia's wedding. Now that he had a settled address, for the foreseeable future anyway, he wondered if he should write and tell Cornelius where he was. He decided not to, in case his letter was intercepted by Aquila. If Caligula found out, it would place Claudius and his family in danger. He shivered, and icy fingers slid down his back. He decided to return inside.

Claudia saw Flavius re-enter the games room. She thought he had a far-away look in his eyes, as if he was remembering something, or someone. She wondered what or who it might be, but was instantly contrite; whatever, or whoever, it was, it was none of her business. Nevertheless, with a worried expression on her face, she walked over to him and said in a concerned voice, "Is anything wrong, Flavius? Are you feeling unwell?"

Flavius was embarrassed. Were his concerns and thoughts so transparent? He gave a half-hearted smile and said, "No, there is nothing wrong, Claudia, I am quite well. I was just hot and needed some fresh air, that's all. But thank you for asking."

Claudius saw the pair talking together and a smile spread across his face. An idea came into his head and his smile grew wider. When the time was right, he would broach the subject and see their reaction.

Lydia Flavia saw the couple talking together. She also saw Claudia's expression as she looked at Flavius. It was obvious she had feelings for him. She decided to keep her thoughts to herself, knowing that if Flavius had anything to say about his intentions towards Claudia, he would come to her and tell her.

CHAPTER TWENTY-TWO

The festival dedicated to the two-faced god Janus, heralding the beginning of another year, was celebrated in style at Claudius' villa. As the winter wore on, Claudius hosted several more receptions for his friends. Flavius noticed that he was always seated next to Claudia at these receptions. He also noted that Claudius was growing ever more attentive to his mother. He wondered what was in the Senator's mind, hoping his mother would not be drawn into something she did not want.

After a wet and cold winter, it was a relief when spring arrived. Flavius was kept busy overseeing the deliveries of olive oil and other goods from Claudius' farm in Latium and keeping the associated bookwork up to date. He had come to know many of the merchants he dealt with by name and they in turn had come to respect him. Claudius was pleased by this, as he was sure that when the time came for Flavius to enter politics, their votes would be assured.

Flavius often felt suffocated and restricted at the villa and was relieved to spend time in the market place dealing with the hard-working merchants. When the business was complete, he would sometimes meet up with Decimus at the Poseidon. Decimus kept him entertained with gossip about Caligula and the latest scandals at the palace.

One particular night, as Flavius was completing his business in the market place, he heard a voice behind him say "So, this is how you spend your nights. A bit different from being an important Tribune, isn't it?"

Flavius bristled at the jibe. He turned round and saw Decimus grinning at him. Surprised, Flavius said, "Where are you off to?"

"The Poseidon, of course. It's been a heavy day and I'm parched. Are you coming?"

Flavius turned to the merchant and said, "I think all is in order concerning the goods I have just delivered to you." The merchant nodded, handed Flavius the invoice and said, "Yes, sir." Flavius gave the invoice to Atticus and saw the suspicious look he was giving Decimus. "It's all right, Atticus, he's a friend," he said quickly. "Take the cart and this invoice back to your master, I'll come home later."

Still looking doubtful, Atticus bowed his head, climbed up onto the cart and urged the oxen forward.

Flavius and Decimus made their way to their favourite tavern. As they walked, Decimus said, "How come you have got mixed up in commercial life? And who are you working for?" Flavius explained that as his army pay had been taken away from him, a family friend had become his patron and this was his way of repaying him. He was careful not to say who the patron was.

They reached the tavern to find that it was busy. They leaned on the counter until a table became available. Flavius asked quietly, "Is there any further news of Pilate?"

Decimus shook his head. "No. But I have other things to tell you that might interest you."

"What things?" Flavius asked, wondering what had happened now. He was staggered when Decimus replied, "It's not common knowledge yet, but we Praetorians have heard a rumour that Macro is dead."

"Dead? How? When?"

A table became free and they walked to it and sat down. Flavius ordered the wine. Making sure he could not be overheard, Decimus continued, "All we know is that a few days ago, he had a blazing argument with Caligula. Apparently the shouting could be heard all over the palace." He hesitated as the wine arrived. He took a drink, then continued. "We heard on the grapevine that soon after, he went home, then took his own life. Whether it was because he had fallen out of favour and would not have the Emperor's backing if he were to face punishment for his many crimes, or whether Caligula, in a fit of temper, ordered him to do it, we can't be sure. Whatever the reason, we now believe the rumour to be true."

"What makes you so sure he is dead?"

"Because no one has seen him since the day he left the palace after the argument."

"If Macro's dead, then who will take his place as head of the Praetorian Guard?"

"We don't know for sure, but Cassius Charea was summoned to the palace yesterday. He served as a Tribune in the legions commanded by Caligula's father, Germanicus, and was commended for his bravery in the Germanic wars, so it's highly likely that Caligula will choose him to take Macro's place."

"Is he a decent officer?"

"Seems to be. I know he's tough, but there's nothing wrong in that. The trick is to try and stay on the good side of him and keep your head down."

"Well, I'm sure you'll find out if he is your new officer soon." Flavius finished his wine. "It's been a long day and a busy night. I'm going home to my bed." He stood up, clasped arms with Decimus, and then made his way home.

CHAPTER TWENTY-THREE

Caligula lay in his bed. He was in a foul mood. Anger and frustration had disturbed his sleep and he was suffering from a bad headache. Since his illness, his headaches seemed to be growing worse; even his doctors could do nothing for him except try different medicines and concoctions, none of which were working.

He blamed his frustration on that disobedient little minx Diana. Last night, during his nightly walk in his gardens, he had called out to the goddess, inviting her into his bed, but she had declined to visit him. Angry that she had disobeyed her lord and master, the supreme god, Jupiter, he resolved to make the Huntress pay. He would order the Consuls, Senators and the people of Rome to ignore her statue and the temple dedicated to her for the next few weeks, or face imprisonment. The order would be announced in the Forum within the hour.

His anger was also directed towards Macro, who had dared to disobey his Emperor's instruction to worship him as a god and had failed to call him Divinity when addressing him. The insult had been too great to bear and had left him no choice but to dismiss him from his service. He frowned. But why did he have to die? Surely the fool could not have taken his Emperor's request to kill himself seriously, could he? Why had he not realised that his master's bad mood had been caused by the excruciating pain in his head, when even the slightest sound caused him agony? Macro should have just humbly kept out of his way until his pain had subsided and he had calmed down.

How he missed the trusted friend who had helped him through so many dangerous situations, as well as ensuring he gained the throne and the Empire from Tiberius. Perhaps they would meet again in the afterworld and Macro would once again serve his master, this time as a protector to Jupiter.

He gave a deep sigh, then called for his slaves, who hurried into the room ready to do their Emperor's bidding. When he had breakfasted and been bathed and dressed, he went to the Audience Chamber ready to receive the first client of the day.

It turned out to be a tedious morning for Caligula. His mood did not lighten, rather it grew darker as each client who presented their case to him seemed to be demanding more and more from him financially and emotionally, bleeding him dry. The last person to see him, an ambassador from

Greece, was unceremoniously dismissed by Caligula before he even opened his mouth. The shocked and embarrassed man quickly left the room. Caligula called for Antonius, who waited, as always, in the secret corridor adjoining the room, in case of any trouble.

Antonius strode into the room and bowed before Caligula. Knowing what had happened to Macro, he was careful to address his master correctly. "How may I be of service to you, Divinity?" he asked.

Caligula lightly touched his forehead to try to soothe the ache in his head, which had been made worse by the chatter and endless supplications of the tiresome people he had been forced to deal with. He said, "I need some fresh air, to take away the smell of those common people. I wish to walk in my gardens. You will accompany me, Leon."

Antonius bowed and followed Caligula outside. Antonius stayed close to his master, for he knew that some of the Praetorian Guards had been angry about the death of their former Commander and might wish to harm the person they blamed for his demise. Caligula was not aware of this, but Antonius had kept his ears and his eyes open. He had seen the scowls on the faces of some of the Praetorians and heard whispers from loose-lipped slaves.

The pain in Caligula's head grew worse. He suddenly announced that he was returning to his apartments and retreating to his bed.

Antonius followed Caligula as he walked down the corridor leading to his bedroom. Antonius felt a cold stab of fear when he saw Calpurnius Aquila hurrying towards them. He knew from the expression on Aquila's face that he had recognised him, despite his beard and long hair.

Aquila stopped in his tracks when he saw who was guarding the Emperor. How in the gods' names had Antonius escaped from the Libyan salt mines and ended up here in Rome, in the palace, and seemingly close to the Emperor? He was obviously here under false pretences and had somehow wormed his way into the Emperor's confidence.

Caligula felt the tension in the air between the two men and turned to Aquila. "Is something wrong?" he asked.

Aquila knew he would have to get rid of Antonius before he told the Emperor about his devious activities. He said, "Antonius, by what miracle of the gods have you escaped from the mines?"

Caligula stiffened at the news. He stared at Aquila and said, "Antonius? The mines? What are you talking about, Aquila?"

Aquila could scarcely look at Caligula. "Divinity, the man standing with you is a disgraced Prefect Alae from your Legions, a convicted criminal and would-be murderer. He was sentenced by Pontius Pilate to serve in the Libyan Salt Mines. How he has escaped and come to Rome only the gods know."

Caligula turned to Antonius. "Is this true? Is your name really Antonius? Are you guilty of the things Aquila has accused you of?"

Antonius was struggling to stay calm. He looked directly at Caligula and replied, "Yes, Divinity, my name is Antonius and Pilate did send me to the mines in Libya, but as far as my so-called crimes are concerned, everything I did was at the request of Aquila. I was one of his agents and brought him news of many things, amongst them the names of people who had conspired against our late Emperor Tiberius, may he rest peacefully amongst the gods." He saw Caligula frown and continued, "I was set free in Libya because I was one of those people pardoned by your own edict when you first came to the throne."

Caligula thought for a moment. "Ah yes, I did pass that edict," he said. He straightened up and said sternly, "How did you get into the palace?"

"By showing my skills as a builder to your Master Builder. He was impressed by my work and offered me a job working in and around the palace."

"I see." Caligula turned to face Aquila. "Did you check to see who the new builder was?"

Aquila tried desperately to keep his voice steady. "No, Divinity. I know the Master Builder to be a careful man, if he thought it fitting to offer this man a job…" He shrugged, then blanched as he saw Caligula's doubtful look. "Besides, Divinity, how could I know that Antonius had been freed from the mines and was able to travel wherever he wanted?"

Caligula gave Aquila a steely glare. "As my Chief Spy, it is your duty to discover and stop any potential threat to my safety. You have failed me."

Aquila bowed. "Forgive me, Divine One."

"I will think about it." Caligula sneeringly replied. He turned to Antonius. "As for you, you have lied to me, your name is not Leon. I placed my safety in the hands of, in Aquila's words, a would-be murderer, and that I cannot allow to go unpunished." He called out for the guards and almost instantly four Praetorians appeared. "Seize that man!" he said, pointing to Antonius.

As the guards tried to grab hold of him, Antonius cried out, "But surely you know, Divine Caesar, that Aquila's word cannot be trusted."

Caligula raised a hand and the guards stood back. "What do you mean by that?"

Antonius smiled as he saw the sweat break out on Aquila's brow. Now! This was the time to tell of his long-held suspicion about where the money had come from to pay for his work as Aquila's spy. If he was wrong it did not matter, because he would have sown a seed of doubt in Caligula's mind. He took a deep breath and said, "I am sure that Aquila has been embezzling money from the Royal Treasury, probably for years, falsifying the accounts so that your auditors would find no trace of his treachery."

Caligula was stunned by this news. "How do you know this?"

"Because, Divinity, it was that money that paid for my services as a spy in Judaea. He told me at the time that what I did for him had nothing to do with the State. Perhaps he has also made a nest-egg for himself."

Caligula turned on a now quaking Aquila and said through tight lips, "Is this true, Aquila?"

"Divine one," Aquila blustered, "surely you do not believe this felon's false accusations? It is obvious that he is trying to deflect the blame from his own guilty secret onto me."

Caligula said, "Can you prove that Leon – Antonius – whatever his name is, is lying?" He studied Aquila's face closely and saw terror-filled eyes staring back at him. "No, I do not believe you can. There is guilt written all over your face. Furthermore, I cannot forgive, or forget, your negligence in failing to check up on a man who might have murdered me." He turned to the guards. "Take them both to the Mamertine. I will decide on their punishments when I am ready."

As the guards dragged the prisoners down the corridor, Caligula shouted after them, "Arrest the Master Builder and the Praetor in charge of the Imperial Treasury too. Let them join the others in prison!"

His head pounding, Caligula went to his bedroom and collapsed on his bed, vowing to make the people who had caused him so much stress that day pay dearly for it. Especially Aquila. Macro had reported seeing the Chief Spy speaking to Flavius. What had he been saying to him? Had he given away his secret? He decided that Aquila would have to be executed as quickly as possible.

When Claudius came home from the Senate, he told

Flavius that Calpurnius Aquila had been arrested and was facing the death penalty. Flavius could find no sympathy for the man, convinced that it was the Chief Spy who had falsely denounced his father to the Emperor Tiberius as a conspirator and was responsible for his suicide.

"But the most interesting part of the story is that the Master Builder will also be executed for negligence by allowing a criminal to work as a builder at the palace, a man who then became a bodyguard to Caligula," Claudius went on. "The criminal called himself Leon, but is in reality an ex-Prefect Alae called Antonius, who had been sent by Pontius Pilate to the Libyan salt mines as punishment for several crimes he committed whilst in the Tenth Fretensis, your old legion, Flavius. Did you ever come across him?"

Flavius was stunned. His imagination had not played tricks on him; it was indeed Antonius he had seen when he had been dealing with the merchant all those weeks ago. How had Antonius reached Rome? And how had he wormed his way into the palace, ending up in the Emperor's service? He frowned, remembering Antonius' cruel behaviour, especially against Julius and Drubaal.

"Yes, I knew him," he said coldly. "He deserved to be sent to the mines. But how in the name of Mars was he set free?"

Claudius shrugged. "When Caligula had the edict published saying that he was giving clemency to certain criminals, it seems this Antonius was one of the people on Caligula's list."

"Is he facing execution too?"

"His name has not appeared on the list of those to be executed, and neither has that of the Praetor, who is also involved. Perhaps the Emperor has other plans for them."

"When are the trials due to take place?"

Claudius replied grimly, "The Emperor has decreed that there will be no trial."

Flavius shook his head in disbelief. Even an Emperor had no right to ignore the Roman justice system that had been adhered to for centuries.

Claudius grimaced. "Caligula thinks he is above the law. He has decided that the men involved are guilty and has demanded they be executed tomorrow morning. A platform is being set up on the concourse leading to the Temple of Concordia Augusta near to the Rostra, Forum and the Senate House so that the general public can watch the show." He said the last word disdainfully. "He thinks the Temple concourse is a fitting place for them to die as the Temple was dedicated by Tiberius, and its construction was paid for by his grandfather, Drusus, to celebrate the harmony, security and prosperity of the Imperial Family. Now that his security has been threatened both financially and personally he can think of no other place." He looked at Flavius. "Will you go to see the executions tomorrow?"

Flavius remembered the horror of the executions of ben-Ezra and the other members of his gang at Skull Place in Jerusalem and suppressed a shudder. He said, "I don't think so."

Claudius was surprised. "I thought you would want to see justice carried out on the man who most certainly had a hand in your father's death."

The barb hit home. "Then I will see it and be glad."

CHAPTER TWENTY-FOUR

Antonius stood before his Emperor. He was worried. Why had he been brought from the Mamertine? What punishment was he to face?

Caligula got up from his throne and walked around him. He squeezed Antonius' arm and leg muscles and stroked his thick neck, then smiled. "I do not want you executed," he said. "It would be a waste of a magnificent body. I have a better idea."

Antonius tensed, wondering what Caligula had in mind for him.

"You will go to Capua to train as a gladiator. You will fight in my name and for every contest that you win, the money you earn will go into my coffers."

Antonius could not help but protest. "But Divine One, I have no knowledge of the arena. What if I do not make the grade as a gladiator?"

Caligula turned on him, shouting furiously, "You will! Capua has the finest reputation for producing the best gladiators in the Empire. The Lanista and chief trainer of the school will be told to train you personally until they think you are perfect. That is my order."

"But..."

"Enough! You fought in the Legions for many years. I know you have the strength, the will and the ferocity to do this." He smiled, "Or perhaps you would rather face execution."

Antonius thought he would die in the arena in any case, but, if properly trained, he might have a chance of survival. After all, he had fought in several battles and survived them. He bowed his head and said, "Let it be as you say, Divinity."

Caligula called for more Praetorians, including Cassius Charea, and barked out, "Take this man away. At dawn tomorrow he is to be transported to the Gladiatorial School at Capua." As the Guards grabbed hold of Antonius, Caligula said, "Stay here, Charea."

Charea listened as Caligula gave him the order concerning the punishment of the Praetor who had been in charge of the Imperial Treasury. Caligula was too angry to give clemency to someone he thought of as the basest traitor. Many of the previous Praetors who had helped Aquila in his crime had died or moved to a different part of the Empire. Tracing their whereabouts would cost the Treasury an enormous amount of money, a price he was not prepared to pay. He decided that it was cheaper to have their crimes added to this present Praetor's own.

As Antonius was beginning his journey under guard to Capua, the Praetor was being taken to the banks of the River Tiber, where the guards forced the struggling official into a large sack. He whimpered as the top of the sack was quickly sewn together, making it impossible for him to escape. Two Praetorians lifted the sack and threw it into the river. The Praetorians laughed as the sack slowly disappeared below the water.

Later that morning, Flavius mingled with the crowd who waited excitedly for the executions to begin. Double rows of Praetorian Guards surrounded the platform, ready to stop the bloodthirsty mob from getting too close and to deter those who might try to rescue the prisoners. Flavius saw Decimus standing in the front row of the guards and noted that although Decimus stood ramrod straight, his eyes were constantly scanning the crowd, watching for any troublemakers.

Flavius looked at the platform. A fixed post stood in the middle, together with a table set to the side on which were laid various instruments of torture. Trying to focus his mind on more pleasant things, Flavius looked up at the magnificent Temple of Concordia Augusta, which stood on top of a large, wide, marble staircase. Two thrones had been placed above the top step of the staircase, obviously one for Caligula who, he thought, would relish the sight of blood, the other for his new Empress, his second wife, Livia Orestilla. He wondered what kind of monster would bring a woman to witness such barbarity, unless, of course, she too revelled in the sight and smell of blood. Four smaller ornate chairs stood nearby.

He admired the beautifully-crafted statues of the goddess of security and stability, Securitas, the goddess of luck, Fortuna, his own family's deity, and of Concordia herself, the goddess of harmony. All stood on the apex of the pediment of the temple. He grimaced at the thought of such beauty being desecrated by the horror he knew was about to take place below those magnificent works of art.

More Praetorians appeared and took their places either side of the staircase. Trumpets sounded and the two elected Consuls of that year, closely followed by the members of the Senate, including Claudius Marcellus, walked out of the temple and congregated to the side of the thrones. They were joined by Praetors, Prefects and other officials. A second fanfare of trumpets sounded and Caligula, dressed in his full Emperor regalia and followed by his lavishly dressed and bejewelled Empress, came out from the Temple where they had been offering prayers to Caligula's ancestors. The crowd gave a mighty cheer as they seated themselves on their thrones. They were followed by the two remaining sisters of Caligula, Julia Livilla and Agrippina the Younger, the third, Julia Drusilla, his favourite sister, having died of an illness some months before. To the horror of the Senate, Caligula had ordered her to be buried with full honours as his wife, then had her deified as a goddess. One of the prayers offered up in the temple today had been for her. The two sisters bowed their heads to their brother and his Empress then sat down on their chairs.

Next came Caligula's uncle, Tiberius Claudius Nero Germanicus, the brother of Caligula's father, Germanicus. The elder member of the Imperial Family limped across to one of the chairs. A pretty young girl walked behind him and sat down on the chair next to him.

Flavius heard a rough voice close by say, "What a vision of loveliness! Such a waste! Fancy Caligula marrying off such a young beauty to that gibbering old goat Claudius." A second voice replied, "Typical of the Emperor. She's a luscious little thing. I'm jealous of Claudius. What's her name again?"

"Messalina," came the first man's reply.

The second man said, "Well, I feel sorry for her. It must be like bedding her father." He made a face.

Flavius had to agree with the men. She was indeed very pretty and innocent looking. Caligula must have once again indulged himself by playing cruel practical jokes on people, 'jokes' that ultimately ruined their lives.

Suddenly all talking stopped as mournful drumbeats sounded in the distance. The drumbeats grew louder as a grim procession made its way down from the Mamertine prison, set on the north eastern slope of the Capitoline Hill. The procession detoured to the bottom of the Sacred Way, so that the condemned might be seen by all those who could not get near to the platform, a dire warning that this is what would happen if they disobeyed their Emperor.

The prisoners, dragged along in chains by guards, were led up the Sacred Way towards the place of execution. Certain members of the public mocked and jeered them as they passed by, but some of the crowd turned their faces away, horrified at seeing the prisoners' tortured bodies as they stumbled along the way.

Flavius noticed that the accused Praetor and Antonius were not amongst the prisoners; only Aquila and the Master Builder were to be executed. Where were they? Perhaps Antonius was already dead and the Praetor had been exiled from Rome, something common for a person of high rank.

Hearing a cheer go up from the mob, Flavius turned his attention back to the platform. The Master Builder was the first to be executed. His face was bruised and bloodied where he had been brutally beaten by the prison guards. He could barely hold up his head as he stumbled up the steps of the platform. Two of the Praetorian guards, waiting on the platform, grabbed hold of him and yanked him towards the post. The chains on his hands were fixed around the post, leaving his back on view sideways to both Caligula and the crowd.

One of the guards went to the table and picked up two iron rods with wicked-looking barbs running down their length. He handed one of the rods to the other guard and the two men began to systematically beat the prisoner with them. A cheer went up from a section of the crowd as they heard the prisoner's screams.

Flavius winced as he saw the Master Builder's blood splatter all over the platform, some reaching as far as the front line of the crowd. The skin of the unfortunate man was gradually being shredded into jagged strips by the cruel barbs. At first he had screamed as the rods connected with his back, but now, through blood loss and pain, his cries were no more than a whimper. Flavius felt immense pity for a man who had only made the mistake of not checking the history of his latest recruit thoroughly enough, but he knew, as far as Caligula was concerned, that mistake was unforgivable.

Flavius was relieved when he saw the Master Builder's lacerated body slump down the post and his blood-soaked head loll to the side, knowing that death for the unfortunate man was a merciful release.

CHAPTER TWENTY-FIVE

Flavius looked up at Caligula and his family. He was sickened when he saw Caligula running his tongue over his lips as if tasting the blood and gore splattered over the platform below. The Empress' face was very pale, but his sisters sat laughing and pointing as the body of the Master Builder was unchained from the post, unceremoniously dragged off the platform and taken away by two more guards. The face of the Emperor's uncle, Claudius, had turned a nasty shade of green. He looked as if he was trying desperately not to vomit. Flavius was sure that Caligula would never forgive his uncle if he embarrassed him in front of the dignitaries and the mob.

Flavius was shocked to see that whilst her new husband sat trying to retain his dignity, Messalina was staring intently at one of the Praetorian Guards who was standing at attention on the staircase. The guard briefly caught her stare and a slow smile crossed his handsome features. Flavius frowned, knowing that if the guard's Senior Officer saw him look upon, let alone smile at, a member of the Imperial family, his punishment would be severe. The guard, obviously realising that, quickly wiped the smile off his face and looked away, forcing himself to concentrate on the crowd.

Flavius felt a light touch on his arm. He turned and saw his brother standing there, smiling. "Hello, Flavius." Marius said in a silky voice. "Come to see the way the Emperor deals with those who would harm him?"

"What do you want with me?" Flavius, scowling, answered abruptly.

"I hoped you might tell me where you are living now, as obviously it is not in *my* home, or anywhere on *my* estate."

Flavius was hard pressed to stop himself from lashing out at his brother to wipe the arrogant, self-satisfied grin off his face."

Seeing his brother's withering look, Marius took a step back and said, "I want you to come and see the improvements I have made to the place. I think you might like them." He smiled with his mouth, but his eyes were cold as he continued, "Although what you think is really of no consequence to me. Anyway, do come, and bring mother with you. I would like her to see the villa too."

Flavius said through gritted teeth, "You can go to Hades as far as I am concerned. I will not tell you where I am living and we will never set foot on the family estate again." He emphasised the word 'family'.

Marius bristled at his brother's answer, insulted that he did not want to come and see his newly-decorated property. He took it as a personal affront and answered in a tight voice, "Please yourself! It wasn't my fault that the Emperor thought I was more worthy of the inheritance than one who had served with the traitor Pilate."

Flavius watched angrily as his brother flounced off in the opposite direction and was lost in the crowd, but his attention returned to the platform as Aquila was roughly pulled up the steps by the two guards who had killed the Master Builder. As Aquila stepped onto the platform, he slipped on the blood-soaked surface, but was yanked upright by his chains. The guards then stood aside as another burly man climbed up onto the platform. He wore a thick leather apron and in his large hand he carried a meat cleaver.

Flavius shuddered as he recognised the newcomer as the Master Butcher of Rome. Flavius had seen him at work, as he had passed by his meat emporium on his way to deal with the olive oil and wine merchants. So Aquila was not to be executed by a skilled swordsman but would die ignominiously, hacked to death by a butcher. He steeled himself. This execution was going to be horrific.

The table had been cleared of torture instruments and moved in front of the post. The guards forced Aquila down onto it and fixed his chained hands to the post. They stood back as the butcher walked forward and positioned himself at Aquila's side. The butcher had been instructed by Caligula to use a blunt cleaver to make the agony of the condemned last longer. He raised the cleaver and brought it down on Aquila's right arm. Aquila screamed as the cleaver struck him. Again and again the cleaver found its mark on Aquila's limbs and body.

Some of the crowd looked away, their hands covering their ears, trying to blot out the sound of Aquila's mournful cries, which grew gradually weaker as his blood loss and pain increased.

Flavius struggled to stop his bile rising. It seemed the butcher was treating Aquila as he would an animal's carcass on his slaughter table. He looked up at Caligula, who was sitting forward on his throne, not wanting to miss a moment of the terrible scene happening below. His Empress, however, had turned her face away.

Time after time the butcher brought his cleaver down onto the dying Aquila's neck until, one last blow and the severed head, eyes wide open, rolled across the platform, stopping at the feet of a Praetorian. The Praetorian picked it up by the hair and showed it to Caligula, who clapped with delight. He turned and held it up to the crowd, who cheered loudly and roared, "Hail Caesar!"

For some it was a thank you to their Emperor for giving them a wonderful day's entertainment; for others, it was fear that if they did not show their support for Caligula, they might end up the same way as the Chief Spy and the Master Builder. For Flavius, it meant the end of the man who had caused his father's suicide.

Later that night, Claudius returned home from the Senate. He went straight to his office and sat with his head in his hands. He looked up as Flavius entered the room.

"I hope I am not disturbing you." Flavius said quietly, noting the pallor of Claudius' face.

"After witnessing such barbarity today in the name of justice, I do not think that anything can ever disturb me again," Claudius replied soberly.

"What can we do?" Flavius said wistfully. "He has the authority as Caesar to do whatever he likes to those who get in his way."

Claudius shook his head. "All we can do is pray to the gods that he will not reach old age."

"If they will listen," Flavius said bitterly. "They have already allowed him to recover from his illness and did not strike him down with a thunderbolt when he called himself Jupiter, King of the Gods."

Claudius grimaced. "For the sake of Rome's people and Empire, we can only hope that one day soon, something will happen to end this nightmare."

CHAPTER TWENTY-SIX

The latest caravan from Jerusalem arrived in Petra. Abdullah, the leader of the caravan, oversaw the unloading of goods, then went straight to the palace to beg audience with King Aretas. Standing before Aretas, Abdullah bowed his head and waited for the king to speak.

"Well, Abdullah, what is it you wish to say to me?"

"I bring news from Jerusalem and Jericho, my king." He hesitated.

"What news?" Aretas asked, keeping his impatience in check.

"It concerns Herod Antipas, Lord."

Aretas sat forward on his throne. "What trouble is he causing now?"

"Lord King, the streets are filled with the news that Antipas' nephew, Herod Agrippa, has been named as a king by the new Emperor of Rome. It is well known that

Agrippa has been a friend of the Emperor for many years. Antipas, being only a Tetrarch, was angry when he heard this news." He took a breath, then said, "Gossip also says that Herodias, the wife of Antipas..." he stopped when he saw the angry look on Aretas' face at the mention of Herodias, but continued when he saw an impatient wave of the king's hand urging him to continue. "Herodias told her husband to complain to the Emperor. It was a bad mistake. When Antipas asked if he too could be a king like his nephew, Caligula stripped him of everything and ordered his banishment to Lyon in Gaul. He has given Antipas' territories to Agrippa."

A wide smile spread across Aretas' face. "No more than that upstart deserves." His smile faded. "What of the harlot Antipas calls wife?"

"She has gone with him."

"Good riddance." Aretas stepped down from his throne and walked towards Abdullah, who stood rigid with tension, wondering if he was to be rewarded or punished for bringing this news to the King. His apprehension soon disappeared. Aretas placed a hand on his shoulder and said, "For this welcome news I will give you an emerald." He called for a servant, who quickly appeared and bowed. "Bring me my jewel box containing emeralds."

The servant bowed again, left the room then soon returned carrying a carved cedar wood box. He held it out to Aretas, who opened the box, chose a large, brilliant green emerald and gave it to Abdullah.

Lost for words, Abdullah bowed low to his master. Then, still bowing, he gradually backed away from his King.

Aretas sat back on his throne and recalled the servant, instructing him to go to Princess Phasaelis' apartments and ask her to attend him.

As Phasaelis' father told her about the downfall and exile of Antipas and Herodias, she could not stop the tears from welling up in her eyes. Even though Antipas had treated her so badly, she still kept a secret place in her heart for him, remembering the love they had once shared.

Aretas saw his daughter's distress and said quietly, "Why do you weep for such a man, one who so badly mistreated and shamed you?"

Phasaelis looked at her father. "Because in the beginning I know that he loved me as I loved him."

Aretas did not comment, for who knew the workings of a woman's heart?

Phasaelis' voice was shaky as she added, "Perhaps their disgrace is divine judgment given by the new god."

Aretas was startled. "Who is this new god you speak of?"

"I think it best you speak to our Jewish visitor from Damascus and to Ruth, father."

"I am intrigued by your words. I will have them sent for." Aretas called for a servant. "Bring Ibrahim's daughter, Ruth, to me; also the Jewish tent-maker who lives in the cave." The servant hurried off.

At first, Saul was worried about breaking Judaic Law,

but this was a king who demanded his presence. How could he refuse?

The servant brought a worried Ruth and Saul to Aretas. Aretas saw the fear on their faces and said, "There is no need to be afraid, I do not wish to harm you. I simply want you to tell me about this new god my daughter speaks of." He gazed at Saul. "Tell me, did you ever have contact with Herod Antipas?"

Saul was bemused by the question. "No, King Aretas. I never had dealings with him." Knowing that Antipas was no friend to Nabatea, he said bluntly, "But I heard many bad things said about him." Aretas gestured for Saul to repeat what he knew about his old enemy. Saul continued. "I know he was responsible for the death of John the Baptiser, whom some named as a prophet."

Phasaelis broke her silence. "I remember that time. It was just after Antipas married Herodias."

"That is true, my lady. John accused Herod of being an adulterer for marrying his half-brother Philip's wife, an accusation agreed with by many people." He paused for a brief moment. "John was a man who tried to bring the people back to our God. If they repented of their sins, he baptised them in the River Jordan to wash those sins away. I am afraid I was not amongst those people, for I thought at the time that he was wrong. As a trainee Pharisee, I spoke out against him and ranted that only God could forgive sins, not a mere man. Now I am not so sure."

Ruth could not help herself from saying, "My friends in

Jerusalem, who knew the Lord Jesus personally and spent years travelling with him, told me that when the Lord was on trial before the Jewish Temple Authorities facing their charge of blasphemy, they were determined that He should die and they sent Him to the Roman Governor, Pilate, accusing Him of sedition and for stirring up trouble. Discovering that Jesus was a Galilean born in Antipas' territory, Pilate sent him to Antipas to either condemn Him or set Him free." She continued, her voice bitter, "Antipas could have saved Him, but he was a coward and sent Him back to the Romans, who crucified Him."

Aretas shook his head and said sarcastically, "How like Antipas to behave in such a way." He looked back at Saul. "Who was this Jesus?"

Saul and Ruth between them explained who their Master was, and Aretas sat astounded. Ruth left out the part where she had been raised from the dead by the Lord, fearing that she would not be believed. When she was sure the King and his daughter fully understood, then she would tell them the truth.

Aretas was curious. "You say, this Jesus was the Son of your God?" Both nodded. "If that is true, then why did your God allow his Son to die like that? I do not understand."

Saul went on with the story, and Aretas grew ever more surprised. "He rose from his grave?"

"Yes, King Aretas," Saul replied. "That is why I am here." At Aretas' insistence, he told the story of his terrible treatment of the new converts in Jerusalem and of his own conversion on the road to Damascus, ending with why he was forced to escape from that city.

When he had finished, Aretas sat still for a long moment, then said, "Please leave me now. I have many things to think about concerning your story."

Saul and Ruth both bowed and left the palace.

Aretas turned to his daughter. "Do you believe this fantastic story?"

"Yes father, I do. When Abdullah first brought Saul to Nabatea, he said he had rescued Saul from the authorities of both Jerusalem and Damascus. Why would they want Saul dead?" She took in a breath. "Unless they were afraid that Saul was telling the truth and felt threatened by this new religion."

Aretas nodded thoughtfully. "We worship many gods, but none that I know of who have cheated death like this Jesus. I will ponder on it."

Phasaelis took her father's hand. "May I leave now, father? I have to get ready for the reception you are giving tonight for the merchants from Sheba."

"I am sure you will look even more beautiful than their fabled queen." He smiled as she blushed. Then she curtsied and returned to her apartments.

Aretas called for a servant. "Bring the Queen to me." He wanted to see what her reaction would be when he told her Saul and Ruth's stories. What was he to believe? Their telling of the story had seemed like a fantastic fable, and yet... He wondered if this new god had somehow caused his old enemy's downfall, after all, Antipas had played a part in the deaths of His prophet and His Son. Although the news had come as a welcome surprise to him, he felt anxious knowing that as the Emperor of Rome had so quickly exiled Antipas for becoming too ambitious, one day that same Emperor, or some other in the future, might grasp Nabatea with their greedy hands and hold it in an iron grip. He hoped that if that day did come, it would not be in his lifetime.

CHAPTER TWENTY-SEVEN

Julia Cornelia sat in the garden of Cornelius' house. The fragrant late spring flowers bloomed all around her, but she did not notice them, thinking only of the happy hours, too few, she had spent with Marcus. It had been almost two years since he had been killed, but every day heartache and loneliness threatened to overwhelm her. Her father and her servant, Martha, had tried everything they could to comfort and encourage her, but to no avail.

Martha came out into the garden. "Forgive me for disturbing you, mistress," she said quietly, "Cavalry Officer Linus is here. He wishes to see you."

Julia sighed. Why would he not leave her alone? She was flattered by his constant attention, knowing that his good looks and strong physical appearance had girls practically falling at his feet, but Linus was not Marcus. He had been one of Marcus' friends and had attended their wedding, where his eyes and manner had made it clear that he'd wished he had been the groom instead of his friend. It was obvious that he had feelings for her, but those feelings were not reciprocated. She wondered if now that she was a widow, he felt he was in with a chance to claim her as his own. She hoped not, for, apart from her father, there had only been two men in her life who had stirred her emotions. One was Marcus, the other Flavius Silvanus.

She remembered the first time she had seen the handsome Tribune. It had been at Pilate's Saturnalia party held at the Caesarea Palace. At the time she had barely noticed him, being more concerned with where her betrothed Marcus was. After his promotion by Pilate, he had disappeared with his friends in the direction of the extensive palace gardens. When he did not return, she went looking for him. She had wandered into the gardens overlooking the sea, and sure that he had abandoned her, she had given way to despair. Tribune Flavius had seen her. He had been so kind to her, had even ordered his litter bearers to take her home. Imagine her surprise when she discovered that he was a friend of her father and that he had invited him to attend her birthday party. Being a Tribune Laticlavius, a much higher rank than her Centurion father, she was sure he would not come. But he had. She had been sitting in this very garden with her friends when her father had introduced him. Her friends had giggled when he had smiled and spoken to her in his deep, rich voice.

A brief smile crossed her face at the memory of her embarrassment at being spoken to by the handsome, godlike figure. Even though she had loved Marcus dearly, she had never been able to fully erase Flavius from her mind.

Julius had written to her father telling him that the Tribune had suddenly left Pilate's staff. There were rumours that he had returned to Rome on family business, but that had been over two years ago. What had kept him in Rome? Had something happened to him? She wondered if she would ever see him again.

She was brought out of her reverie by Martha's insistent voice saying, "Mistress, Linus is waiting to see you."

Julia forced herself to concentrate. "I am sorry, Martha, I was thinking of…" she stopped.

"I know, mistress. You were thinking of Marcus."

Julia did not correct her. She said, "It is such a lovely day Martha, please bring Linus to me here."

Martha went back into the house, soon reappearing with Linus in tow. She then retreated back into the house, leaving them alone.

As Martha stood in the kitchen preparing food ready for the evening meal, her heart was filled with hope. It would be a relief for her poor father, as well as for herself, if Julia accepted Linus as her second husband. It was obvious to anyone that Linus was deeply in love with her. Besides, she was worried by her young mistress' melancholy, which had gone on for far too long. If marrying again solved that emptiness in Julia's heart, she would be glad.

Linus did not stay long. Martha frowned as she saw the young officer come back into the house with a grim expression on his face. He nodded to Martha, then left the house, retrieved his horse and rode quickly away. Martha sighed, then went outside to her mistress.

Julia looked at Martha with tear-filled eyes. "I cannot marry him, Martha," she said. "I admire him greatly, but I do not love him. Our marriage would be a sham." She dried her eyes. "Linus will not come here again."

Martha guessed correctly that Julia had turned down Linus' marriage proposal. She shook her head. Would her poor mistress ever be happy again?

Later that night, Cornelius came home. He was greeted by Martha, who told him what had happened between Julia and Linus. Cornelius was unhappy at his daughter's decision. He liked Linus and had hoped that he would be the one to bring Julia out of her melancholy state. He went to see Julia, who had retired to her room.

"May I come in?" he asked softly. When she replied that he could, he entered her room. She was lying on her bed, her face wet with tears. He went to her and held her in his arms. He said softly, "Oh, Julia, Julia! I cannot stand to see you like this. Marcus has been gone for two years, is it not time to marry again?" He looked into her eyes and saw the pain there.

"Please understand father, I do not love Linus." She delicately wiped her tears away with her fingers and asked pleadingly, "Why must I marry someone I do not love? For the sake of an old law passed years ago by Emperor Augustus that all widows should be remarried within two years? Well, I will not. You never married again after mother died."

"That is true," he replied. He had never wanted anyone else to take his beloved Helena's place. How could he admonish Julia for doing the same?"

An idea came to him. "Look, perhaps I can prove to you that there is more to life than sorrow and regret. I know someone who can give you words of comfort in a way I cannot. If you will allow, I will go to this man tomorrow and ask him to visit you."

Julia was surprised, but she knew her father had her best interests at heart. She also knew that her situation was hurting him too. She nodded and said, "Very well, father, I will see this man."

Cornelius smiled. "Good. I am sure his words will soothe you." Relieved, he left her. He knew where Philip usually preached and he would find him, the follower of Jesus of Nazareth, and ask him to come home with him.

Early the next morning, Cornelius, on his way to the garrison, went to the marketplace where he was sure Philip would be. He was not there. For a brief moment he panicked, fearing that Philip had been arrested and imprisoned by the authorities. He scoured the surrounding area. Breathing a sigh of relief, he suddenly saw Philip come out of a nearby house. He hurried towards him.

Philip felt Cornelius' hand on his shoulder and spun round, his face a mask of fear. He was relieved to see a face he knew, but his voice was tight as he spoke. "Centurion Cornelius. What do you want?" he said.

"I'm sorry, I didn't mean to startle you. I need your help."

Philip raised his eyebrows in surprise at the Roman's request. There had been many times when he had escaped arrest by legionaries by the skin of his teeth, and now here was one of them asking for his help. "How may I help you?" he said.

"My daughter is filled with melancholy after the death of her husband. It has gone on for too long. It is as though she has given up on life." He took a deep breath. "I have tried everything to console her, but to no avail. I have listened to your words about your Lord Jesus and I have seen how you have comforted the sick and the oppressed. Will you come home to my house and speak to her?" He looked at Philip earnestly. "You are my last hope."

Philip could see the man was distressed and worried about his daughter. It was clear to him that he loved her very much, but there was an obstacle in the way. "I am sorry, Cornelius, but I cannot come home to your house. I am forbidden by Judaic Law to enter the house of a Gentile." He felt a pang of guilt as he saw Cornelius' expression of sorrow and tried to ease it by offering an alternative solution. "If you can bring her to me, I will speak to her." He saw the Roman's look of hope and added, "I no longer go to that original marketplace because it has become too dangerous for me there. These days I move around more. My followers know where to find me. As I have learned to trust you, Cornelius, I will tell you that tomorrow I will be speaking close to the hippodrome. Until tomorrow." He walked away.

Cornelius felt a wave of relief sweep over him. Having studied many Jewish scrolls, he should have remembered the Judaic Law concerning Gentiles, but in his haste to help Julia he had pushed that information to the back of his mind. He hoped that tomorrow, she would agree to go with him to see Philip.

At first Julia had refused outright to have anything to do with a Jewish preacher. How could he help her? But on seeing the look of anguish on her father's face, she relented, and the next morning, daughter and father made their way to the hippodrome. As she neared the racetrack, she grew nervous, but Cornelius assured her there was nothing to worry about.

They found Philip standing in the shadow of the hippodrome, speaking to a group of people. Philip saw Cornelius join the eager listeners with a young woman he took to be his daughter. When he had finished what he had been saying, he turned his attention to the words of comfort spoken by the Prophets and the Lord. He began, "My friends, we live in dangerous and uncertain times, filled with anxiety and fear, but I tell you, the Most High God and His Son, the Lord Jesus, are with us, and if you truly believe, they will never leave us. Hear the words of the Prophet Jeremiah: 'For I know the plans I have for you, declares the Lord God, plans to prosper you and not to harm you. Plans to give you hope and a future.' And on the night before Jesus died, as we were sitting with Him at the last supper we shared together, He knew that He was going to die but He was still concerned for us. He said, 'Do not let your hearts be troubled. Trust in God and trust in me.' Later, He said, 'this is my parting gift to you: my own peace such as the world cannot give.' Then He repeated, 'Set your troubled hearts at rest and banish your fears'."

Philip looked directly at Julia and said, "I urge you to hear those words and believe them." Julia felt uncomfortable at this. Philip turned back to the others and said, "My friends, after Jesus was crucified, we Disciples and followers of the Lord were very afraid, wondering what would become of us. Then, after His resurrection, it was as though a great weight had been lifted from us. The Lord was victorious over death itself. We were no longer afraid, for He had bestowed His wonderful peace on us." He took a breath, looked earnestly at the eager listeners. "Do not give up hope, for surely these days will pass. Remember the Lord's words and put your trust in God and in Him." Holding up his hands in blessing, he said, "Now, I wish the Lord's peace on you all."

Some of the listeners, visibly uplifted by Philip's words, intoned, "Amen." Philip smiled as the people walked away.

All except Cornelius and Julia. Cornelius went up to

Philip and said, "Your words are like balm to a troubled mind. I hope they have had that effect on my daughter."

Philip studied Julia's face. It was clear to him that she had suffered greatly, as her eyes mirrored her troubled soul. He placed his hands on her head and quietly intoned a prayer, ending with, "May the Lord have mercy on you, may you find consolation in His enduring love."

Cornelius escorted his daughter back home, then made his way to the garrison. He desperately hoped that Julia had found comfort in the preacher's words. Julia, however, felt confused, wondering how her father had come to know this man who had spoken of love and endurance. Who was this God he spoke of? She had never heard of Him, or his Prophets and supposed Son Jesus. Would this deity take pity on her and give her the peace she so desperately needed? After Marcus had died and she had lost her home, she had prayed to Venus to help ease her tortured mind, but if the goddess of love *had* heard her prayers, she had obviously chosen to ignore them. All she wanted was for someone, one day soon, to come and ease the ache in her heart and take away her loneliness.

CHAPTER TWENTY-EIGHT

Flavius and Atticus were instructed by Claudius to ride to his farm to make sure everything was in order there. Flavius reached the farm first. He dismounted from Saturn and patted the horses' withers, and the magnificent black stallion tossed his mane in reply. It was obvious to Flavius that Saturn had enjoyed the journey, which had given him the chance to stretch his limbs and delight in the feel of the fresh breeze cooling his flanks as he galloped through the countryside. Although he had exercised Saturn as often as possible, this was the furthest they had travelled together for some time.

Atticus arrived a few minutes later. Saturn had been so fleet of foot that Atticus' horse had found it hard to keep up with him.

When the horses had been stabled Flavius walked to the farm manager's office, while Atticus went to check on the slaves working in the olive groves, the vine fields and general agriculture. Both were satisfied with the farm manager's accounts and the work of the slaves. They shared the evening meal with the manager, then stayed at the farm overnight. The next morning they rode back to Rome.

Claudius and Lydia Flavia enjoyed watching the ceremony honouring the god Jupiter. When the ceremony ended, they made their way down the Capitoline Hill. As they reached the bottom of the hill, Lydia Flavia suddenly stopped.

"Is something wrong?" Claudius asked in a concerned voice. He looked to his left and saw Marius watching them, his eyebrows raised in a quizzical stare and a sly grin on his face. He approached them and said, "Hello, mother. Where is Flavius today?"

His grin grew wider as Lydia Flavia turned her face away. Without looking at him, she replied brusquely, "He is attending to his own business."

Marius clearly wondered what his brother's business was. He must be living in Rome, as Marius knew he would never abandon their mother.

"What do you want?" said Claudius coldly.

Marius shrugged. "I am simply saying hello to my mother, not that it is any of your business, Senator." He turned back to his mother and said sarcastically, "So, mother, you have taken up with my late father's friend. Have you forgotten his memory so soon?"

Enraged by this insult to Lydia Flavia, Claudius was hard pressed not to hit the insolent young braggart, but remembering the high office he held, he refrained, with supreme effort, from doing so. Instead he said calmly, "Go home, Marius, you are making an exhibition of yourself."

Marius sneered, "It is you who are making an exhibition of yourself, Senator, by publicly flaunting your association with my mother." He saw the murderous look on Claudius' face. Filled with self-importance, he said, "I do not have time to stand here talking with either of you, I must go and ready myself for the Emperor's banquet in honour of this festival. I have been invited as his special friend." He emphasised the word 'friend'. He grinned at Claudius. "You do know I am Caligula's best friend?"

Claudius shook his head in disgust. Then Marius turned to his mother and said, "Goodbye, mother, it was nice seeing you again. Give my regards to my brother if you see him." He could not resist a final barbed comment. "Take my advice, mother, be wary of who you are seen with in public. People do love to gossip, you know."

He walked away, laughing, while Claudius ground his teeth in anger. He looked at Lydia Flavia and saw the tears rolling down her cheeks. In that split second he came to a decision. He would make an offer and he hoped that Lydia Flavia would agree to it.

Soon after Claudius and Lydia Flavia returned to the villa, Flavius and Atticus arrived. Claudius was pleased to know that his farm was in good order. He decided not to tell Flavius about the encounter with Marius and the insults he had given to his mother, knowing that Flavius would seek his brother out and confront him. Besides, there were more important things he had to say to him. Smiling at Flavius he said, "Take some refreshment, rest, then prepare yourself for dinner. We'll speak later."

That night, after dinner, Claudius approached Flavius and asked him to go with him to his office. Flavius readily agreed, but wondered why Claudius needed to talk to him in private. Had he mishandled one of Claudius' business deals?

Claudius came straight to the point. "You must know that I have developed deep feelings for your mother, Flavius. In fact, this afternoon I asked her if she would do me the honour of becoming my wife." He saw the surprised look on Flavius' face but ploughed on. "She has intimated to me that she would be happy to accept my proposal, but first, she would like you to give an opinion on the matter. Do you consent to this marriage, Flavius?"

Flavius was shocked by this unexpected revelation. How strange it felt to be asked this by someone he looked upon as his guardian; usually it was the younger man who asked for permission from the elder. He knew Claudius was a decent and clean-living man, one, who he was sure, would look after his mother and give her back her deserved status. She would also gain protection as a Senator's wife.

He had seen her eyes light up whenever Claudius entered the room, and she had begun to laugh again. Her happiness was important to him. If she wished to marry Claudius, he would not stand in her way.

He looked straight at Claudius and said, "If my mother wishes to be your wife, then I am truly happy for you both."

Claudius clasped Flavius' arm. "Thank you, Flavius." He stepped back and looking intently at the younger man, he said, "Now, there is something I wish to ask you."

"You may ask me anything, sir," Flavius replied

"What are your feelings towards my daughter?" said Claudius.

Flavius found himself struggling to find a reply that would not sound insulting. He said carefully, "As you know, sir, I have been friends with both Claudio and Claudia since childhood." He did not say that back then he had sometimes felt irritated when Claudia had interfered in his and Claudio's boyish games.

"Yes, Flavius, but do you like her?" said Claudius.

Flavius hoped this was not leading to somewhere he did not wish to go, but he had to give an answer. "Yes, sir, she has grown into a lovely young woman."

Claudius smiled. "Good, because I know she has feelings for you. I would be very happy if you two were to marry." He ignored the look of consternation on Flavius' face. "I know she could have her pick of any senator's son, but I don't think I could trust them, they are all so power mad and self-seeking. I do know that I can trust you, Flavius, and I am sure you will make a good husband for Claudia."

Flavius was dumbstruck. What could he say to the man who had saved himself and his mother from penury and starvation, had given them his protection, as well as giving him important work to do, along with a generous allowance? If he declined the offer, Claudius might decide to take away those privileges, or worse, throw him and his mother out. It seemed he had no choice in the matter. He eventually found his voice.

"Sir, I would be honoured to become a member of your family."

Claudius was delighted. "That's settled then. May I suggest, if your mother is agreeable, of course, that we plan a double wedding. What do you say?"

Flavius swallowed. "If my mother is agreeable, then yes sir."

Claudius beamed. "Good. Now, go and give my daughter your answer, she's waiting for you in the garden. I'll tell your mother that both matters have been settled. I am sure she will be delighted."

Claudia was sitting on a marble bench, close to the fountain. She turned as Flavius approached her. Looking at him, she said, "Has my father spoken to you?"

"Yes, he has," Flavius replied, trying to keep his voice pleasant.

She stood up and walked towards him. "Do you agree with his plan?" she asked expectantly. She was relieved when he nodded in reply.

Claudia knew that it would not be a love match, but then patricians rarely married for love, usually only for a combination of joining wealth, gaining power and acquiring land, but she had loved him since childhood, she would do all in her power to be a good, dutiful wife to him, so that one day he might come to love her too.

Flavius felt guilty and tried to hide his lack of feelings for her. It was not her fault her father had placed him in an impossible position. He knew that she was of impeccable character, her father and brother had seen to that, and was certainly attractive to look at. She carried herself with grace and dignity and he knew she would never bring disgrace on him. Most men would be proud to have her as their wife.

He looked at her expectant face and said, "I will now ask you formally to be my wife. Will you agree?"

Her reply came quickly, "Yes, Flavius."

He took her in his arms and kissed her forehead, saying, "Then we will speak with your father and make arrangements for our forthcoming wedding."

Sleep eluded Flavius that night. His agreement that he would marry a woman he did not love played on his mind. Claudia was every inch the Roman patrician maiden, one who had been trained to keep her deepest desires in check. He wondered what it would be like to bed her. Would she be cold and aloof? Or would she be insatiable, like Marcia Virilis? He winced as he remembered his liaisons with Marcia and the trouble that had caused, trouble that had ultimately changed his life. Whenever her father, Senator Virilis, had been out, he had gone to the family villa to see her; until Virilis had come home early one day and caught them in Marcia's bed. Virilis had complained to his father, who had threatened to disinherit him, and had forced him to join the army. That was how he had come to join the Legion 1 Italica, based close to Rome, where it had been easy to continue his dissolute behaviour. Finally, almost giving up hope that his elder son would ever change, his father had asked his mother to write to her cousin, Pontius Pilate, the Governor of Judaea, asking him to find a place for Flavius in the legion there. Pilate had placed him as a Tribune in the Legion Tenth Fretensis based at the Fortress Antonia in Jerusalem, under the Command of Quintus Maximus.

It was in Jerusalem that he had met Farrah, the only woman he had ever truly loved, but she had been cruelly taken from him. Even though that terrible event had taken place almost three years ago, he had not been able to erase the memory of her beautiful face, her voluptuous body and the powerful feelings she had awakened in him. Nor had he wanted to.

He felt for the gold talisman around his neck and sighed. It was no use thinking about those past days now. He had to force himself to concentrate on his forthcoming unwanted marriage.

A few days later the betrothals of Claudius and Lydia Flavia and Flavius and Claudia were announced. Claudius and Flavius placed iron rings on the third fingers of the left hands of their respective brides-to-be, thereby proving their commitment to each other.

CHAPTER TWENTY-NINE

The double weddings took place one month after the betrothals. Lydia Flavia had no one to give her a dowry, but Claudius told her she would not need one, as he had added a codicil to his will that if he died first, she would inherit part of his estate and fortune. She would never be left destitute and penniless again. However, Claudius settled a generous dowry on his daughter, and bought, as a wedding present for her and Flavius, a small villa, complete with a doorkeeper. It was situated further down the Caelian Hill. Claudius knew how much Flavius treasured his horse, so he had made sure there was also adequate stabling adjoining the property and had employed a suitable groom and stable lad, both of whom had been recommended by his own head groom. He had also informed Claudia and Flavius' present slaves that they would be accompanying their new master and mistress to their new villa.

Flavius went to see the villa, which was situated in an area that suited them all. It would be easy for him to carry on overseeing his business interests without having too far to travel, and Claudia would be able to visit her father without having to make her way through the busy, and sometimes dangerous, streets of Rome. Having inspected it and the stables, making sure they were up to standard and easy to keep clean, he thanked Claudius profusely for his wonderful gift.

Their wedding ceremonies were different from the traditional occasions, as Flavius and his mother were already living at the prospective groom and bride's house and, apart from Decimus, Flavius did not have any friends to escort him to his new villa to wait for his bride. As the two brides did not have living mothers, they were dressed by their senior female servants. Both brides wore simple white woollen tunics, tied around the waist by a white belt with a 'Hercules' knot, said to ward off evil. Their feet were placed in saffron-coloured shoes and saffron-coloured wedding veils were draped over their elaborate hairstyles.

Claudia had one trusted friend who agreed to be her Matron of Honour. Lydia Flavia had not dared to contact any of her old friends, so Claudia's friend would act for both of them. As there were not ten bridesmaids to witness the marriages, Claudius arranged for seven of his Senator friends and three business associates to be at the marriage ceremony.

As Claudius and his daughter were among the upper

echelons of society, the Chief Priest of Jupiter, the *flamen Dialis,* and the *Pontifex Maximus,* the highest of all of the Priests of Rome, came to their beautifully-garlanded villa to conduct the ceremonies. Flavius felt anxious that as the Great High Priest was part of the Imperial set-up, Caligula might put a stop to the proceedings, but nothing happened. This left him with the conclusion that if Caligula had known about the ceremonies, he had either not bothered to stop them or had not cared. Or perhaps the Emperor was busy with his latest wife, his fourth: Milonia Caesonia, who, one month after their wedding, had given birth to Caligula's first child, Julia Drusilla, named in honour of his dead sister.

Everyone gathered around the atrium rainwater pool. The water sparkled like diamonds as the sunlight shone down through the skylight above. When all was ready, the wedding ceremony began. Prayers were said, an animal was sacrificed and the omens were read. When the priests were satisfied that they were favourable, they continued with their offices. The Matron of Honour took Claudia's right hand and joined it to Flavius' right hand, then repeated the act for Lydia Flavia and Claudius. The Priests intoned the sacred words and both couples exchanged their vows, sealing them with a kiss.

After the ceremony was concluded, the wedded couples lit torches to Ceres. Lydia Flavia hid a wry smile, for this was done by newly-married couples hoping that the goddess would grant them fertility, something she was too old to care about now. However she dearly wished that Ceres would look upon her son and his new bride with favour. She would delight in once again hearing the patter of tiny feet running over tiled floors.

Later, the feast given by Claudius was magnificent. Along with Claudia's friend and his ten witnesses, several more of his friends had been invited, and to his relief, they had all come.

The night wore on and soon it was time for the guests to depart. With much merriment, they escorted their host and his bride to their bedchamber and with ribald comments, watched them go in. Next they escorted Flavius and Claudia to their bedchamber. It had been agreed that they would stay at the villa that night and go to their own villa the next day.

Flavius closed the door behind them. He saw how nervous Claudia looked and tried to put her at her ease. He knew she was a virgin and that he would have to take great care not to upset her or cause her any unnecessary pain.

As was a husband's right, he untied the knot on her belt, gently removed her dress and studied her naked body. Embarrassed, she turned her face away as he undressed himself and sat on the bed. She felt uncomfortable at the sight of his nakedness and superb physique. When Flavius encouraged her to join him, she hesitated, but when he held out his hand to her, she took it and let him pull her down onto the bed.

Flavius took her in his arms and kissed her, hoping to kindle a dormant fire to life. He gently laid her back on the bed, hoping that once she got over her nervousness she would relax and willingly take part in the act of love, but she remained tense and still like a cold statue. Flavius realised that this was going to be more difficult than he had anticipated.

Flavius and Claudia soon settled into their new home. At first Flavius had visualised Farrah's face and body as he had made love to Claudia, but guilt had overcome him and he had forced himself to banish that illusion and concentrate on his wife. After infinite patience and tenderness, he saw Claudia begin to relax and become eager to accept his advances.

Claudia had noticed that he never removed the golden amulet he wore around his neck. One night she said, "Do you ever take that off?"

Flavius answered emphatically, "No! It is precious to me."

Shocked by his stern reply, she knew not to raise the subject again.

To Flavius' delight, his mother seemed like a young woman again and he could not help smiling when he saw that Claudius had developed a new spring in his step. All seemed to be going well.

Then Claudio came home.

Claudius found himself staring at the empty space where his son's lower right arm should have been. Shocked by the sight, he ushered Claudio into his office and called for wine to be brought to them. Claudio sat down wearily, and Claudius sat beside him. After taking a long drink, Claudius said, "I am sorry to see that you are injured, Claudio. If it is not too distressing, will you tell me what happened?"

Claudio looked down at the heavily-scarred stump just below his elbow and said coldly, "There was an uprising by some of the local hill tribes, and two cohorts of the Sixth Victrix were sent to put it down. I had been placed in charge of one of them." He gave a deep sigh at the remembrance of the battle. "A tribesman came at me. I killed him but I was concentrating so hard on him that I did not see another man approach me from the side. He slammed his huge club down hard on my sword arm, rendering it useless.

He gulped down his wine then said, "Filled with pain and rage, I turned and rammed my shield boss into his face. The man went down, but he was still alive and dangerous. Fortunately, a Centurion who had witnessed the attack came to my rescue. He thrust his sword into the belly of the tribesman as he lay on the ground. He then shouted for some legionaries to encircle us to protect us on all sides." He shook his head, "Had it not been for that brave Centurion, I would have died on that battlefield."

He took another drink. "I must have passed out with shock and pain, for the next thing I remember was waking up in the camp hospital. Later, the Centurion came to me and told me that the rebellion had been put down successfully. I asked him how I had been brought back to camp and he said, 'I ordered legionaries to carry you to the cart where the wounded had been placed and well... here you are, sir.' When I told him I owed him my life he just grinned and said 'Tribune, sir, you are liked and respected by both myself and the legionaries. They would have strung me up if I had not done my best to protect you'."

Claudius made a mental note to find out who that Centurion was. He would make sure that the man who had saved his son's life would be well rewarded.

Claudio continued, "Unfortunately, the surgeon could not save my arm, the bones had been shattered beyond repair." He began to weep as he remembered the pain and terror of the operation to remove the damaged part of his arm and hand. The poppy juice he had been made to drink had barely dulled the pain. He wiped away his tears and began again. "Because I was no longer of any use to the legion, I had to give up my commission." He turned his stricken face to his father and said dolefully, "I am no longer of any use to anyone, least of all to you, father." He held up his wounded limb and said, "I am sorry father, I do not think I can pursue the political career you had hoped for me, not after this."

Claudius was overwhelmed with pity for his son. He placed a consoling hand on his shoulder. This was not the time to say it, but he did not think Claudio's injury would be a stumbling block to a career in the Senate. He said, "We will not speak of that now. You have had a long and tiring journey, so I suggest that you eat something and then rest."

Claudio shook his head. "I am not hungry."

"Nevertheless, you must eat. You need to regain your strength."

Knowing deep down that his father was right, Claudio stood up and let Claudius lead him to the dining area. As instructed, the dining room slave, trying not to look at his young master's injury, brought Claudio a bowl of broth and some bread. Despite himself, Claudio soon demolished the contents of his bowl. After another cup of wine, he announced that he wanted to retire to his room.

A slave came in and spoke quietly to Claudius. Claudius dismissed him then said, "I have just been told that your bedchamber is ready."

Claudio nodded, stood up and said, "I am so glad to be home, father."

Claudius smiled. "Try to get a good night's sleep, son." He placed an affectionate arm across his shoulder. "We will speak tomorrow. I have many things to tell you."

Claudio went into his room, closing the door behind him. Claudius instructed a slave to sleep outside the room that night in case his son needed anything. He also told the slave that on no account was Claudio to be disturbed in the morning, but should be left asleep until he wished to get up.

The slave bowed and settled himself on a chair outside Claudio's bedroom door. If the young master required anything during the night he would be ready to help.

CHAPTER THIRTY

Claudio rose out of bed at midday. He had spent hours tossing and turning before sleep had rescued him from his turbulent thoughts. He called for a slave to attend to his needs. The slave outside his door quickly came into his room and helped him to the bath house. After he had dressed, he presented himself to his father.

Claudius had already quizzed the slave about Claudio's night and was concerned when the slave had replied, "The young master seemed to be having a nightmare, master, I heard him groan and shout 'No!' several times." Claudius decided that he must do everything in his power to help to ease his son's troubled mind. When Claudio came into his office, he said, "Ah, Claudio. Let us go to the dining room and eat. It is too late for breakfast now, and although it is too early for the main meal of the day, I am sure whatever you want will be brought to you. Afterwards, we will go out into the garden, it's a lovely day and I have many things to tell you."

Although Claudio was pale with dark shadows under his eyes, his father was pleased to see that he seemed to have regained some of his appetite and soon finished off a plate of cold meats and bread, washed down with a light wine. He decided that now was the time to tell his son that he had married Lydia Flavia and that his sister had married his best friend. He wondered how Claudio would react.

Claudio smiled. "Are you and Lydia Flavia happy, father?"

"Yes, very," Claudius answered, smiling. "As are your sister and Flavius."

"Then I am happy for you all." He looked around. "Where is my stepmother?"

Lydia Flavia was waiting anxiously in her room for news of Claudio's reaction. A slave arrived and bowed to her, saying, "Mistress, your husband is waiting for you in the dining room and asks you to go to him there." She followed him nervously. When she reached the dining room, Claudio went to her and greeted her affectionately. A wave of pity swept over her as she saw her stepson's injury, but she kept her thoughts to herself and said "Welcome home, Claudio."

"And where are Claudia and Flavius? Can I see them?" he asked.

Claudius replied, "Flavius will be here tonight. I am sure he will answer your questions."

A look of apprehension crossed Claudio's face. What would Flavius say when he saw his injury?

Later that night, Flavius arrived at the villa with the latest invoices from the sale of olive oil to the market dealers. He was surprised when a slave led him to the dining area, and even more so when he saw Claudius sitting there with his son. "Claudio!" he gasped, "I did not expect to see you here. I thought you still had four months left to serve in the Legion."

Claudio held up the remnants of his arm. A shocked Flavius stuttered, "I am so sorry."

Claudio was surprised to see his friend at that time of night, and dealing with business paperwork. When he felt stronger, he would ask his father what was going on. For now, he would change the subject.

"I was very pleased to hear of my father's marriage to your mother and I am delighted to know that my sister is in safe hands with you," he said. "I could not have asked for a better husband for her." He stifled a yawn. "I am sorry, Flavius, but I am very tired. Forgive me, but I would like to go to bed now." He looked at his father.

Claudius nodded. "Yes, son, you need your rest. You and Flavius can tell each other your news another day.

Claudio stood up, turned to Flavius and said, "Will you bring Claudia to see me soon?"

"Of course. I'll bring her tomorrow."

"Thank you." Claudio smiled. "It's good to see you again,

old friend. Now I wish you both good night." He turned and left the room.

There were many questions Flavius wanted to ask Claudius, but seeing the weary look on his father-in-law's face, he held back. There would be time enough later when the initial shock of seeing Claudio's injury had passed. He handed the invoices to Claudius, bade him goodnight and left.

On the way home he wondered how he would tell Claudia the disturbing and sad news about her brother. When he arrived home, he was relieved that she was already fast asleep in bed, so it was not until the next morning he gave her the news. She was distraught, and asked Flavius to take her to her father's house so she could be with her brother. Flavius readily agreed.

Claudio had suffered another disturbed night, wondering if his sister would come. His hopes were fulfilled when he heard her calling his name. He left his room and went to greet her. Seeing her brother's distress, she wrapped her arms around him. Flavius left them alone and went to see Claudius.

"I must do everything in my power to see that my son does not slide into morbidity," said Claudius. "I have tried to tell Claudio that the loss of his arm is no barrier for him to serve in the Senate, but he has convinced himself that it is impossible." He passed a weary hand over his forehead and sat down heavily in his chair. "It has been a long time since I served in the legions, but you, Flavius, have had more recent experiences. Tell me, what can I do to help my son?"

Flavius frowned, remembering the battle at Beth-Horon and his inability to save Farrah. "It will take time, care and patience, sir," he said. "If it will help, and if Claudio is willing to do so, I am happy to let him unburden himself on me."

Claudius nodded. "Thank you, Flavius. Maybe he will listen to you."

Just then Claudia came into the room, her eyes wet with tears. "Where is Claudio?" asked her father.

"He is in the garden," she replied. "He wants to speak to you, Flavius."

Flavius found Claudio standing staring up at the blue sky. He approached him carefully, not wishing to startle him. Claudio became aware that he was standing there and turned to face him. Flavius said quietly, "You wished to see me?"

Claudio nodded. "I don't know where to turn, Flavius," he said. "My life is over."

Flavius said calmly, "If you wish to tell me what happened I will gladly listen. If you are not yet ready, I will wait until you are." He looked deep into Claudio's troubled eyes. "Just know that you are not alone, Claudio. You have a family who care deeply for you, and remember, I will always be here for you."

Claudio grasped Flavius' arm and said, "I know that. Give me a little time and I will come and see you, father has told me where you are living." He watched as Flavius walked back inside.

A week later, Claudio went to see Flavius and his beloved sister at their new villa. Flavius had told Claudia about his conversation with Claudio and his offer of help. After warmly embracing her brother and making sure refreshments had been served, she excused herself and beat a hasty retreat to the kitchen, saying that she needed to discuss with the cook the food needed for their evening meal.

Flavius sat patiently waiting for Claudio to speak. When he did so, Flavius was surprised by his chosen subject.

Claudio said, "My father told me how badly and unfairly Caligula treated you. It is a disgrace. He also said that he asked you to take over the running of his business interests."

Flavius answered warily, "Yes, he did, and I accepted his offer. If you wish to take that job for yourself I will understand."

Claudio shook his head. "You know, Flavius, that I have never been interested in my father's business affairs. I am glad he has someone he can trust and knows will do the job properly. Please keep on doing that."

"Then I am happy to carry on for as long as your father wants me to."

Claudio grew silent. Flavius waited for him to speak further, but he could see that his brother-in-law was not yet ready to talk about what had happened to him. Obviously embarrassed, Claudio made his excuses and left, leaving a worried Flavius watching him go.

Several days passed before Claudio came back, and this time he seemed more at ease with himself. Flavius sat waiting for him to speak. When he was ready, he told Flavius the whole sorry saga, ending with, "How can I enter the Senate now?"

Flavius' voice was gentle. "May I speak plainly, Claudio? If you say no, I will not be offended."

"Yes, speak, Flavius, I welcome your view."

Flavius was heartened by his friend's reply. "Then I will come straight to the point. I cannot see how your injury could possibly affect your becoming a Senator. You have all your faculties intact, and we need men such as you to speak up for the rest of us."

Claudio grimaced. "My father tells me that our Emperor has done some terrible things and everyone is scared to stop him for fear of their lives. Who is brave enough to combat such tyranny?"

Flavius sighed. "My hope is that one day people will band together and see an end to the cruelty and slaughter. That is why strong, honest men are needed in the Senate. Men like you, Claudio." He saw the ghost of a smile spread across his friend's face and ploughed on. "I know it is your father's dearest wish that you keep up the family tradition by following him into the Curia, just as he followed your grandfather."

He saw Claudio's doubtful expression and added, "All I ask is that you think about it and do not waste the chance to make your mark. Remember the code of the legions: 'Courage, Strength and Honour'. Your honour has never been in doubt, and I know you have the courage and the strength to see this through."

Claudio smiled wistfully. "I'll think about it." He stood up, said goodbye to Flavius and Claudia, and then made his way back home to his father's villa. On the way, he thought about Flavius' words. Could he make his mark in the Senate? He would discuss it with his father.

The next day, Flavius went to see Claudius. "After much thought, if you will agree, sir, I think it best I discontinue training to be a Senator," he said. Claudius began to protest, but he cut his father-in-law short. "I know you had me in mind for the Quaestor's position at the forthcoming elections. However, I feel it is Claudio's right to stand. After all, it is his future at stake."

"Now look..." Claudius began, but Flavius interrupted him. "If you are in agreement, sir, I should like to continue overseeing the merchandising side of your business dealings. I think that is a role I am more suited to." He waited for the Senator's answer.

After a long moment of thought, Claudius replied, "Perhaps I should put my son first and concentrate on him to fulfil the career he was born to." He looked at Flavius. "But do not forget, Flavius, had it not been for your father's untimely death, you would have already taken your first steps into the Senate House."

"Sir," Flavius said earnestly, "I have never really been interested in politics. I do not think I would make a good Senator, whereas I know Claudio will make an excellent one."

"Well, if that is what you wish Flavius, I am more than happy for you to continue handling my business affairs, for you are certainly good at doing that." Claudius smiled. "Thank you for being honest with me."

Flavius returned home pleased at the outcome and relieved that he would not have to entangle himself in the dangerous game of politics.

CHAPTER THIRTY-ONE

A month went by, and Flavius and Claudio continued to talk together. Flavius could see a small improvement in his friend, but he knew things would not change overnight.

After the distress of Claudio's unexpected homecoming, the family needed some happy news to restore their good humour. That news came when Claudia told Flavius that she was expecting their first child. Flavius took her to see her father, who was ecstatic to know that he was soon to be a grandfather. Even Claudio smiled when he heard that he was going to be an uncle. Lydia Flavia was delighted. She congratulated them and wished them every happiness.

A few nights later, Flavius and Atticus went to the market with the latest consignment of grain. The deal with the merchant was done quickly so Flavius told Atticus to take the invoice back to Claudius. He then went to the Poseidon Tavern.

"Castor and Pollux! Did I hear right? You? *Married?*" Decimus almost choked on his wine. He wiped his mouth with the back of his hand and shook his head in disbelief. "I never thought you, of all people, Flavius, would ever settle down, and you say you are to be a father too?"

Flavius laughed at his friend's reaction. "Yes, it is true," he said.

"Well, I hope your new wife knows how to keep you under control. She's a Senator's daughter, you said." Flavius nodded. "Not Marcia Virilis?"

"No!" Flavius quickly replied.

"Did you get your wife pregnant before the wedding? Is that why you married her, before her father killed you?"

"Certainly not!" Flavius said indignantly. "My wife is a virtuous, well-brought-up patrician. She would never behave like that." He drank the wine Decimus had bought him in honour of his news. "She is the daughter of Senator Claudius Marcellus."

Decimus put his wine cup down on the table and blew through his teeth. "You lucky... he is the most distinguished of all our Senators in the Curia."

Flavius thought it best not to say that it had been Claudius who had approached him about marrying his daughter. He shrugged and changed the subject. "How are things at the Palace?"

"Bad as ever," came Decimus' reply. "In fact, after his sister's death, Caligula has become even more ruthless."

"I saw you at the executions."

Decimus shook his head and said grimly, "A bad business that. Caligula has chosen a new Chief Spy and Master Builder. I wish them luck, because who knows what he is going to do next? He is very unpredictable."

"I also saw Caligula's uncle with his new wife."

Decimus grinned. "Ah, the delectable Messalina. One to watch there, I think. Half of the Guard are already in love with her. Beautiful to look at, but dangerous to tangle with."

Flavius remembered the guard she had stared at, the one who had dared to smile at her.

Then he realised that it was getting late. He did not want to upset Claudia, especially now that she was pregnant. "I suppose I had better go home, I don't want Claudia worrying about me," he said.

Decimus nodded. "Yes, you do that. We mustn't have wifey getting herself in a stew wondering which woman you are with."

Flavius bristled at that remark, but when Decimus broke into a smile, he knew he was just joking with him. He punched his friend lightly on the arm, smiled and said, "I'll see you soon." He left the Poseidon with a grinning Decimus looking after him.

Decimus shook his head. Who would have thought that the man who had once been the most notorious womaniser in Rome was now married with a child on the way?

Finishing off his wine, he headed back to the Praetorian barracks.

CHAPTER THIRTY-TWO

Over the past months, Antonius had been put through a rigorous training programme at the Gladiatorial School in Capua. Day after day, hour after hour, he had strained muscles, suffered deep bruising, lost copious amounts of sweat in the heat of the day and shivered in the chill of the last of the daylight. All of this under the direction of Thorg, a retired gladiator originally from Thrace, who had specialised in fighting Thracian style.

Antonius was well muscled, had sturdy legs and was quick on his feet, so the *Provocator* or 'Challenger' style of fighting had been chosen for him. This pleased him, because this class of gladiator had originally stemmed from Roman soldiers and the Provocator's weapon was the gladius, the short sword with which he was all too familiar.

When Antonius had first arrived at the school, his guards had handed Albanus, the *Lanista*, the owner and manager of the school, a scroll holding the Emperor's personal seal. Albanus had opened the scroll and read Caligula's commands. They were: the newcomer was to be called Leon. His training was to be relentless, because the Emperor wanted him fully trained and ready for the forthcoming games in Capua's area, so that by the time Leon appeared in the arena in Rome he was experienced enough to fight and more importantly, to win.

Albanus had frowned when he read that Leon was not to be promoted by him for his own profit; he was the personal property of the Emperor and would fight only for his benefit. The communication ended with the words 'Leon's identity and purpose must not be made known to the other trainee gladiators in case of jealous retaliation.' He was slightly bemused by these directives, but he knew he could not argue against the Emperor's decree, so he had nodded and told the guards that he fully understood his orders.

Several weeks on, Antonius hated his situation, his trainer, most of his fellow pupils, and one man in particular: the young Gaul Katurix, whose slim but athletic build marked him out as a future *Retiarius*, a gladiator who used a trident and a net. Antonius looked upon Katurix with disdain. He was very handsome, almost feminine in his looks and movements. He was not surprised to discover that he was the lover of a huge German named Gundhram, a trainee *Postulati gladiator*, a heavily-armed and armoured fighter who had almost completed his training.

One night, when Antonius was sitting eating his supper in the canteen, Katurix sat down opposite him and made suggestive advances to him. Disgusted, Antonius angrily rebuffed him. Katurix felt humiliated by Antonius' reaction. No one had ever turned him down before, and the urge for revenge was strong. Knowing Gundhram's jealous nature, Katurix told him about it and claimed that it was Antonius who had made the approach.

This drove Gundhram to seek out Antonius to punish him. When Gundhram tried to punch him, Antonius' temper got the better of him and he fought off the German's attack, causing damage to his arm. For that, Albanus ordered Antonius to be whipped by the Roman guards who protected the school. Bearing in mind that Leon belonged to the Emperor, he told the guards to go lightly so as not to cause too much damage. Left to him, he would not have had Leon whipped at all, and would have been happy just to confine him to his cell for a few days, but he had to show the others that he would not tolerate violence between the trainees.

The taste of the whip on his back made Antonius realise the suffering he had caused those men in the legion who had not obeyed him and had met the same fate. He could not sleep on his wounded back for many nights after. There had been one consolation though: Katurix and Gundhram never came near him again.

On certain nights women would be brought into the men's sleeping quarters. Antonius was given a small, dark-haired girl, a slave, who told him she originated from Lycia. She was seventeen years old and as he roughly satisfied his lust with her, she did not complain but seemed to enjoy him. When it was time for the girl to leave, he hoped that he would see her again, but he never did. The next time it was a completely different, older, woman who just let him do what he wanted without uttering a single word. Albanus obviously did not want emotional attachment to interfere with the training of his protégés.

There had been times when Antonius had seen leg and facial injuries suffered by some trainees because of misjudged ducking or jumping over moving wooden obstacles, or being knocked senseless by mistiming their runs between large swinging metal balls. Antonius watched each mistake carefully, concentrating on learning the timing to overcome these obstacles.

It was his arm that ached the most. The main part of his training had been spent in hitting a large wooden post with a wooden sword, one much heavier than the legionary sword he had been used to. The legionary *gladius* had been introduced when the trainees were more skilled. After all his years in the legions, Antonius felt comfortable with it in his hand.

Sometimes he saw an angry Thorg lash out with his whip at those who he thought did not learn quickly enough or were lazy. Some had sustained injuries to their faces or eyes as the whip had struck them. He did not want to suffer their fate. One taste of a whip had been enough.

The day of Albanus' test arrived. Those who passed would be sent to arenas across Italy to take part in professional contests before a paying audience. Those who failed would be either dismissed or their training resumed.

Albanus faced the gladiators lined up before him and said, "Put on a good show. Small injuries will make your contest look more authentic, but under no circumstances are you to seriously maim or kill each other. It has cost a lot of time and money to train you, and I do not want to waste either. If there is already a quarrel between you, put that aside. This is not the time to take out your vengeance on each other. Remember, the winner will be the one who draws blood first by inflicting a slight wound, or who forces the other to the ground. Do I make myself clear?" He pointed to Thorg. "Or do I have to let Thorg deal with you?"

Knowing that if they disobeyed their master Thorg would not be merciful to them, the gladiators shouted as one, "Yes, we understand."

As Caligula had ordered, Antonius had been speedily trained. Now, eight months on from his arrival here, he was about to enter his first contest in the arena of the Capua School's small, wooden amphitheatre. He had hoped he would face Gundhram to further humiliate him in front of the other trainees, but in fact he was pitted against another Provocator from the school, as members of this class of gladiator were always paired together.

It was time. Antonius adjusted his round-topped, full-faced, neck-protecting helmet, making sure he could see properly through its bronze circular lattice-work eye protectors. The small breastplate covering the middle of his upper body and the large grieve protecting his forward leg made him feel awkward, but he would have to get used to them. He moved his arm, making sure that the bronze, cloth-padded arm sleeve did not hinder his movements. Adjusting his leather and metal belt above his loincloth, he picked up his *gladius* and hefted it in his hand. Holding his large, square shield, he took a deep breath, and with his Provocator opponent by his side, he walked out into the arena.

They were greeted by cheers from the rest of the gladiators watching from the raised seating tiers above.

A light breeze ruffled the two tall feathers placed one either side on the top of his helmet. Antonius was grateful for this, as it helped to cool the blisteringly hot sun beating down on the oval arena.

The two opponents stood before the box where Albanus and several local dignitaries sat. They lifted their swords in salute, then walked back to the middle of the arena.

Albanus signalled for the contest to begin.

Antonius' opponent, Dario, originally from Hispania, made the first move. He thrust his gladius at Antonius' uncovered leg, but Antonius knocked the weapon aside with his shield. He circled Antonius, who turned with him so as not to be struck from behind. For a while both men sparred defensively, then suddenly Dario sprang forward, aiming for a second time at Antonius' leg. Antonius was too quick for him and quickly moved aside, causing Dario's sword to slash at thin air. This brought howls of derision from the watching gladiators. Some yelled out, "Come on, you useless Spaniard!" While others chanted "Leon! Leon!"

Albanus sat forward in his chair, watching both gladiators closely. He heard one of the dignitaries say to another, "I hope this contest livens up soon, I am becoming bored." Hearing that comment, Albanus signalled to Thorg, who stood on the perimeter of the oval arena. Thorg nodded and moved further into the arena. He cracked his whip close to the contestants, careful not to touch them. The threat of the whip spurred the combatants on. Dario quickened his pace, but Antonius was faster.

Antonius suddenly dropped to one knee. Dario moved towards him, confident that victory was his. He raised his sword ready to strike, but Antonius, with a surge of speed and using a legionary move, lifted his shield and rammed it up under Dario's chin, hard, but not hard enough to kill him.

Reeling from the impact, Dario staggered back. Antonius took his chance. He sliced his sword across Dario's leg, inflicting a small, but not lethal, cut, causing him to fall to his knees on the sandy, gritty ground. Antonius stood up. Placing his boot down hard on Dario's feet, keeping him on the ground, Antonius lifted his sword and held it over the back of Dario's neck as if he would strike the killing blow.

The other gladiators began shouting and swearing at

both fighters, waving their arms around angrily. Then they looked at Albanus.

Albanus ignored them. He stood up and applauded his two contestants, pleased that the dignitaries who had complained that the contest had been slow were now praising the spectacular ending.

The dignitaries applauded the contestants and began slapping Albanus on the back. Smiling, he led them inside, where a feast awaited them.

As the school's doctor worked on Dario's injuries, Antonius, after bathing, was having his muscles massaged and anointed with oil. Later, he was fed well and given a woman for the night.

The next day, Albanus informed Dario that he needed further training. To Antonius he said, "You have passed the test. You are ready to leave here and fight in the main arenas." Later he wrote to the Emperor telling him that his personal gladiator was now fully trained and ready to fight for him.

A few days later Caligula's guards arrived to escort Antonius back to Rome. He was to stay at the finest training school in the city to perfect his skills as Caligula's gladiator.

Antonius arrived in Rome to find that Caligula had gone to Germania. He wondered how long he would have to wait for his first professional contest and his chance to win fame and glory.

CHAPTER THIRTY-THREE

Caligula arrived in Germania with his legions, Praetorian Guards and auxiliary forces, gathered from throughout the Empire. The expedition was not a success, so he moved on to Gaul. After a disastrous campaign there, where he almost instigated a mutiny amongst his legions, he hurried back to Rome so quickly that the Praetorian Guards struggled to keep up with him.

He was met on the outskirts of Rome by three Senators, one of whom was Claudius. Caligula shouted in a threatening tone, "Why has the Senate sent only three Senators to greet me on my return to Rome? And where is my Triumph? I have been cheated by the Senate!"

Claudius replied calmly, "But, Divinity, you yourself said that on no account were we to honour you, on pain of death. So we obeyed your command."

Caligula turned on Claudius and said murderously, "Do you think I would order a Triumph for myself? No! It is for *you* to honour *me.*"

Shortly afterwards, a Senatorial delegation met him and begged him to return to the city. Caligula shouted, "I am coming!" He tapped the hilt of his sword and said threateningly, "And this is coming too!"

The following day, he ordered the Senators to come to the Palace and appear before him. He looked with disdain at the men lined up before him and angrily shouted, "You are a disgrace! You revelled in feasting and drinking, idling your time away at theatres, whilst I was facing death in barbarian lands!"

The Senators stood silent, afraid to speak. Caligula ordered his guards to lift the lids of several enormous chests standing behind him. The Senators gasped when they saw what was inside them.

"These are my spoils of war!" he declared to the stony-faced Senators. "I have instructed my agents to organise my Triumph, and I have demanded that it must be more lavish than any Triumph has ever been before." He laughed. "But have no fear you greedy Senators, I have told them that it must be done as cheaply as possible." He ran his hand through his hair, then said abruptly, "Get out, all of you!"

The stunned Senators hurried out of the Palace. None returned to the Senate House. All hurried back to their homes.

Claudius' thoughts were in turmoil as he stormed into

the atrium of his villa. What would the public reaction be when they saw Caligula's 'spoils of war' paraded through the streets of the city? It might lead to an insurrection, and despite what Caligula had said, he knew that this mockery of a Triumph would cost a fortune.

Lydia Flavia came out of a side room ready to greet him, but when she saw the anger on his face, she hurried back into the room. Perhaps he might tell her later, but if not she would not question him. That was something she had learnt from her first husband a long time ago.

It was Caligula's birthday, and the day of his Triumph. Claudius advised Lydia Flavia to stay at home in case of trouble. Flavius stayed with Claudia, as the day for the baby's birth was drawing near.

That day came sooner than anticipated. Just after midnight on the day of the Triumph, Claudia went into labour. The hours passed by and the child had not appeared. Flavius could see that Claudia was becoming more and more distressed and her screaming was relentless. He called for his slave.

"You must go into the city and find Scribonia, the midwife," he said sternly. "Tell her she must come at once as I fear for my wife and child."

The slave bowed and hurried off towards the city. As he reached the bottom of the hill, he saw that the streets were filled with people eagerly waiting to see the Triumph. Scribonia lived in the middle of the city. He frantically shoved his way through the crowd, desperate to reach her, praying that she was at home and not attending another birth elsewhere, or had decided to watch the Triumph and was lost amongst the throng of people.

Eventually, the slave reached the midwife's house. Thank the gods, she was at home. He quickly gave her his master's message.

Scribonia had overseen the birth of many children, some to wealthy families. To be asked to attend the birth of an important Senator's first grandchild filled her with pride. She packed her instruments and instructed the slave to carry the birthing chair. Then they made their way through the bustling city.

The journey back to the Caelian Hill was frustrating. They had a hard time trying to get through the Praetorians and legionaries who lined the streets, but Scribonia was well known in Rome and when she said who she was and that she was on urgent business, they let her and the slave through. Once through, the portly midwife and slave hurried to Flavius' villa.

Claudia was now in great distress, and Flavius was relieved when Scribonia arrived. Red-faced and puffing with the effort of climbing up the hill, she smoothed back her greying hair and went into the bedroom. She told the slave to place the birthing chair in front of the bed. He did so, then hurried out of the room.

"Hold your mistress' hand." Scribonia ordered Claudia's handmaid. She quickly examined Claudia and frowned. This would not be an easy birth.

Scribonia went out into the main living area and found a worried Flavius pacing up and down. She said, "I insist that you stay away from the birthing room, sir. I do not want to be interrupted by a worried man who will only distress the mother more. I suggest you find something else to do, preferably somewhere else." Ignoring the look on Flavius' face, she hurried back to Claudia.

Flavius thought the midwife was a little too abrupt, especially when speaking to someone of a higher class than herself, but he did not argue. He went to the stables and stayed with Saturn, knowing Scribonia would tell him when the child had been born.

Scribonia ordered Claudia's handmaid to fetch a bowl of warm water. The handmaid hurried out of the room, soon returning with the bowl which she placed on a small table nearby. Scribonia told her to support Claudia while she, saying words of encouragement to the frightened mother-to-be, helped her off the bed and onto the birthing chair. She instructed the handmaid to support Claudia's back, then sat down on a low stool in front of the birthing chair ready to help Claudia to deliver a healthy child.

CHAPTER THIRTY-FOUR

The Praetorians and legionaries lining the way of the Triumph told the people that they must loudly cheer the Emperor as he rode by. Some had infiltrated the crowd to make sure they did so.

The crowd's excitement grew as they saw the Senators and dignitaries approaching at the head of the Triumph. They were followed by musicians playing flutes and trumpets. The cheers died away when they saw how few hostages Caligula had brought back with him from his two campaigns, but, spurred on by the threat of a sword in their belly or back, they began to cheer again.

The crowd stared wide-eyed with shock as cart after cart passed by carrying mountains of sea shells, Caligula's 'spoils of war'. Caligula had insisted that the Triremes used in his campaigns must also be part of his Triumph, so they had been transported, mostly overland, to Rome.

The crowd gasped as they trundled by on their massive wheeled vehicles.

Behind them came Caligula, dressed in purple and gold and standing proudly in his golden chariot, led by three white horses. He was accompanied by two slaves, one holding a golden crown of victory above his head, the other holding a large branch of laurel. He looked straight ahead, ignoring the crowd.

With whispered threats all around them, the crowd gave a rousing cheer as he passed by. When they heard the horns and drums of the approaching victorious legions, their cheers increased. The legionaries marched past, proudly displaying their standards, but with anger and frustration clearly etched on their faces.

The Triumph ended at the Temple of Jupiter Best and Greatest on the Capitoline Hill, where sacrifices were made and prayers were offered to the god for the safe return of the Emperor. When all was complete, Caligula returned to the Palatine.

Cassius Charea scanned the crowd and saw that they were growing restless. Some of them had begun to loudly voice their disapproval of Caligula's mockery of a Triumph. He ordered some Praetorians to arrest the trouble-makers before they caused a riot, then told others to escort the Senators to their homes. Two were ordered to escort Claudius home, one of them Decimus.

Sitting in Claudius' office, Claudius angrily described Caligula's Triumph to his son.

"Can the Senate do anything about this?" Claudio asked, horrified.

Claudius stood up and began to pace back and forth. "Some Senators have already been executed, so, understandably, the rest of us are wary of speaking out publicly against Caligula. In any case, the Senate has become a toothless dog now that he oversees everything we try to do."

Claudio shook his head and said sadly, "Then we are doomed."

"Not necessarily. I saw the hateful look in some of the legionaries' eyes as Caligula passed by in his golden chariot, and the faces of the army marching in the Triumph clearly showed how they felt about their Emperor. If men such as these rise up against Caligula, we may yet have a chance." He stopped pacing and looked at Claudio. "Tell me, Claudio, what do the men of the Sixth Victrix think about Caligula?"

Claudio shrugged. "Some are disgruntled and want desperately to complain, but like the Senators, they fear for their lives."

"Then along with what I saw in those legionaries' eyes today, that means there is hope," Claudius said. A sudden thought had entered his head.

"What do you mean, father? How can there be hope? You just said yourself that the Senate can do nothing..."

Claudius raised a hand and said, "Hear me out. With the discontent I saw today, along with the men of the legions in Germania and Gaul who were almost driven to mutiny by Caligula's treatment of them, and if, as you say, those legionaries and officers you served with are also feeling disgruntled, then the Senate may not have to worry. Perhaps, if he drives them too far, the legions will turn on Caligula and kill him for us. After all, he will not be the first ruler to die by his own troops."

"But what will happen to the people of Rome?"

"Don't worry about them, Claudio. If they do kill him, I know the people will support them and celebrate his death, for they too have had enough of his cruelty and insane actions." He smiled. "But enough of that for now. Come Claudio, let us have some refreshment. I want to talk to you about standing as a candidate for the position of Quaestor at the upcoming election."

As father and son discussed the matter, Flavius was receiving devastating news.

CHAPTER THIRTY-FIVE

Scribonia shook her head. "Go and find your master. Tell him he must come now!" Claudia's handmaid fled the room and went in search of Flavius. She found him in the stables. Trying to hold back her tears, she gave him Scribonia's message.

Anxious, Flavius hurried back to the house and entered the bedroom. The new-born child had not been placed on the floor ready for him to pick up and claim as his to rear, as was the custom. He looked at Scribonia and said, "Where is the child?"

Scribonia pointed to a small, carved wooden crib close by the bed. Flavius peered into it. A clean cloth covered the baby. He lifted it off and saw the lifeless form of his son laying on the silken sheet. He reeled back with shock.

He heard a sobbing Claudia say over and over again, "I'm sorry." He replaced the cover over the baby and turned to her. Seeing her tear-stained, chalk-white face, Flavius went to her and took her in his arms. As he looked over her shoulder he saw laid out on the nearby table a bowl of bloody water, Scribonia's blood-soaked apron and bloodstained cloths and a tool with a sharp hook on the end of it. Seeing his shock, Scribonia hastily gathered her apron, cloths and hooked tool together and bundled them into her bag.

He scowled at Scribonia. "What happened?"

"It was a difficult birth, sir. It took too long for the child to enter this world. When he did, he was stillborn." Seeing Flavius' angry face, she whined, "I tried my best, sir." She held out her hand ready to receive payment for her efforts.

Disgusted, Flavius said, "Do you think I would speak of your payment now? Tell my slave how much I owe you and I will have him bring it to you tomorrow."

Scribonia picked up her things and asked if the slave could help her with the birthing chair. Flavius nodded, then said, "Now get out!" And turned his back on her.

All night, Flavius sat by an exhausted Claudia, holding her hand and whispering words of comfort, assuring her that in time, they would have another child. But she would not be comforted. She wept and blamed herself for their lost son until, worn out by pain and grief, she fell into a troubled sleep. Flavius tried to stay awake in case she needed anything, but try as he might, he could not stop himself from drifting off into a restless slumber.

As dawn cast its early light into the room, Flavius woke up with a start. Claudia was moaning incoherently and thrashing around, entwining herself in the bed sheet in her delirium. He looked at her colourless face, her wide open, staring eyes, and panicked. He called for his slave.

"Go and get the Greek doctor. Your mistress is ill," he snapped.

Without a word, the slave did as ordered.

The Greek doctor, Alexander, lived in a villa not far from Flavius' house. He had made a fortune by administering treatment to wealthy Romans, amongst them Claudius and his family. Flavius knew he could be trusted. He was relieved when the doctor arrived and followed Alexander into the bedroom.

Alexander was extremely sad to see Claudia in this terrible condition. He had known her since she was a child and had often treated her for childhood illnesses. He gently drew the sweat-stained, blood-soaked sheet to the side and procceded to examine her. His expression was grave when he saw the extent of the internal injuries she had suffered.

He turned to Flavius and asked, "Where is your child?" Flavius pointed to the crib. Alexander shook his head when he saw the lifeless form within and said gruffly, "Who was the midwife?" When Flavius told him, he grimaced and said angrily, "She is a barbarian! I will make sure she never acts as a midwife again!"

Flavius asked earnestly, "It is too late for our child, but can you save my wife?"

With down-turned mouth, Alexander said, "I am afraid your wife has a serious infection. I will not bleed her, she has lost enough blood already. All I can do is try to bring down her fever and get her to drink some infused herbs." He hesitated for a brief moment, then said, "I suggest you pray to Divine Juno and Carmentis, goddess of protection in childbirth, asking for their help in seeing your wife through this ordeal. Now please ask Claudia's handmaid to bring in some clean cloths, a bowl and a jug filled with clean, boiled water, after which, I must ask you to leave the room." He opened his doctor's case and pulled out a mortar and pestle and various bags of healing herbs.

Holding back his tears, Flavius left the room, praying to Juno, Carmentis and most of all, to the Silvanus family goddess, Fortuna, that they would have mercy on his wife.

Alexander eventually emerged from the bedroom. Seeing the grim look on his face, Flavius knew that the news was bad.

Alexander shook his head and said sadly, "I am sorry. I did all that I could, but I am afraid your wife has succumbed to her injuries and loss of blood."

The statement hit Flavius like a hammer blow. Claudia and his child - both dead! In a dreamlike state, he thanked the doctor, scarcely hearing him say that he would waive his fee as he knew both deaths would come as a terrible blow to Claudia's father.

Alexander picked up his case, offered his condolences to Flavius, then quickly left.

Flavius went into the bedroom and looked at Claudia. He wept as he saw her white, pinched face and the purple shadows under her closed eyes, evidence of the great suffering she had endured. He held her lifeless hand and kissed her forehead, whispering "May Divine Juno take you into her loving care." He walked over to the crib and, his heart breaking, picked up his lifeless son and hugged him to his chest. Then, laying the baby back down in his crib, he covered him with the cloth. He had to let Claudius know about the tragedy, but how could he tell him that he had lost both daughter and grandson? He would have to find the words somehow.

He called out to Claudia's handmaid, who came hurrying into the room. "Stay with my wife and son until I return," he said sadly.

The handmaid nodded and sat down next to the bed, too upset to look at her mistress. Leaving the tragic scene, Flavius went to the stables and ordered the groom to ready Saturn. When all was ready, he mounted the horse and rode to the Claudii estate.

Claudius' spirits soared when he saw Flavius come into the villa. Surely, he thought, Flavius was here to tell him that he was a grandfather. When Flavius told him of his daughter and new-born grandson's deaths, he collapsed onto a couch. Shaking his head in disbelief, he covered his face with his hands and wept bitter tears.

Hearing her husband's distress, Lydia Flavia came to see what had happened. When Flavius told her the sad news, she gathered him into her arms and said through her tears, "My poor Flavius." She whispered a prayer, "May Claudia and your son dwell with the gods in peace forever."

Claudio was out in the city, so Flavius told his mother that he would wait for his return. He wanted to be the one to tell him, for he knew Claudio would be devastated by the news.

When Flavius told Claudio, the shock was too great for his already disturbed mind. Flavius understood when he shut himself away in his room to grieve for his beloved sister in private.

Later, that same day, Flavius and Claudius arranged the funerals of Claudia and her son. Claudius made sure it would be a grand affair, befitting the daughter and grandson of a Senator and the wife and son of an important administrator of his business affairs.

CHAPTER THIRTY-SIX

The following morning, after the ritual preparation of their bodies was complete, Claudia and her child were placed in two elaborate and costly coffins, one for an adult, the other befitting the size of the tiny child. Although new-born infants were not usually given funeral rites and cremation, Flavius and Claudius had demanded that their dead son and grandson would be suitably honoured.

The coffins were carefully placed on hand barrows ready to be borne through the city by professional bearers, as no matter what your station in life, no wagons were allowed in Rome during daylight hours.

The funeral procession was led by musicians and mime artists. They were followed by a large number of professional women mourners who wailed loudly and scratched their faces, some also pulling out their hair, as they walked along. Hired actors wearing the ancestral masks of the family of the deceased came next. Dressed in dark-coloured funeral togas, Flavius, Claudius and Claudio, walked grim-faced behind the coffins. Lydia Flavia, wearing a deep wine-coloured gown, walked with them. As a mark of respect for their Patron, some of Claudius' clients joined the back of the procession.

When the sad procession arrived at the Necropolis, the City of the Dead, set outside the city walls, the coffins were taken off the barrows and placed on the funeral pyre. Claudius could not hold back his tears as the flames ignited. Lydia Flavia took his hand and tried to comfort him as Claudio stood ramrod straight, desperately trying to control himself.

White-faced, Flavius closed his eyes, unable to bear the sight of Claudia and their son being consumed by the flames. His thoughts were tormented. First Farrah, now his wife and child. It seemed to him that he brought death to those he cared for. He had prayed to the goddesses to save his family but they had abandoned him. He began to wonder if they existed at all.

When the pyre grew cold, the ashes of the dead were collected and put into two funerary urns. Both were handed to Flavius. He held Claudia's out to her father, saying, "I think Claudia's remains should be placed in her family's tomb."

Claudius took the urn and said in a voice choked with emotion, "I thank you, Flavius."

Flavius declared that his son would be placed in the Silvanus family's ancestral tomb.

The family then went to the cemetery, situated not far from the place of the cremations. Because the Marcellus and Silvanus families' ancestors had been wealthy Patricians, both tombs were far more elaborate than the resting places of the middle classes and plebeians.

Whilst prayers for the dead were being intoned by the onlookers, the funeral urn containing Claudia's ashes was interred in the Marcellus ancestral tomb, quickly followed by the internment of the deceased baby's urn in the Silvanus family tomb.

The family and some of the clients returned to Claudius' villa to eat the small repast prepared by the female slaves in honour and memory of their dead young mistress. When it had been eaten, Claudius declared a time of mourning which would last for nine days.

An hour after eating, tired out and overwhelmed by people he barely knew offering their condolences on his loss, Flavius politely excused himself, telling Claudius and his mother that he needed to be by himself for a time of private grieving. Perfectly understanding that he needed time alone, Claudius clasped his arm and said gravely, "May Pax, the goddess of Peace, be with you."

Lydia Flavia gathered her son into her arms and kissed his forehead, trying vainly to stop her tears. Without saying another word, Flavius left Claudius' villa and returned to his own. When he arrived, he saw that the slaves had observed the ancient custom of hanging yew and cypress tree branches on the walls outside, warning people that there had been a death in the house and that for a time it was tainted.

Later that night, Flavius walked into the bedroom he had shared with Claudia. He looked at the bed on which she had breathed her last and wept. Although he had never passionately loved Claudia, he had felt a deep affection towards her and had tried to be a good and faithful husband to her. But for her untimely death, he knew they might have stayed together for many years.

He knew he would never sleep in that bed again.

He turned to the crib, then looked away, unable to bear the sight of the empty space where his son should be peacefully sleeping. He had hoped that the boy would continue the Silvanus family line, but the goddess Nemesis had intervened and declared otherwise.

He came to a decision and called for his slave. In a voice choked with emotion, he said, "Go and fetch the groom and the stable lad from the stables and bring them here to me."

The slave bowed and went out, then returned with the other two. They stood before Flavius, waiting for their instructions. They were shocked when Flavius said, "Take the bed and the crib outside and burn them."

Flavius watched as the slave and groom heaved the bed out of the room. The stable lad picked up the crib and followed them.

For the time being, knowing that the bedroom held too many bad memories, Flavius decided that he would sleep on a couch in the living area until the mourning period was complete, and then purchase a new bed.

The next few days dragged by for Flavius. On the ninth and last day of the mourning period, Claudius hosted the traditional feast for the departed. After, they went to the cemetery, where libations of wine were poured over the two urns. Flavius' house was then swept clean in order to dispel the ghosts of his dead wife and child.

Flavius was not in the mood to go to the Poseidon to meet Decimus. He would see his friend when time had healed his heartache.

The next day, Flavius approached Claudius and offered to return the villa he had purchased for Claudia and himself. Claudius shook his head and said, "The villa was not part of Claudia's dowry, Flavius. I bought it as a wedding present to you both. I do not want it back. It is yours now."

Flavius was relieved that he would not be homeless again. Grateful for Claudius' generosity, he said, "I thank you with all of my heart."

Laying a hand on Flavius' shoulder, Claudius said, "You are still part of my family."

CHAPTER THIRTY-SEVEN

There followed a time of mourning in Nabatea too. Ruth, Mary-Farrah and Hagru were shopping in the marketplace. Ruth noticed that a man leaning against a palm tree was staring at Hagru. When he saw Ruth looking at him, he quickly turned his face away.

Ruth had seen him watching Hagru on previous trips to the marketplace, and had sometimes seen the woman shyly return his smile. Ruth wondered who the man was. Worried, she asked outright, "Who is the man who keeps staring at you?"

Embarrassed, Hagru replied, "His name is Obodas, and he was the husband of my friend who died last year. He has spoken to me and asked if I would marry him, but I am your servant, ordered by Sheikh Ibrahim to take care of you and Mary-Farrah. I will not disobey my master and leave you."

Ruth felt guilty. She did not wish to be the reason why Hagru could not fulfil her personal happiness.

That afternoon, Ruth sat with Princess Phasaelis in her garden. Ruth was telling the Princess about her time with the Disciples and all the things they had done, even though they faced great danger every day. Her thoughts turned to John Mark. She knew that he loved her and had one day hoped to marry her, but her mission to work for the Lord had been far more important to her and she had left Jerusalem with few regrets.

She decided that the time was right to tell Phasaelis about the miracle Jesus had performed on her and her daughter after Mary-Farrah's birth.

Before she could begin, a servant entered the garden, bowed and said, "A thousand pardons your Highness, but the latest caravan has arrived back from Egypt."

"Does my father know?" she asked the servant.

The servant nodded. "Yes, Highness. Sheikh Ibrahim is with him now." He bowed and left the room.

Phasaelis turned to Ruth. "The Sheikh has been gone for weeks. When my father has finished speaking with him, I'm sure you would like to greet him."

Ruth was pleased that Ibrahim had returned safely to his homeland. "Thank you, your Highness, I would very much like to see him," she said.

Phasaelis smiled, knowing the great affection the Sheikh and his adopted daughter shared. "Well I suggest you go to his house and wait for him there. We will speak again soon."

Ruth had left Mary-Farrah with Hagru, and now she returned to her house to collect her. A tired-looking Hagru sighed with relief as she handed Mary-Farrah back to her mother. She was getting too old to keep up with such a mischievous and energetic child. All three then went to Ibrahim's house to await his arrival.

An hour later, followed by Drubaal, Ibrahim entered his house. Mary-Farrah was about to run to her grandfather when Ruth stopped her, shocked by what she saw. Ibrahim had grown very thin and had a debilitating cough. He seemed to have aged since his departure to Egypt. She immediately sent Hagru to fetch the doctor.

Ibrahim sank down gratefully into his silk-covered chair, and Ruth gave him a refreshing drink of grape juice and water. As he drank it, a violent burst of coughing racked his body. A worried Drubaal carried him into his bedroom and laid him down gently on his bed.

The doctor came and examined Ibrahim. His expression was grim as he turned to Ruth and said quietly, "Your father is very ill. He is suffering from a bad infection, probably picked up somewhere along his latest caravan route." He reached into his leather bag and handed her some vials containing potions and medicines. "I have already given him the first dose. It is up to you now to see that he receives the medicine a further three times today and thereafter, four doses at regular intervals for the next few days." He picked up his bag and shook his head. "I can do no more for him. He is in the hands of the gods now." With that he left the house, leaving a distraught Ruth looking after him.

Day and night, for the next four days, Ruth, Drubaal and Hagru took turns to nurse Ibrahim, with Hagru muttering prayers for his recovery to the gods of Nabatea, while Ruth and Drubaal prayed constantly to the Lord Jesus.

On the fifth day, Sheikh Ibrahim, once the proud warrior and leader of the greatest trading caravan in the Roman world, finally succumbed to his illness. Ruth clutched a distressed Mary-Farrah to her breast and wept bitter tears as she watched Drubaal undress Ibrahim, carefully fold his clothes and put them on a side table. Then a weeping Hagru washed her master's body with perfumed water, finally covering him with a silken sheet.

Drubaal went to inform Aretas of his valiant warrior's passing. When the King heard the sad news, he was deeply upset. He called his servants to him and told them to immediately begin the preparations for the state funeral of his most treasured warrior and friend, and declared a time of mourning.

When Drubaal returned, Hagru removed the silken sheet covering Ibrahim. Drubaal dipped his hands into a bowl containing various ingredients prepared by Hagru and began to anoint his master's body. When this was completed, Drubaal dressed Ibrahim in a clean robe and tied his gold belt, holding his ceremonial dagger, his mark as a warrior, around his waist. Hagru then helped him to wrap Ibrahim in three different layers of shroud, two of linen and one made from animal hair, each layer being spread separately with the mixture. All three were then secured with leather straps.

Usually the body of the deceased would be taken straight to their final resting place, but Aretas decreed that his trusty and faithful envoy would receive a state funeral in the Temple of Winged Lions the next morning.

When he heard of the death of Ibrahim, Saul was sad and offered prayers for the soul of his Nabatean friend. Although he had become friendly towards Ibrahim and Drubaal as converts to the Nazarene faith, he would not attend the Sheikh's pagan funeral, but would not try to stop Ruth from going to honour her much-loved adopted father.

The next morning, watched by a weeping Ruth and Hagru, Drubaal and Abdulla placed their master in a leather wrapper. They carried the body outside, where two further drovers waited, and laid it on the bier, ready to be taken to the Temple. Many people had gathered waiting to pay their respects to the owner of the most important caravan in Nabatea, and to a renowned warrior.

The funeral procession was led by the King and his family. Ruth, with silent tears rolling down her face, held Mary-Farrah's little hand as they and Hagru followed the funeral bier. As they slowly walked along, Ruth cast her mind back to the time when, as a child of the streets in Jerusalem, Sheikh Ibrahim had rescued her from a life of squalor and shame by taking pity on her and placing her under his wing. He had taken her to be a maidservant to his beloved niece, Farrah, and ever since that day, had shown her nothing but loving care.

As they approached the Temple of Winged Lions, Ruth handed Mary-Farrah to a weeping Hagru, saying she did not think it appropriate for a small child to witness what was about to happen to her adopted grandfather. Hagru nodded in agreement and led the child back to the house.

Ruth watched Ibrahim receive a similar Nabatean religious ceremony to that of Farrah's, but with slight changes due to his warrior status. She turned her face away as the young camel was sacrificed, still not being able to bear the sight, and said silent prayers for Ibrahim's soul, asking the Lord to receive him in Heaven.

When the religious ceremony had finished, Drubaal, Abdullah and the two drovers wheeled Ibrahim's bier to his family tomb. Ruth and some of the Sheikh's drovers followed on. Drubaal opened the door to the rock tomb and the bier was taken inside. Ibrahim was lifted off the bier and his body was placed near to the remains of his brother, Hassan, and his brother's wife, son and baby daughter. Ruth fought back tears as she saw the cedar wood casket containing Princess Farrah's ashes. The whole family were together again.

The Nabatean drovers said their final prayers, asking their gods to welcome the spirit of their dead master into their kingdom. Then Drubaal closed the door to the tomb.

Ruth turned away and went back to Ibrahim's house,

where she saw several of the Sheikh's clothes and weapons stacked on tables and placed on shelves. Picking up one of his robes she hugged it to her, weeping bitter tears. Life without Sheikh Ibrahim would never be the same.

CHAPTER THIRTY-EIGHT

It was early September, time for the annual games paying honour to the god 'Jupiter Optimus Maximus', Jupiter Best and Greatest. The games were organised by the Curule Aediles, the magistrates responsible for the care and supervision of the markets, and were extremely popular with the populace, especially pickpockets and cut-purses, who gained a fortune by mingling with the crowds and robbing them whilst they were distracted.

The excited crowds, filled with anticipation, made their way to the Circus Maximus where the games were being held. When most of the people had gained their places, the Consuls, Senators and Magistrates seated themselves in their prime position seats. Claudius had been obliged to join his fellow Senators, but his heart was not in it. Claudio had declined to go, while Flavius, who had seen too much blood recently, refused outright, a decision Claudius fully understood and sympathised with.

A blast of horns and trumpets sounded. The officials, together with the crowd, looked up to see Caligula and Caesonia, surrounded by German and Praetorian Guards, appear on the Palatine balcony overlooking the stadium below. Caligula gave a half-hearted wave as thousands of voices shouted as one "Hail Caesar." After Jupiter's priests had intoned prayers to the god, Caligula and Caesonia sat down, waiting for the games to begin.

The first event was a chariot race, followed by young men showing off their skill and horsemanship in exhibitions of horse riding. This concluded the first part of the games. Next, half-naked athletes came out onto the track and began to show off their agile, supple bodies and well-honed muscles by performing a number of different movements, and by engaging in running races, wrestling and boxing. The athletes completed their programme. As they ran off the track, they heard seductive pleas from several young women who shouted out their names and offered their addresses in the hope of future assignations.

Then came the beast hunts, where professional hunters and condemned criminals hunted down wild animals. The crowd loved to see the professional hunter's skills, while the novel forms of execution for the condemned were for them, pure entertainment.

After the event, the human and animal carcasses were hauled out of the arena by slaves wielding large hooks.

The empty, blood-soaked track was then smoothed over by slaves using rakes and long-handled brushes.

There followed an interval, after which it was time for the gladiatorial contests. Antonius stood in the tunnel leading to the arena, waiting for his turn to fight. He did not pray to the gods to keep him safe because he did not believe in them; he believed only in himself, and put his trust in the strength of his arms and legs and his determination to win.

He had watched as several pairs of gladiators of different classes had entered the arena, had heard the roar of the crowd as they had fought and parried blows, and then seen them stagger back into the tunnel exhausted and badly bruised.

This was to be his first professional contest, and he was glad that the contests were only to show off the gladiators' skill and not lead to their deaths. He was annoyed that any money he earned today would not be his to keep but would go straight into the Emperor's coffers, for Caligula had demanded that he fight as his personal gladiator and not for his own prestige or fortune. He knew that unless he gained his freedom by winning many contests, or died in the arena, his situation would not change. He was as much a prisoner now as he had been in the mines.

A blast of trumpets sounded. It was time to show the crowds what he was capable of. He took a deep breath, faced forward as his opponent joined him and together, they entered the arena.

The response from the crowd was lukewarm; nobody knew who the two opponents were. Antonius decided that he would change that. After saluting Caligula, they walked into the centre of the arena.

At first, Antonius was put off by the sheer size of the arena and the crowd watching him. He hesitated. A bad mistake, for his fellow Provocator gladiator sensed he was distracted and moved in to successfully strike a blow. His sword glanced off Antonius' shoulder but did not cut it. Furious, Antonius hit back, his sword aiming for his opponent's thigh. It struck low and bounced off his opponent's metal leg greave. Incensed by his mistake, Antonius struck out time after time, hitting his opponent's shield, breastplate, leg greave and enclosed helmet, but still the man would not give in.

Antonius knew he had to win this contest for the Emperor's sake as well as to save his own life. In desperation, he decided to use the same trick he had performed at his test contest in Capua. He moved backwards as his opponent began his onslaught, then suddenly stopped, dropped to one knee and waited. His opponent, confident of his victory, brandished his sword and moved towards him. When he was close enough, Antonius, in a burst of lightning speed, lifted his shield and rammed it up under the man's helmet, into his throat. The man was caught off guard, and the sudden impact made him stagger back. Antonius rose up and charged. Using his shield, he knocked his opponent onto the ground. Flat on his back, it took a moment for the stunned opponent to realise his predicament. Too late! Antonius was upon him.

Antonius stamped his foot down onto the fallen gladiator's stomach and held the point of his sword at his throat. As the crowds yelled and shouted their approval, a red mist descended over Antonius. He had to force himself to remember that this contest was an exhibition and not a fight to the death. He took his sword away from his opponent's throat, lifted his foot from his stomach and walked away.

The crowd erupted with delight, thrilled that they were watching the debut of a new champion. Caligula leaned forward on his chair, happy that, thanks to Antonius, he would be adding funds to his dwindling coffers. He stood up and beckoned Antonius to approach the balcony.

Breathing heavily, Antonius looked up at Caligula and raised his sword in salute.

"Leon, today you have proved yourself a worthy victor," said Caligula. "I salute you."

Antonius saluted Caligula again, then walked out of the arena. As he walked down the tunnel, he felt a presence behind him. He turned to see his opponent following him.

The man grimaced, "You play dirty, you cunning bastard."

Antonius smiled. "No hard feelings."

The opponent replied angrily, "You may have outwitted me today, but I warn you now, you will not be so lucky next time."

"What is your name?" Antonius asked.

"My name is Dagon, what is yours?"

"Leon," Antonius replied.

"Well, Leon, I want you to know that your dream of glory and fame in the arena will not last long. I will make sure that one day we are matched together again, this time in a contest to the death, and then I will kill you."

Antonius did not reply. He just grinned at Dagon, then turned away and swaggered down the tunnel, exhilarated that he had won his first public contest.

Outside, those who had heard the Emperor call the new star gladiator Leon were busily repeating it to their neighbours, and soon the whole of the stadium was buzzing with the name. Everyone was vowing that they would bet heavily on Leon in any future contest he featured in.

CHAPTER THIRTY-NINE

Three weeks after the death of Ibrahim, Nabatea endured another unexpected time of grief. The aged King Aretas, the most accomplished and longest-reigning ruler Nabatea had ever known, took to his bed and died. The family and the nation went into deep mourning.

The funeral of Aretas was the most magnificent occasion. The Queen, Phasaelis and other members of the family, led the people, including Ruth and Drubaal, in a sad procession to the Temple of The Winged Lions. After the funeral rites had been held, the King's body was borne to a magnificent painted sandstone tomb which had been erected by the King's own orders several years before his death. As Aretas was interred in the tomb, the Royal Family stood with bowed heads, quietly intoning prayers to the gods to accept Aretas into their divine presence while the people wept and wailed at the loss of their great King.

Ruth and Drubaal, who were still mourning for the Sheikh, found this loss of a second great man hard to bear. They wondered if life in Nabatea would change now that the great King was no longer the ruler.

Drubaal accompanied Ruth back to her house, where Hagru had cooked a meal for them all. When she saw her mother, Mary-Farrah ran to her and wrapped her little arms around her leg. Ruth smiled down at her, trying to ignore her terrible headache brought on by the overpowering smell of dozens of static incense burners and censers being swung on chains by the priests over and around the body of the king.

After their meal, Ruth told Drubaal her news. He sat, shocked and surprised when she said, "Sheikh Ibrahim bequeathed to me a great deal of money as well as his house." When Drubaal said immediately that he would leave his quarters there, she gently silenced him. "No. Mary-Farrah and I are happy here in this house. I do not need two houses. I would like you to have it, as a thank you for all the years you looked after and protected the Sheikh. You deserve it."

Stunned into silence by her generous offer, Drubaal bowed his head, not wanting Ruth to see the unshed tears stinging his eyes. When he could speak again, he looked at her and said, "I thank you from the bottom of my heart. As I protected my master, so too will I protect you and Mary-Farrah. This is my pledge to you."

Ruth took his hand and said quietly, "From now on, Drubaal, wherever Mary-Farrah and I go, you will go too."

Drubaal kissed her hand. Hagru got up from the table and turned away so they would not see her tears.

It was announced soon after the funeral of Aretas that his son, Malichus, would be the next king of Nabatea. Malichus was the son of Aretas and Chuldu Huldu and the brother of Phasaelis. He was welcomed by the people, but they knew he could never replace his father. They would never see the like of King Aretas again.

Over the next few days, Ruth and Drubaal visited Saul several times. On one visit, Saul told them that now that Aretas had gone, he no longer felt secure in Nabatea. He explained his reasons. "Aretas was understanding, and he often invited me to the palace to speak with him about the Lord. I don't think Aretas' son will be interested in Jesus, or be as generous as his father."

Ruth empathised with his feelings, for she had begun to feel the same. She was sad that she would no longer see Phasaelis at the palace now that she had lost most of her power to her brother and his Queen. Phasaelis had been a good and trusted friend to her. And now that the Sheikh, who had once held a powerful position working for his king, was no longer there, she felt afraid and vulnerable to the whims of someone who did not know her.

As the three of them talked together, they came up with a plan. They decided that when the next caravan was journeying to Jerusalem, they would be travelling with it.

Ruth asked Abdullah, who was to lead this caravan, when it would be leaving. She was delighted when he told her it would be the following week. When he asked Ruth why she wanted to know, she told him of their plan. Abdullah was shocked and said, "But, Ruth, you have many friends, wealth and a lovely house here, why do you want to go back?"

"It is something I feel I must do."

Abdullah shrugged. "Well, if that's what you want, then I will make sure there is room for you and your child. Given the child's age, I will try and arrange a horse-drawn carriage for you both."

Ruth thanked him, then said hesitantly, "I know I am asking a lot of you, Abdullah, but can you make room for Drubaal and Saul too?"

Abdullah frowned, scratched his forehead and sighed. "I will try to find room as a favour to you, the daughter of my former master the Sheikh, may he rest with the gods."

"Thank you." Ruth stood on tiptoe and kissed Abdullah's cheek. He blushed, and touching his cheek, he smiled as he watched her walk away.

Over the next few days, Ruth, with a tearful Hagru helping her, packed everything she could into bags which Abdullah said could be fitted over a camel's back. Knowing that Drubaal no longer needed the Sheikh's house, she told him to sell it and keep the money for himself. He sold it to a wealthy Nabatean merchant.

When she told Hagru that she could either come to

Jerusalem with her or stay in Nabatea, Hagru replied, "I thank you, mistress. But I should like to stay here. Now that you are returning to your friends in Jerusalem, you will no longer need me and I will be free to marry Obodas. He has asked me many times and says he will not give up until I say yes to him."

"Do you love him?"

"Oh yes, mistress, he is a good man."

"Then I wish you well and I truly hope that you and Obodas will be very happy together. When I am gone, I will no longer need nor want this house. Will you accept it as a wedding present from me? If you do not want it, then sell it and keep the money for yourself and your new husband."

Hagru bowed her head, too overcome to speak. When she had calmed herself, she kissed Ruth's hand in gratitude, uttering prayers to the gods asking them to protect Ruth and Mary-Farrah on their long journey to Judaea.

Drubaal hoped to see Tribune Flavius in Jerusalem, so, having the money now, he decided to buy him a present in remembrance of his promise that one day he would repay Flavius for the beautiful sword he had asked the Antonia armourer to make for him, the replacement for the sword broken in the attack by ben-Ezra's gang in Bethany. He bought an expensive dagger complete with a beaten silver and jewelled sheath.

The next morning, it was with a mixture of sadness and pleasant memories of her time in Nabatea that Ruth settled Mary-Farrah into the carriage, then climbed in by her daughter's side. Saul was balancing precariously on his camel. He was not looking forward to the journey, remembering his uncomfortable experience on a feisty camel's back when escaping from Damascus. Drubaal, on the other hand, had travelled by camel with Sheikh Ibrahim on several occasions, so it was no bother to him.

As the caravan pulled away amidst camels' bellows and the shouts of the drovers, Ruth settled back on her cushions, knowing that soon she would be with Mary and the other Disciples, especially John Mark. She was going home.

When the caravan eventually arrived in Jerusalem, Ruth climbed out of the carriage, glad that the jolting vehicle had stopped. She stretched her aching back and then, leaning inside, she picked up Mary-Farrah and carried her out. Drubaal instructed his camel to kneel and climbed off its back, shaking his head as he saw Saul struggling to control his beast. One of the drovers came to Saul's assistance. Laughing, he tapped the camel's legs with his stick and with a grunt, the camel sank down onto its belly, almost throwing Saul over its head.

Abdullah walked over to Ruth and said, "Praise the gods, we have arrived safely." He studied Ruth for a brief moment then said, "Now that we are here, have you somewhere to stay?"

"I have some very good friends who I know will welcome Mary Farrah and me into their home," replied Ruth.

"And my late master's bodyguard?" Abdullah pointed to Drubaal. He nodded when Ruth said that he too would be welcomed. "What about Saul?" he asked.

Standing close by, Saul heard the question and replied, "I will make my own arrangements. I know I won't be welcomed in the house of Ruth's friends." Seeing Ruth's worried face, he turned to her and said, "Don't worry about me, Ruth. I have many places to stay. I will manage."

Saul thanked Abdullah, nodded to Drubaal and, stroking Mary-Farrah's hair affectionately, smiled at Ruth, saying so that only she could hear, "Please don't tell Peter and the others that I have returned to Jerusalem. They will be afraid of me as they don't know about my conversion."

"But surely you can tell them?" Ruth protested.

"I have done so many bad things to the followers of Jesus." He hung his head. "Especially to their friend Stephen of Alexandria. I don't think they will ever trust my word, and who can blame them?" Before Ruth could say another word, he turned away and was quickly lost amongst the bustling crowds.

With a final smile, Abdullah turned to his drovers and ordered them to begin unloading the goods, ready to be taken to the appropriate merchants and wealthy customers.

Ruth sighed and took Mary-Farrah's hand. Drubaal picked up their luggage and followed them to Mary's house.

CHAPTER FORTY

Mary was humming a tune as she busily swept her house. She heard a loud knock on the door, and grumbling at the interruption of her housework, she leaned her broom against a cupboard and went to open it. She stared wide-eyed when she saw Ruth and a little girl standing there.

"Can it be?" she asked incredulously, "Is it really you, Ruth?"

Ruth smiled. "Yes Mary, it is me."

Mary gave her a hug, then looked at the child, who had buried her face in her mother's skirts. She said kindly, "And is your name Mary-Farrah?"

Ruth encouraged her daughter to look at Mary and answer her. "Yes," answered Mary-Farrah immediately burying her face in her mother's skirts again.

Drubaal stepped forward. He had stood to the side of

the door so that Ruth and Mary-Farrah would be the first people Mary would see. Mary gasped when she saw him.

"And you, Drubaal! It is so good to see you all. Come in, come in." She stepped away from the door and ushered her friends into the house. She pointed to the table benches. "Please sit down," she said. She poured out two cups of watered wine for Ruth and Drubaal, then gave Mary-Farrah a cup of goat's milk. Shaking her head, she said, "I can't believe it's you. Have you returned to us?" She smiled when Ruth nodded. She looked at the little girl sitting quietly beside Ruth and said "You have grown so tall, Mary-Farrah. How old are you now?"

Mary knew exactly how old the little girl was as she had helped to bring her into the world in this very house. Memories of the traumatic birth came back to her. If the loving Lord had not shown mercy, both mother and child would have perished.

She forced her attention back to the present as Mary-Farrah replied proudly, "I am almost four years old."

"Well, you have grown into a lovely young girl," Mary said, smiling.

Mary-Farrah giggled at the compliment.

Mary wondered what Peter would say when he saw Ruth looking so well and dressed in an expensive Nabatean garment. What too would her son, John Mark, say when he saw the girl he loved sitting there?

As if she had read Mary's thoughts, Ruth asked, "Are Peter and the other Disciples well?"

"Yes, they are fine," came Mary's reply.

"And how is John Mark?"

"He too is well," Mary said. "He has never married you know."

All Ruth could say in reply was, "Oh."

"Peter, John Mark and those of the Disciples who are still in Jerusalem will be home soon. If you can wait for them, I know they'll be so happy to see you, and they'll want to know what you've been doing these past few years."

"We can wait for them," Ruth said, nervous at the prospect of seeing John Mark again.

An hour later Peter, John Mark, James, John, Andrew and Barnabas came home. John Mark was speaking with Peter and, at first, he did not see who was sitting at the table. When he turned to greet his mother and saw Ruth, he stood rooted to the spot, open-mouthed with surprise. Taken aback, he hesitated in greeting her, not knowing what to say.

Seeing the look of shock on her son's face, Mary said, "Peter, all of you, look who has returned to us?"

Peter and the other Disciples were delighted to see their friends again. Peter sat down next to Ruth and said, "May the Lord be praised. I, I mean we –" he glanced at John Mark – "thought we would never see you again." He looked at Mary-Farrah and said kindly, "Hello, my name is Peter." Mary-Farrah gave her mother a nervous look, obviously afraid of the big man who was speaking to her. "You are so pretty, Mary-Farrah, so like your mother."

Mary-Farrah gave him an astonished look. "You know my name!"

"Yes, I know your name, because you see, you were born in this house." He saw Mary-Farrah's wide-eyed look but did not elaborate. If the child did not know the circumstances of her birth and what had happened after, it would be up to Ruth to tell the child the truth. He looked across the table at Drubaal. "And you, our dear Drubaal, are you well?" Drubaal nodded. "But how did you reach Jerusalem from Nabatea?"

"We travelled from Petra with the latest caravan, arriving in Jerusalem this morning." Drubaal answered.

"Of course, you have returned with Sheikh Ibrahim."

Ruth looked down and said sadly, "I am afraid Sheikh Ibrahim died a few weeks ago."

Peter frowned. "I'm sorry to hear that. Is that why you have come home?"

"Partly," Ruth replied.

Seeing Ruth's distress, Mary began to lay bowls on the table, saying kindly but firmly, "Peter, I'm sure all of you are hungry. The broth is ready and I think we should eat now. There will be plenty of time to talk after supper."

Peter nodded, understanding her meaning. The other Disciples sat down at their places around the table, and Mary poured the broth into their bowls. Peter took the bread from its wooden platter, broke it and blessed it, then passed it around for all to take their share.

Mary-Farrah looked on in wonder. She had never seen

or heard anything like this before. What kind of words had the big man said when he broke the bread and passed it around? She did not understand; she only knew that mealtimes here were conducted differently from those in Nabatea.

After they had eaten, Mary asked Ruth if they had a place to stay. When Ruth said they had not had time to arrange anything yet, Mary immediately said, "That is settled then. You will stay here with us."

"Do you have enough room for us?" Ruth asked.

"Yes, of course. Some of the other Disciples have left Jerusalem for the time being, so we have enough spare sleeping mats and there's enough room in my bedroom for you and Mary-Farrah." She looked across at Drubaal and said, "I'm sure you will not mind sleeping in this room, Drubaal." She pointed to a corner of the room which was big enough to take a large-sized sleeping mat.

"I'm happy to do that," said Drubaal, smiling.

Ruth helped Mary to wash the dirty bowls, and then Mary organised the sleeping mats. Seeing her daughter practically falling asleep at the table, Ruth carried her into Mary's bedroom and settled her onto her sleeping mat, staying with her until she was fast asleep.

Ruth looked around the room where she and Mary-Farrah had been saved by the Lord. She had answered His request for her to travel to Nabatea, but she did not know why she had gone to the Sheikh's homeland. She had not done much to spread God's word there, but she had met Saul of Tarsus and heard his miraculous story. He too had been anxious that he was not doing the Lord's work. Perhaps the Lord had different plans for them. She would have to wait and see.

She wondered where Saul was now and if he had found somewhere to stay. It was his choice not to come here with her, so there was nothing she could do. She knew only that she had to keep her promise to him and not tell Peter that he was back in Jerusalem.

She went back out into the main room and sat down at the table, where Drubaal was talking with the others. Peter leaned across the table and asked her about her stay in Nabatea. Leaving out the part about meeting Saul of Tarsus, she told him of her adoption by the Sheikh, of her friendliness with the daughter of King Aretas, the Princess Phasaelis, and of her talks about Jesus with both the King and the Princess.

"And did they believe?" asked Peter hopefully.

"They were certainly interested in the stories about Him," Ruth replied, "and I think, given more time, they would have become true believers, but unfortunately, King Aretas died soon after Sheikh Ibrahim, and his son became King." She sighed. "He's a different man from his father and I don't think he could ever be swayed from his own gods. The new King would no longer let me see the Princess so we could talk together." Knowing that she would never see Phasaelis again made her feel sad. "Things were changing quickly in Nabatea," she continued, "and without the Sheikh's protection, I no longer wished to stay there with Mary-Farrah. That's why we returned here."

The evening passed by pleasantly. They spoke of political changes concerning Herod Antipas, which Ruth said Phasaelis had told her about, and mentioned the sudden disappearance of Pilate, which Ruth did not know about.

"We had a new Governor, Marcellus," Peter explained, "but he did not last long. Now we have Herod Agrippa, a friend of the Roman Emperor." He shook his head. "I fear we will fare no better under him than under Pilate."

They talked some more, but it had been a long day and Ruth felt exhausted and hot. Stifling a yawn, she excused herself and went outside. She climbed the stairs leading up to the flat roof of the house. At the top of the stairs she stopped and gratefully breathed in the cool night air, then walked out onto the roof.

She saw a man standing in the shadows, looking up at the stars. Suddenly nervous, she called out, "Who's there?"

Surprised at the sudden interruption, the man turned his head and looked straight at her. It was John Mark.

He walked over to Ruth and said, "I was praying to the Lord, thanking him for your safe return." He took her hand, "Oh, Ruth, I've missed you so much. I wondered if I would ever see you again, and now here you are standing before me. The Lord has answered my prayers." He looked into Ruth's face, saw her eyes shining with tears, and said, "I have always loved you. I was going to ask you to marry me before you went away, but it seemed the Lord had other ideas." He gently wiped away her tears with his fingertips and said, "Did you accomplish His work in Nabatea?"

"No, not really." Ruth shook her head sadly. She looked earnestly at John Mark and said, "I truly do not know what I have to do, or where I have to go to do the Lord's work. I feel lost."

John Mark gathered her into his arms and kissed her forehead. "Then stay here with me, marry me and we will work for the Lord together."

It was so comforting to be held in John Mark's embrace; she felt safe and loved. It would be so easy to say yes to his plea. She pulled away from him, looked up into his eyes and said, "Please give me time to give you my answer. I'm so tired I can hardly think straight."

"You can have all the time you need, Ruth," he replied, but he desperately hoped her answer would be yes. Relieved that Ruth had not given him an outright no, he stepped away from her and watched as she walked back down the stairs.

When Ruth entered Mary's bedroom, she looked at Mary-Farrah, who was sleeping peacefully. As Mary was still talking with Drubaal and the others, she had time to think about John Mark's proposal. She lay down on her sleeping mat, her thoughts in turmoil. She would never regret the time she had spent with her adopted father in Nabatea, nor forget the honour he had bestowed on her, but she had been arrogant and foolhardy to think she could go to the

Sheikh's homeland and spread the Lord's message. Was marriage to John Mark what the Lord had really intended for her? She tossed and turned, her thoughts reeling. She saw Mary enter the bedroom and prepare herself for bed. Not wishing to enter into conversation, Ruth lay still pretending to be asleep.

Soon Ruth heard Mary gently snoring. Ruth whispered, "Please Lord, tell me what I must do to serve you."

No answer came.

CHAPTER FORTY-ONE

They had been back in Jerusalem for two weeks, during which time Ruth had found it hard to keep Mary-Farrah occupied within the confines of Mary's house. Mary-Farrah had been used to playing outside in the sunshine with the Nabatean children in the relative safety of Petra. Ruth knew from her own experiences that the narrow streets of Jerusalem were no place to let a child run free; there were too many people constantly bustling up and down, as well as columns of patrolling Roman legionaries marching through the streets, knocking aside those who got in their way.

This morning, she decided to take her bored daughter out, accompanied by Drubaal. An excited Mary-Farrah held her mother's hand as they began their sightseeing tour of the city. The first place they visited was the Valley of the Cheesemakers. Ruth smiled as she saw Mary-Farrah stare wide-eyed at the vast amount of shops situated there, shops ranging from those selling food, to those selling luxury items and expensive clothes. Mary-Farrah had never seen anything like it; how different it all was from the Nabatean marketplaces. Only one thing was the same: the noise. Mary-Farrah covered her ears as the sound of bargaining from both shop owners and their prospective customers resounded everywhere around her.

When they came to a dress shop, Drubaal waited in the street while Ruth took her daughter inside. Mary-Farrah looked around in wonder at the beautiful garments displayed there. She fixed her eyes on a pale blue dress hanging up on the wall. The dress had silver thread running through it; above it were a matching headdress and a pair of dainty slippers. They all looked as though they would fit her. She sighed and said, "They are so beautiful, like the clothes of a princess."

With the large sum of money Sheikh Ibrahim had left her, Ruth felt that she could hardly refuse her daughter. Mary-Farrah squealed with delight when Ruth told her she would buy the outfit for her.

Clutching the parcel of clothes under his arm, Drubaal followed Ruth as she led her daughter along the street. Ruth stopped and pointed, "If you look up there, you'll see Herod's Palace and the viaduct which leads from the palace to the Temple area."

Shading her eyes from the brilliant sunshine, Mary-Farrah looked up and said, "It is wonderful."

Ruth did not tell her daughter that before His crucifixion, the Lord had been sent to that palace where Herod Antipas, who could have saved Him, had instead mocked Him and returned Him to Pilate and certain death. Feeling uncomfortable, she said, "Let's go to the Temple."

Drubaal could not enter the Temple, so he waited outside while Ruth and Mary-Farrah went to see the beasts being sold for sacrifice. When she saw that a priest was about to slaughter a young bull as an offering to God, Ruth hurriedly moved her daughter away. Outside the Temple, they looked up at the Fortress Antonia looming above and saw Roman legionaries patrolling its perimeters. The sight of the soldiers frightened Mary-Farrah. She held her mother's hand tightly and began to cry. They immediately returned to Mary's house.

Seeing the fortress had brought back mixed memories for Drubaal. He wondered if Decurion Julius and Tribune Flavius were still there, and decided that he would go to the fort and make enquiries.

From the first day of their arrival, Ruth had offered Mary money for their keep, which she had refused to take, saying that she was delighted that Ruth and her daughter were staying in her house and pleased that Ruth seemed happy there.

Ruth had listened eagerly to Peter and the others when they came home in the evenings and spoke of their successful conversion of people to the Lord. On this night, when the Disciples returned, Ruth decided to ask Peter some questions.

"Where do you meet these people?" she began. She was shocked when Peter gave her the answer.

"We go to the Pool of Bethesda and to areas where the poor and beggars live, places we know the Priests and Temple Authorities call 'unclean' and would never visit."

"Aren't you afraid of catching a disease, or being robbed by the beggars?" Ruth asked incredulously.

Peter shook his head. "No. Jesus was never afraid to give comfort to people such as these. We Disciples saw Him cure their illnesses or, in some cases, cast out the demons that tormented them. The poor and the dispossessed never hurt Him, rather they hung onto His every word and clamoured for Him to heal them."

Ruth sat silent for a moment, then said, "How I would have loved to have seen Jesus and hear His words when I was a child of the streets."

A sudden thought came to her. "Peter," she said, "can I come with you and help these poor people too?"

Peter scratched his chin, wondering if it would be wise for such a pretty young woman to be in the company of beggars and rough men.

"Please," Ruth said. "I know Mary will look after Mary-Farrah while I am with you."

Drubaal, who had been listening to the conversation, said immediately, "I will accompany her and make sure no harm comes to her."

Ruth wore such an earnest look that Peter felt he could not refuse her request. He said, "I could do with extra help giving out bread and tending to the people…but you must both stay close to me, I do not want you to be harmed in any way."

"Oh thank you!" A grateful Ruth gave him a hug, as Drubaal looked on smiling.

Peter gave a silent plea: "I hope I am doing the right thing, Lord."

For the next few days, Ruth and Drubaal accompanied Peter and John Mark to the Pool of Bethesda. John Mark watched admiringly as Ruth gave out bread to those who were hungry, while Drubaal helped to bathe their sores, both speaking words of encouragement to those who were downhearted by their troubles. Afterwards they would sit and listen to Peter. How inspiring he was. How he made their heart sing with his stories of Jesus. Ruth thought that if only she could speak up for the Lord like him, then perhaps she would have had more success in Nabatea. How could she know that Princess Phasaelis had kept Ruth and Saul's words in her heart, and had begun secretly to pray to the Lord?

After a particularly hard-working but fruitful day, Ruth, Drubaal, John Mark and Peter returned to Mary's house, where they heard about the other Disciples' successes. They were preparing for the evening meal when Barnabas came rushing in and said excitedly, "I have brought someone to see you." Barnabas gestured to the visitor to come into the house.

When the man walked nervously into the room, the others saw a man dressed in ragged clothes; his beard was matted with grime and his face and hands were encrusted with dirt. At first they thought it was a beggar Barnabas had taken pity on and brought home to be washed and fed.

Peter looked warily at the beggar and asked, "Who are you, stranger?"

The man did not reply.

Barnabas said, "He is Saul of Tarsus."

Speechless with shock, the group stared at Saul. Mary was the first to speak. She looked at Barnabas and said coldly, "How dare you bring that man here to my house! Get him out. Now!"

Saul turned to leave, but Barnabas blocked his way, saying firmly, "Stay here, Saul." Barnabas turned to the others and said with a pleading voice, "Please, let me explain."

"Your excuse had better be a good one," John Mark said, narrowing his eyes.

"If you will allow me, I will tell you the circumstances in which I found Saul."

"Yes, Barnabas," replied Andrew, "I think you should."

CHAPTER FORTY-TWO

Barnabas began. "I was walking through the city making my way home when I passed by an alleyway and heard a man's feeble voice call out my name. Fearing someone was hurt, I walked down the alleyway to see if I could help them." He took a breath. "As I approached the man, he said, 'Barnabas, do you recognise me?' When I shook my head, the man whispered, 'I am Saul of Tarsus. Please help me'. Looking closer, I could see that it was indeed Saul and he desperately needed help. So I brought him here." He looked at Peter and said, "Will you help him?"

Peter looked at the bedraggled figure standing head bowed before him and said, "Are your clothes and appearance a trick to gain Barnabas' pity? Were you hoping he would bring you here so that you could arrest us?" Saul shook his head. Peter continued: "Are you going to arrest more converts and cause them more misery?"

Saul shook his head again. Peter was becoming annoyed at Saul's lack of answers and said gruffly, "Then why exactly are you here?"

"I know you will find it hard to believe after all the bad things I have done, but I want you to know that the Lord Jesus…"

Andrew interrupted Saul, "You dare to say the name of the Lord?"

"Yes, I dare," came Saul's reply, "you see, the Lord forgave me. I have repented of my sins and I am a reformed man."

Ruth blurted out, "Yes, he has repented. He has done some good things in the name of the Lord."

Peter turned to her and said, "How do you know this, Ruth?"

Ruth looked squarely at Peter. "Because Drubaal and I met him in Petra." She saw Peter's quizzical look and explained. "I'm sorry I didn't tell you before, but Saul was with us when we arrived in Jerusalem with the caravan. He told me I was not to let you know he was here. He was afraid of what you might do." She looked imploringly at Peter. "Please, Peter, let Saul tell you his story."

Peter sighed, then looked at Mary and said, "Mary, please fill a bowl with water and give Saul a towel to dry himself." Mary protested, but Peter held up his hand and said, "Please, Mary." Then he turned to Andrew. "You look to be the same size as Saul, would you give him one of your spare undergarments and a clean tunic?"

Andrew was horrified, but did as his brother asked.

Later, freshly washed, his hair and beard clean and combed and wearing Andrew's clothes, Saul sat down to eat with the group. It was the first good meal he had eaten in a long time. When the meal was finished, they listened intently as Saul explained what had happened to him.

"When I returned to Jerusalem, I went straight to some old friends, but they wanted nothing to do with me and shut the door in my face." He sighed. "My fear of being arrested stopped me from seeking out my old tutor, Gamaliel."

"Why should you be arrested?" Andrew asked.

"Because of my conversion."

"Your conversion?" Peter said warily.

"Let me explain," said Saul. He told them what had happened on his journey to Damascus, how he had been converted by the Lord, how he had been hunted and beaten in that city and of his escape to Nabatea through the help of Ananias, who had been sent by the Lord to restore his sight and baptise him. He also spoke of the brave converts: Mordecai, the wine merchant and Jonathan and Calisto.

He sighed. "So you see, if the High Priests knew I was here, they would arrest me. That's why I am homeless and reduced to living hand to mouth every day."

When he had finished, John shook his head and said, "Do you believe this fantastic story, Peter?"

Peter sat pondering on Saul's story. He made up his mind when Ruth, backed up by Drubaal, told him how she and Saul had taught about Jesus to Princess Phasaelis and her father, the King of Nabatea. He looked straight at Saul and said, "Very well, Saul, you may stay here with us."

Despite the scowls on the others' faces, Saul was jubilant. "I cannot thank you enough, Peter. I promise you all, from now on, my life will be dedicated to the Lord."

Ruth and Drubaal looked at each other, then at Saul, and smiled.

The next day, after helping Ruth and Peter to feed the beggars, Drubaal went to the Fortress Antonia. Drubaal approached the fortress gate and was challenged by the two legionaries guarding it. "What do you want?" one said, appraising Drubaal carefully.

"I wish to see Decurion Julius Cornelius Vittelius."

"What do you want with the Decurion?" he asked suspiciously.

"We are old friends," Drubaal replied.

The guard searched Drubaal for hidden weapons. Satisfied there were none, he said, "Wait here!", then went into the fortress to find Julius. He was soon back with him in tow.

Julius was overjoyed to see his old friend. "Drubaal! What are you doing in Jerusalem? I thought you were in Nabatea with Sheikh Ibrahim?"

Drubaal gave a wan smile and said, "A lot has happened since I last saw you".

Julius was intrigued. "Look, I am off duty in a couple of hours. Come back here then and we will go to The

Charioteer's Tavern. It's near the chariot race track and Roman friendly."

Drubaal nodded, then walked away. Julius went back inside leaving the guards looking after Drubaal, and wondering how the Decurion could be friends with a Carthaginian.

Two hours later, Drubaal went back to the fortress. He was amazed at how busy the tavern was. It was filled with off-duty legionaries and foreign merchants. Julius laughed, saying, "You think this is busy, you should see this place on race day." He took a long drink of wine, then said, "It is good to see you, old friend. Tell me, how are the Sheikh and the servant girl – what was her name?"

"Ruth," Drubaal replied. When Julius asked how they had fared in Nabatea, he told him the whole story and gave the reason why he and Ruth were back in Jerusalem.

"I'm sorry to hear about the Sheikh," said Julius, "but it's good to see you again."

"How is Tribune Flavius?" Drubaal asked before taking a mouthful of watered wine.

Julius shrugged. "All I know is that he was recalled to Rome, something to do with a family problem, but he never returned. That was almost four years ago. The Commander, Sextus and Governor Pilate have gone too." He went on to tell Drubaal about Pilate and the Samaritan massacre.

Drubaal leaned forward and said quietly, "Do you know the Tribune's address in Rome?"

Julius shook his head. "No, but Flavius did say once that his family lived on the Caelian Hill." He decided to change the subject. "I'm glad I've seen you, Drubaal. I'm being transferred soon." He saw Drubaal's surprised face and said, "To the Caesarea Garrison." He smiled. "I'm going home. Hopefully I will get to see my father and sister. I cannot wait!"

"I wish you well," Drubaal replied.

"You too, Drubaal. Perhaps one day you will visit Caesarea."

Drubaal nodded, thinking it unlikely that he would.

Over the next few days, Ruth and Drubaal continued to work with Peter and John Mark at the Pool of Bethesda. From time to time, as Ruth was handing out bread to the beggars, she would look up and catch John Mark looking at her. She would return his smile, knowing that his feelings for her had grown, as had hers for him. If he asked her again to marry him, she would probably say yes.

One night after supper, John Mark spoke to his mother. "Mother, you know that I love Ruth, and I know that she loves me, so I'm asking you if you will agree to my marrying her."

Mary's eyes shone. "Yes, son. It would make me very happy."

John Mark kissed his mother's hand and said, "Thank you. Then tomorrow, I will ask her to be my wife."

That night, Ruth dreamed a strange dream. A dream that would change everything.

The next morning, before John Mark had risen from his bed, Ruth saw Peter sitting at the table. She sat down by his side. When he saw her troubled expression, he said, "Is something wrong?"

"I'm not sure," Ruth said. "Last night I dreamed a strange dream."

"Would you like to tell me about this dream?" Peter asked kindly.

Ruth nodded. "I dreamed that I was in a large open-air space, standing before a faceless man seated on an ivory throne. He was laughing at me. Above his head was a banner with the word 'Babylon' written on it. Suddenly I was lying on sand, my dress was torn and bloody and I could hear a cheering mob."

She stopped briefly, trying to remember every detail of the disturbing dream, then resumed. "Then it was the faceless man who was lying on the sand covered in blood and I was standing over him. My bloodstained dress had changed into a pure white robe and I had a golden crown on my head." She looked quizzically at Peter and said, "Please, Peter, can you tell me what it means?"

Peter shook his head. "I don't know, Ruth. But the banner with 'Babylon' written on it may be significant."

"I know about the Jews' captivity in Babylon hundreds of years ago," Ruth said, "but what does Babylon mean now?"

Peter stared at her, frowning. "Babylon is the name the Jews call Rome."

"Peter," Ruth said excitedly, "I think the Lord wants me to go to Rome."

CHAPTER FORTY-THREE

When Ruth told Drubaal she was going to Rome, he readily agreed that he would accompany her as her bodyguard. This might be his chance to find Flavius and give him the dagger.

Mary, Saul and the Disciples were shocked when Ruth told them her plan. John Mark was stunned. Later, he found Ruth in Mary's bedroom, packing clothes into a bundle.

"Am I to lose you again so soon?" he said sadly.

Ruth saw the sadness in his eyes. "John Mark, please let me go to Rome, I know the Lord has a purpose for me there." She told him about her dream.

Horrified, John Mark argued, "Are you so sure that it was the Lord speaking to you? Rome is such a dangerous place. It might have been a warning." He held her close.

"I love you and want to marry you. I could not bear it if I never saw you again."

Ruth smiled. "I love you too, John Mark. I will not be gone forever. Let me do what I believe I must. Then, when I return, I will gladly become your wife."

John Mark held her tightly, not wanting to ever let her go.

Early the next morning Ruth sent Drubaal out to hire a donkey and a cart. This would be their means of transport to reach the northern Port of Akko.

When Drubaal returned with the donkey and cart, a tearful Mary kissed Ruth and Mary-Farrah goodbye. Saul and the other Disciples wished them all a safe passage to Rome. Peter took Ruth's hand and said, "Ruth, Mary-Farrah, once again we must say goodbye. May the Lord bless and keep you, and may He protect you in the days to come." He turned to Drubaal and said, "May He bless you too, Drubaal."

Drubaal smiled. "Don't worry, Peter, I will take care of Ruth and Mary-Farrah."

John Mark agreed to go with them to Akko; when they had boarded their ship, he would return the donkey and cart to their owners.

Drubaal climbed up onto the cart. John Mark sat next to him as Ruth and Mary-Farrah settled down on the interior seat. When all was ready, Ruth gave a final wave to her friends, and Drubaal urged the donkey forward. This was the beginning of a new adventure.

When they reached Akko, John Mark helped Ruth and Mary-Farrah down from the cart while Drubaal climbed down from his seat, removed his curved swords and wrapped them in a cloth, securing the cloth with leather straps. He placed them with their luggage, then, with Mary-Farrah walking up the gangplank behind him, he took the luggage onto the ship leaving Ruth and John Mark alone.

John Mark took Ruth into his arms and whispered words of love. Ruth, tears streaming down her face, said, "I love you dearly, John Mark. When I return, if you still want me…"

"Want you?" John Mark exclaimed. "I can hardly draw breath when I am away from you." He kissed her and held her close. Finally he released her, saying, "Hurry back to me." Just then they were interrupted by the vessel's captain warning passengers that the ship was about to set sail, with or without them. Ruth boarded the ship and, with a last wave to John Mark, she joined Mary-Farrah and Drubaal.

Heartbroken, John Mark's eyes followed the ship until it disappeared from view. With a heavy heart, he climbed up onto the cart and began the long journey back to Jerusalem.

It was a long, tiring journey to Rome, and Ruth sometimes

found it difficult trying to keep Mary-Farrah occupied. She was grateful when, seeing the child's boredom, one of the sailors, who said he had children of his own, offered to keep her busy. When he had the time, he showed Mary-Farrah how to tie knots in the many ship's ropes and kept her entertained by telling her stories about his adventures at sea. He explained to her how the ship travelled, sometimes by using oarsmen and sometimes by sail. She was fascinated when he told her about navigation by the stars. When she told her mother and Drubaal about this, Drubaal said, "When I was a child, my father told me that long ago, the Carthaginians were the masters of the seas and he explained to me how they used the stars for guidance. Tonight, if you wish, I will show you."

Ruth nodded, saying, "I too would like to know."

Ruth and Mary-Farrah looked up as Drubaal pointed to the stars which sparkled like diamonds set in a background of black velvet. Drubaal showed them Polaris, the North Star, Orion's Belt, commonly known as the Three Sisters and the various shapes made by the constellations. He gave some of them names: Taurus, the Bull, Sagittarius, the Centaur and Scorpio, the Scorpion. Later, a tired but happy Ruth and Mary-Farrah retired to their beds, leaving Drubaal looking up at the skies and dreaming about his long-lost homeland.

Although Saul's conversion had made the Disciples' lives easier, they knew that the High Priests' agents were still searching for converts, especially Saul. Peter was worried. Over the last few weeks Saul had placed them in great danger. Unconcerned, Saul had begun to walk about freely in Jerusalem, speaking boldly about Jesus and debating with the Greek-speaking Jews, not knowing that they secretly planned to murder him. Fearful that the High Priests would become involved, the Disciples decided that Saul could no longer stay in Jerusalem. Peter and Barnabas offered to escort him to Caesarea and find a ship that would take him back to Tarsus.

When the ship carrying Ruth, Mary-Farrah and Drubaal arrived in Ostia, Drubaal asked the Captain what the easiest way to reach Rome was. The captain answered, "You have a small child with you, it would be impossible for you to walk to Rome, and if you travelled by cart, you would have to wait until dark before you could enter the city." He thought for a moment, then added, "However, there are barges constantly sailing up the River Tiber delivering merchandise to the merchants' warehouses in the city. You may be lucky and catch one."

Drubaal told Ruth this, and they hurried to the mouth of the Tiber, where they saw a barge loaded with amphorae waiting by the river bank. Drubaal approached the barge owner and asked if they could come aboard and travel on it to Rome. The owner agreed – for the right price. Drubaal handed him the money and the three weary travellers boarded the barge. With a sharp order from the owner, the barge began its journey to Rome.

Sometime later, the barge manoeuvred into a dock. The owner announced to Drubaal, "We have reached the Emporium, the Port of Rome." He turned and shouted at his crew, "Lift these amphorae of durum wheat off and carry them up to the wheat merchants' warehouse. He turned to Drubaal. "This is where you get off. We are not too far from the Aventine Hill district, you'll be safe there."

The weary travellers thanked the barge owner. They looked up and saw separate walls and ladders leading up to the quayside. They followed the members of the crew up a ladder until they reached the paved stone walkways of the Emporium, where some legionaries and Praetorians stood watching the goods being taken to the various merchants. When they saw three strangers, they stared at them, especially at Drubaal. Ruth instinctively covered the lower half of her face with her scarf and held Mary-Farrah's hand tightly.

One of the legionaries saw the large bundle of cloth carried by Drubaal. He stepped forward. "What have you got there, stranger?"

Drubaal hesitated, knowing he had no option but to show his swords to the legionary. When the legionary saw them he exclaimed, "By the gods, look at these monsters." The other legionaries came to have a look. "You can't walk about the city wearing these," the first legionary warned, "You will have to leave them with us."

Gambling that they did not know who the Sheikh was, Drubaal pulled himself up to his full, impressive height and said, "I am Drubaal, bodyguard to His Illustrious Highness Sheikh Ibrahim bin Yusuf Al-Khareem, Chief Envoy to the Nabatean Royal Family, and these," he pointed to Ruth and Mary-Farrah, "are his daughter and granddaughter. They are on a personal visit to Rome and I have been instructed by the Sheikh to guard them."

A Praetorian stepped forward, demanding to see the weapons. He looked at them, then at Drubaal, then turned to the legionary and said, "Leave those swords with me. This is Praetorian business." The legionary shrugged and handed them over. The Praetorian said to Drubaal, "Before you leave Rome, come to the main Praetorian Guard House and I'll make sure you get these back. Now, you had best be on your way."

Drubaal was disappointed but also relieved as he led Ruth and her daughter away from the Emporium. They came to the base of the Aventine Hill, hoping to find suitable lodgings. They looked at several apartment blocks, finally deciding to rent a room in one that looked clean and safe. It was close to sunset and Drubaal knew it would be dangerous to walk the streets in the dark, so he decided to wait until morning to try to find Flavius' family estate.

The next morning, Drubaal said to Ruth, "Stay here, while I go in search of Flavius."

The sun was shining as he walked into the city. Where was the Caelian Hill? He asked a passer-by, who pointed him in the right direction. He came to the hill, looked up at the massive aqueduct high above it and began to climb. The higher he climbed, the more impressive the villas became. But which one belonged to the Silvanus family?

Near the top of the hill, he came to the edge of a large estate. Perhaps this was the place. He entered the estate, walked to the front door of the villa and knocked. The doorkeeper opened the door grille and looked out.

Drubaal said, "Is this the Silvanus residence?"

The doorkeeper replied "What do you want?"

"Is Tribune Flavius Silvanus at home?"

"No!" The doorkeeper slammed the grille shut.

Drubaal trudged down the hill until he came to the next wealthy villa. The doorkeeper challenged him. When Drubaal said he was a friend of Flavius and gave his name, the doorkeeper said, "Wait there!" A few minutes later, the grille reopened and a man looked out.

It was Claudio.

CHAPTER FORTY-FOUR

"Are you the Carthaginian?" Claudio stared incredulously at Drubaal. When Drubaal nodded, Claudio said, "Flavius has told me a lot about you. Why do you wish to see him?"

"I have urgent news from Nabatea and Judaea," Drubaal replied.

Claudio was curious, but this news was for Flavius alone, so he directed him down the hill. "Look for the villa with the red door and the bronze horse-head knocker." Drubaal thanked him and set off.

Flavius' doorkeeper looked Drubaal up and down, and said, "Name?" When Drubaal told him, he said, "I will inform my master." The doorkeeper shut the grille.

Flavius was stunned when he heard Drubaal's name. He came to the front door and looked through the grille. "Drubaal? It is you! Come in, my friend." He unlocked the door and ushered him in.

After ordering his slave to bring wine, he said, "What are you doing here?"

"Ruth and her daughter are here too. We are staying in an apartment in the Aventine Hill District."

Flavius was filled with curiosity. He had many questions, but they would have to wait. "You are most welcome to come and stay with me," Flavius offered.

"Are you sure, sir?" Drubaal replied, surprised.

"Of course, I have plenty of room. Go and get them and bring them here."

"Thank you, Tribune."

Drubaal left the villa and returned to Ruth. When he told her about Flavius' offer, she immediately agreed to go there. Soon they were being welcomed into Flavius' home.

He asked Ruth's daughter her name. When she replied shyly, "Mary-Farrah," he smiled; it kept alive the name of his lost love.

Flavius ordered the surprised slave to bring refreshments for him and his guests. While the refreshments were being prepared, he showed them their rooms. Leaving their luggage there, they returned to the dining area.

Flavius listened as Ruth and Drubaal spoke about Sheikh Ibrahim and life in Nabatea, and why they had returned to Judaea. He was sorry to hear of Ibrahim's death. He remembered the first time he had seen him and Drubaal in the tavern in Jerusalem where Farrah, the Sheikh's niece, had danced so exotically. Only later had he discovered that she was a spy working for Pilate. He tried to banish the vision of the beautiful girl who had captured his heart, and concentrate on what Drubaal was saying.

When he heard Drubaal say that he had seen Julius, his response was immediate.

"How is he?"

Drubaal replied, "He is well, and happy to be transferring to Caesarea."

Flavius smiled. "That's good news. It means he will be able to see his family again."

Ruth was about to ask Flavius why he was not living on his family's estate, but then the refreshments arrived.

"Come, eat and drink," Flavius said, smiling.

After they had eaten, Ruth asked her question.

Flavius frowned. "It's a long story." He began with his father's suicide, then went on to tell them about his stolen inheritance. Drubaal shook his head, angry that Flavius had been the victim of such unfair treatment.

Flavius continued, "Senator Claudius has been very generous to me and to my mother. He gave us shelter and made me the manager of his business affairs. He married my mother, and I married his daughter, Claudia." He sighed. "Unfortunately, Claudia died after giving birth to our son, who also perished."

Ruth was shocked. "Life has been so hard for you," she said sympathetically.

Flavius did not respond to that. "How long will you stay in Rome?" he asked.

"I'm not sure," Ruth replied.

Trying to lighten the atmosphere, Drubaal took the opportunity to give Flavius the dagger. As Flavius unwrapped the cloth, he smiled. "This is magnificent!" he said, "Thank you Drubaal, for such a beautiful gift."

"I told you sir that one day I would repay you for your generous gift of my sword," Drubaal replied, smiling.

"Where are your swords?" Flavius asked.

"When we reached the Emporium, I had them confiscated by a Praetorian Guard."

"Of course, you would not be allowed to wear them in the city. Do you know who the Praetorian was?" Drubaal shook his head. Flavius decided he would ask Decimus when he next saw him, for surely such swords as those would be the talk of the guardhouse.

"Rest yourselves today, and if you wish, tomorrow I will show you some of the city," said Flavius.

"Yes please!" said Mary-Farrah. They all laughed.

The following day Flavius took them on a tour of the Palatine area, pointing out the Emperor's palace, the Circus Maximus and several of the Temples. They also visited some shops, where Ruth purchased a doll for Mary-Farrah.

After a while, Flavius saw that Mary-Farrah was tired and said, "I think that's enough sightseeing for today, we'll see more of the city another time," adding, "Tomorrow, I should like to take you to meet my mother."

They returned to Flavius' villa and after eating a hearty

meal, Ruth put a sleepy Mary-Farrah to bed and then the three adults sat and talked.

Lydia Flavia was delighted to meet them, particularly Mary-Farrah. She introduced them to Claudius and Claudio. Claudio took Drubaal aside and asked him to tell him about some of the adventures he had shared with the Sheikh. Claudius gave his apologies, saying, "I'm sorry, I have to go to the Senate, but please do visit us again." He left the room.

At first, Ruth felt shy in front of Lydia Flavia, but her hostess soon put her at her ease.

When it was time to go, Lydia Flavia said, "I would very much like you all to come to supper tomorrow evening." She smiled when her invitation was graciously accepted.

The next evening, Flavius, Ruth, Mary-Farrah and Drubaal went to Claudius' villa. Lydia Flavia welcomed them, saying to Mary-Farrah, "How pretty you look in your lovely blue dress and slippers."

Mary-Farrah proudly lifted her little chin and said, "Thank you."

The evening was a success. After dinner, Flavius asked Claudius if he might loan Drubaal one of his horses so that he and Drubaal could ride out into the surrounding countryside. Claudius agreed, saying, "Take Draco, he's a good horse. Have him for as long as you like."

The next morning, Flavius and Drubaal rode through the countryside, breathing in the fresh, late-autumn air, happy to be temporarily free of the claustrophobic city. Flavius knew that Saturn too was relishing the wind rushing through his luxurious mane as he galloped along.

Ruth and Mary-Farrah had a restful day. They sat in Flavius' garden until the wind blowing off the Tiber became too chilly. Back inside the villa, Ruth kept her daughter happy by playing blind man's bluff and hide and seek.

When Flavius and Drubaal returned, their faces were red and their hair windswept from the chill wind, but they were happy, and hungry.

When Peter, Barnabas and Saul reached Caesarea, they stood on the side of the harbour.

"I have failed the Lord," Saul said disconsolately.

Peter shook his head. "No, Saul, you just need time to think about how best to serve Him. Perhaps, while you are in Tarsus, the Lord will speak to you and show you what He wants you to do."

Saul smiled weakly, "Perhaps." He listened as Peter intoned a prayer for his safe passage, said farewell, then boarded the ship.

Peter wondered if they would ever see him again. He turned to Barnabas and said "I am staying in Samaria for a while, I want to see some of the converts here."

"If you don't mind, Peter, I will return to Jerusalem," Barnabas replied.

The two Disciples said farewell, then went their separate ways.

Days passed by and Ruth waited for a sign from the Lord, but none came. She contented herself with going into the city, or visiting Lydia Flavia. One day, when Flavius and Drubaal were out with Claudio, Ruth and Mary-Farrah sat with Lydia-Flavia. Now feeling she could trust Flavius' mother, she decided to tell her about her past life and the reason why she had come to Rome.

Lydia Flavia was amazed by her story. "It's an epic tale," she said, "You have been through so much." She added a note of caution. "You say you wish to tell people about this Jesus, who you call the Son of God?" Ruth nodded. "I warn you, the Emperor will not like it, for in his mind he thinks he is Jupiter, Rome's most powerful god." She took Ruth's hand. "He delights in vicious acts of cruelty. If he heard that you had been spreading tales about a new god…"

Ruth smiled. "I know it's dangerous, but there is a hunger in my heart to spread the good news about the Lord to others, and I cannot ignore it."

Ruth sounded sincere in her beliefs. Lydia Flavia asked her about Jesus. She sat entranced as Ruth told her everything she knew about Him: His stories, how He had worked miracles on sick people, His death and Resurrection, and lastly, how He had saved her and her daughter.

Lydia Flavia was stunned. She looked at Mary-Farrah, happily playing with her doll, and thought, if only Flavius' wife and son could have been granted that same mercy.

The Saturnalia Festival was a quiet affair for Claudius and the family. Claudius did not invite any of his friends and clients to his home, feeling that it was inappropriate to celebrate after the death of his daughter and grandson. The family observed the religious acknowledgement to Saturn, followed by a dinner. There were no entertainments after.

Flavius did not celebrate the season either, but stayed quietly in his own villa with Ruth, Mary-Farrah and Drubaal.

In early January, after the Festival of Janus, Flavius asked his guests if they might like to visit the Theatre of Marcellus to see a play performed by Greek actors. They said yes. Flavius then visited his mother and asked her if she would look after Mary-Farrah.

Lydia Flavia replied, "Mary-Farrah would be bored watching a Greek play. If Ruth is agreeable, I would be happy to let her stay here until you return."

When Flavius told Ruth, Mary-Farrah looked expectantly at her mother and said pleadingly, "May I, mother?"

Ruth smiled at her daughter then said, "Yes. But you must be on your best behaviour."

Mary-Farrah squealed with delight. "Thank you! I promise I will be good."

The next morning Mary-Farrah waved her mother goodbye and watched as the three adults walked down the path of

Claudius' villa. When they were out of sight, Lydia Flavia said, "Would you like to see our new songbird? He lives in the garden, in a pretty golden cage."

"Yes please," came the excited reply.

Lydia Flavia smiled as Mary-Farrah skipped back into the villa.

CHAPTER FORTY-FIVE

Simon Magus bowed to the adoring crowds applauding him. Wearing a self-satisfied grin, he relished the knowledge of how far he had come from that day when those busybody Apostles, Peter and John, had caused him to flee from Caesarea with Peter's curse ringing in his ears. Since then he had travelled far and wide, fooling gullible people with his tricks. Now, here he was in the Forum in Rome, the centre of the world.

On their way back to Claudius' villa, Flavius, Ruth and Drubaal were discussing the Greek play they had just seen. They came to the Forum, where they saw a crowd of people standing watching something. Intrigued, they made their way through the crowd, stopping in front of a man dressed in a robe designed with suns, half-moons and stars. They heard the crowd gasp as he pulled coins from out of thin air and watched as Simon then took a man's belt off his tunic and made that disappear, only for it to reappear from out of his own pocket.

Raising his voice so that all could hear, Simon announced that if the crowd stayed there, they would see him jump off the tower of a high building and fly through the air.

The crowd mumbled amongst themselves, then a man shouted, "He must be one of the gods."

"If I can fly, then I am indeed a god, and you must worship me," said Simon. The crowd laughed at this.

Angry by the man's arrogance and lies, Ruth stepped forward. Without thinking, she pointed at Simon and said, "You are no god, you are just a man. There is only one God, the Creator of the universe and the Heavenly Father of the Lord Jesus."

The man who had shouted said, "What about Divine Caesar?"

Ruth looked at him and said, "He is no more divine than you or me!"

Horrified, Flavius cried out, "Ruth! No!"

It was too late. The man turned and quickly left the crowd, shortly returning with two Praetorians in tow. "Here she is," he cried, pointing at Ruth. "This is the one who said that Caesar is not divine and there is only one God."

Drubaal instinctively moved to protect Ruth as the Praetorians grabbed hold of her.

Flavius protested loudly, "Leave her alone. Her brain is addled, she does not know what she is saying."

Alerted by the jeering of the crowd, more Praetorians appeared, one of whom was Decimus. One of the Praetorians who had hold of Ruth pointed at Flavius and Drubaal and said, "Arrest these men too!"

Flavius cried out, "Where are you taking us?"

The Praetorian laughed and said, "To Caesar, so your girlfriend can repeat her words to him."

Simon stood with a sly grin on his face as he watched the Praetorians dragging the prisoners away. "Serves them right for interfering with my performance," he muttered to himself. "When the mob see me fly, they will know that I truly am a god."

After performing more tricks, Simon Magus entered a tower, eventually re-appearing on the roof high above where the equipment he needed had been stored. He picked up a winged contraption and put it over his head, then put his arms through leather straps fixed to the wings and secured it to his belt. The crowd applauded as he launched himself off the edge and flapped his wings. The thermals lifted him up, and for a few moments he seemed to be successfully flying through the air. Then he began to drop.

Simon frantically flapped his arms up and down, but the wings did not respond. The crowd gasped as he plummeted to the earth and landed with a sickening thud.

Some of the crowd rushed over to him. They looked at his tattered wings and shattered body. One man shouted, "He was no god! He was a charlatan!" Angry at being duped, the crowd quickly dispersed.

"On your knees!" The burly Praetorian forced Ruth to the tessellated floor in front of Caligula's throne. Four Guards held Flavius and Drubaal nearby. One of them punched Drubaal in the mouth as he struggled to get free.

For a long moment Caligula sat on his throne just looking at Ruth. Then he suddenly got up, stepped down from the dais and walked around her, like a lion prowling around its prey. He ordered the guard to grab her by her hair, forcing her head backwards, then loomed over her and stared at her.

With an icy voice he said, "So, you are the girl who doubts my divinity."

Ruth stared back at him.

Caligula slapped her face. "Do you know who I am?" No answer came. Through gritted teeth Caligula said, "I am the one who has the power of life or death over you."

"There is only one God who has that power over me, over you, over everyone," Ruth replied. The Praetorian kicked her in the middle of her back and she crumpled with pain, causing her grabbed hair to be torn out by the roots.

Incensed, Caligula shouted, "Yes, there is only one god, and that is me!" He circled her again and said, "Because I am a magnanimous god, I will give you one more chance. I will free you if you publicly worship me as a god in the Temple of Castor and Pollux."

Ruth tried desperately to hide the pain in her head and back and whispered, "No matter what you do to me, I will never worship you."

The Praetorian kicked her again.

Furious, Caligula said, "So be it! You leave me with no choice. Cassius Charea!" Charea stepped forward, "Take her away, let the Praetorians do what they want with her, but tell them that I want her alive for the Palatine Games tomorrow."

Drubaal tried desperately to free himself as Ruth was led away, but the Praetorians held him in an iron grip. Flavius shook his head, knowing that her death would be terrible.

Caligula walked over to Flavius and said mockingly, "We meet again, Flavius Silvanus. I thought you might have tried to stay out of trouble, after all, I let you live... once! How do you know the condemned?"

"We are friends," Flavius replied curtly.

He received a vicious slap from the Emperor. "You must call me Divinity!"

Flavius looked away trying to hide his anger.

Caligula moved on to Drubaal. "By Jupiter! That is to say by myself," he preened, "what a colossus you are." He ran his hand up and down Drubaal's arm muscles. "What a superb gladiator you would make." He grinned as an idea came to him. "Yes, a perfect plan. I am a genius."

He turned to the Praetorian Guards holding both prisoners and ordered, "Take them to the Mamertine. Bring them to the Circus early tomorrow."

He watched, laughing, as the guards dragged both men out of the chamber.

In a back room of the guardhouse, several Praetorians were lined up ready to rape Ruth, each one becoming more and more excited as their turn neared.

Cassius Charea shook his head in disgust at the sight of Ruth's cruel abuse. His eyes met those of Decimus, who had refused to take part in the monstrous act, and both nodded.

Decimus immediately left the room and rode up to Claudius' estate.

"I must speak to the Senator," Decimus told the doorkeeper. Seeing a Praetorian standing outside, he at first refused to open the door. Decimus said angrily, "Look, it's a matter of great urgency. It concerns the Senator's son-in-law."

The doorkeeper shut the grille and went to fetch Claudio. When Claudio heard that Flavius was in danger, he ordered the doorkeeper to let Decimus in. He called for his father, then led Decimus into his father's office.

Claudius stood grim-faced as Decimus told him what had happened. "Is there anything we can do to save him and his friends?" he asked.

"Yes," came Decimus' quick reply. "I know you are one of the few Senators who can be trusted. Please listen to what I have to say. Cassius Chaerea has a plan." He saw Claudius' mouth tighten into a thin line as he told him what it was. He looked straight at Claudius and said, "Now is the perfect time for him to put that plan into action. But you too, Senator, must play your part." Decimus told him what he must do if he wished to save Flavius.

"I will do everything I can," Claudius replied.

"And so will I," said Claudio.

Claudius called for Atticus. The slave was worried. Why was a Praetorian standing there? Was his master in trouble?

Claudius reassured Atticus that he was not, then opened his desk drawer and took out a key. He walked over to a padlocked cupboard, unlocked it and pulled out a bag of money. Securing the cupboard, he turned to Atticus, gave him the bag and said, "This is what you must do." He spoke to him for a few more moments. The slave bowed, then, securing the money in a shoulder bag, he took a horse from the stables and galloped out of the estate.

Decimus made his way back to the city.

Flavius and Drubaal were thrown into the dungeon of the Mamertine Prison, both frantically worried about Ruth and her fate.

Decimus entered the grim prison and approached the prison guard, saying authoritatively, "I must see the condemned prisoner Flavius Silvanus." The guard refused. Decimus offered him a bribe. The guard shook his head. Decimus drew his dagger and held it against the guard's throat. The guard, fearing for his life, said, "Go down to the lower level and tell the guard there that the Emperor has sent you. He cannot refuse you."

Decimus said threateningly, "If you say one word about this, I will kill you." He withdrew his dagger and made his way to the stairway leading down to the lower level.

"What are you doing here?" Flavius said, surprised to see Decimus enter his dank cell.

Decimus spoke in a low, urgent voice. "Listen to me, Flavius, I cannot free you, or your friend, now, but whatever happens tomorrow, hold on and be ready for my sign."

"What sign? What do you mean?"

Decimus saw his confusion. "I cannot explain now, but for Mars' sake, just be ready!" He left the cell, pleading silently to the Goddess of Justice to be with those involved in tomorrow's desperate plan.

All that night, Flavius kept turning Decimus' words over and over in his brain. Why should he hold on? Why be ready for Decimus' sign? What was going to happen at the Games tomorrow?

Lydia Flavia was worried. Flavius and his friends should have returned from the theatre hours ago. Where were they? She tried to sooth Mary-Farrah, who was crying for her mother. Then Claudius told her the devastating news.

Antonius picked up his wine cup and smiled. Since his first victory, he had appeared several times in arenas in Rome and the surrounding districts, winning every contest, including a rematch with Dagon. His previous fighting technique had become too well known, so he had adapted his style, using ever more inventive ways to gain victory over his opponents. His only disappointment was that he was not allowed to kill them, a rule that when his blood lust was up, made him feel frustrated and angry.

The only time that lust was satisfied was when he fought against untrained, condemned criminals, who were dressed in minimal gladiator costumes and given a sword and a shield or a net and trident, none of which they knew how to use, and were forced into the arena to fight against the cream of the gladiatorial world. These contests were to the death; a cheap form of execution loved by the mob.

Antonius' fame was growing throughout the city, and he revelled in the glory. The women he had been given after his victories had told him that graffiti about him had begun to appear on the walls of various buildings throughout Rome. Some graffiti, they said, was in admiration of his skill, while others showed lewd imaginings of his manhood, accompanied by indecent proposals from amorous females, proposals that would make a battle-hardened Centurion blush.

Antonius finished his wine, thinking that perhaps a gladiator's life was not so bad after all.

CHAPTER FORTY-SIX

An air of excitement reverberated around the packed public tiers overlooking the arena as the priests sacrificed a white bull and two rams. A cheer went up when the priests announced that the entrails showed the gods wished the games to go ahead. The ceremony completed, the priests, swinging incense burners, filed out of the arena, while slaves removed the altar and the sacrificed animals.

Fanfares, mixed with the cheers of the mob, created a cacophony of sound as, led by groups of musicians, the Editor, the Producer of the Games, a wealthy young man named Gnaeus, entered the arena riding in a golden chariot. Dressed in purple and carrying an ivory sceptre, he was desperate to impress Caligula. He hoped that if the games were successful, Caligula might grant him a Magistracy.

Gnaeus was followed by floats pulled by horses, mules and elephants, each carrying a statue of a god or goddess, with their own priests and altars in attendance, or carrying young men and girls re-enacting scenes from mythology.

Caligula walked through the covered tunnel leading from the palace to the Circus, closely followed by his German bodyguards, Cassius Charea and two Praetorian Guards. A trumpet fanfare greeted him as he entered the Imperial Box set above the Podium, his guards taking up their stations around him. The parade circled round the arena then went out, leaving Gnaeus looking up at Caligula.

Gnaeus bowed low and said obsequiously, "I am honoured, Divinity. I have carried out your orders and I trust that you will enjoy the result."

Caligula gave him a sneering look, then, pointing to the centre of the arena, he said, "I had better! If not, you will find yourself in the arena with the rest of the criminals."

Gnaeus bowed again, quickly climbed out of the chariot and retreated to the Podium, praying to the gods that Caligula would be satisfied with his efforts.

Caligula turned to face the mob and stood for a moment absorbing the adoration emanating from them. They should be grateful to him, for was he not their god? He waved a perfumed silk handkerchief at them, then put it to his nose, trying to blot out their rancid smell. He sat down on his silk-covered chair, followed by the Vestal Virgins in their box opposite. The Consuls, Senators, including

Claudius, and other dignitaries then sat down in their seats.

There was a second fanfare of trumpets. Cheers and applause erupted as, led by half-naked young girls, the contestants entered the arena. The girls scattered rose petals under the feet of charioteers, gladiators, wild animal trainers and professional hunters as they marched around the arena. A detachment of Praetorian Guards in gold armour marched at the rear of the procession. The whole procession formed up before Caligula and saluted him, shouting as one, "Hail Caesar!" They then saluted Gnaeus, who bowed in reply. Most of the procession marched off, but some of the gladiators, including Antonius, stayed behind, flirting with the women. After they had left the arena, another fanfare sounded, announcing that the Games were about to begin.

The chariot races were the first event. The people cheered as the charioteers appeared, their four teams of horses tossing their manes proudly as they trotted towards the Imperial Box. The charioteers saluted Caligula.

Caligula shouted down to his favourite Green Team charioteer. "Aulus! A purse of gold coins is yours if you win for me today."

Aulus bowed and replied, "Never fear, Divinity, the race is already won!"

Caligula waved him away. The charioteer laughed and saluted again, and the teams rode over to the starting line, their horses obviously eager to begin the race.

An almighty roar went up as the race began. The teams manoeuvred their horses around the massive *spina*, the huge barrier running down the middle of the track, separating its two sides. This was where the structure holding the seven golden dolphins stood, each dolphin being lowered one at a time as each lap finished and another began.

The last golden dolphin was lowered, heralding the final lap of the race. The crowd rose from their seats, shouting and screaming for their teams. The Green Team were so far in front of the others that they could not be overtaken. Aulus was ecstatic when he crossed the finishing line.

Aulus stood proudly in his chariot before Caligula, who picked up the promised purse and threw it down to him. Aulus caught it and opened it. It contained nothing but stones.

Seeing the disappointment on Aulus' face, Caligula laughed and said, "You will get your proper reward when you have completed another challenge for me. Now go and rest your horses. You will need them later."

Embarrassed, the charioteer turned his horses and left the arena.

The next event was the beast hunt. The mob cheered when the professional hunters came into the arena, then booed at the condemned criminals following them. The professionals would hunt down the wild animals and kill them, whereas the criminals would be hunted down and killed by the animals.

There was a deafening roar as tigers, leopards and bears burst out of the tunnels. The hunters fought and slaughtered many of them. Some of the criminals put on a good show, but most were eventually killed and devoured by the angry big cats. The bears rampaged through the survivors, ripping them apart. The crowd laughed when a huge bear picked up one of the condemned men, ripped his arm off, then proceeded to maul him to death. Maddened by fear, the remaining animals turned on each other. The arena soon became littered with dead and dying humans and animals. This ended the first part of the games.

During the interval, slaves cleared away the dead carcasses, then others raked over the blood-soaked sand, ready for the afternoon events. Those who had backed the Green Team to win went off to collect their winnings. The Consuls and most of the Senators went home for lunch, while some of the crowd stayed in their seats eating theirs while watching criminals being crucified or suffering other forms of violent executions.

Caligula was suffering from a bout of indigestion. He wished he had not eaten and drunk so much the night before. While he was debating if he wanted any lunch, a Praetorian came into the box, saluted and said, "Divinity, your guest has arrived."

"Good, bring him to me." Caligula smiled as his guest was shown into the box. "Sit here, by my side, Marius," Caligula said, pointing to a chair close by. "I have arranged something special just for you."

Marius gave Caligula a broad smile. "Just for me? Oh, thank you, Divinity, how thoughtful you are. May I ask what it is?"

Caligula stroked Marius' thigh. "Wait and see." He clapped his hands.

A Praetorian came out from the tunnel, dragging Flavius behind him. He brought Flavius to the Imperial Box, then took the rope binding his hands and fixed it to a post overlooking the arena. He saluted Caligula and disappeared back into the tunnel.

Bewildered, Marius asked, "Why is my brother here, Divinity? Please tell me, I am bursting with curiosity."

"Oh very well," Caligula sighed, then said loudly so that Flavius could hear, "I want him to see what is going to happen to his friends. Then after the gladiatorial contests, I have arranged a special treat for you and the mob." He looked directly at Flavius. "The animal trainers have a new, supposedly, ferocious Nubian lion and I need to know if it is worth the expense, so I am going to use your brother to test it."

Marius blanched. "Oh" was all he said.

Claudius gasped as he saw Flavius enter the Imperial Box. He saw Caligula turn to Flavius's brother and say something, but he could not hear the words. He hoped desperately that Charea's plan would work.

CHAPTER FORTY-SEVEN

The mob cheered as a fanfare announced the start of the afternoon programme featuring the highlight of the day: the gladiatorial contests. There was a murmur of disappointment when, instead of the contests beginning, a young woman dressed in a short filmy dress, her hands bound by a thick rope held by a Praetorian Guard, staggered into the arena. Her face and body were covered in scratches and bruises and her thighs were stained with dried blood. The Praetorian dragged her towards the Imperial Box.

Flavius felt sick when he saw that the woman was Ruth.

Ruth looked up at Caligula and said, "I know that death awaits me, but I forgive you and I pray that the Lord Jesus will forgive you too."

In reply to her insolence, Caligula ordered the guard to force her to her knees, then said sarcastically, "Where is this Lord Jesus you hope will forgive me?" He made a show of looking around the arena, then laughed and said, "You foolish woman, he does not exist! But I do, and it is only I who can save you."

He studied his fingernails for a moment, then pointed to the mob, who were growing restless. "But I will not, for how can I disappoint all of these people who have come here today seeking entertainment?" He called for one of the Praetorians standing nearby and whispered instructions for Aulus to him. The Praetorian hurried out of the box and made his way to the charioteer stables.

As Flavius stared at Ruth, he saw a halo of bright light surrounding her head. Where had he seen such a phenomenon before? Then he remembered. It was when he had first arrived in Jerusalem and had witnessed the stoning of the young Nazarene called Stephen. Before his death, his head too had been surrounded by light.

As Flavius watched, the light began to disappear. He wondered if Caligula had seen it. If so, he had not acknowledged it.

Ruth was dragged away from the Imperial Box. The Green Team's chariot thundered into the arena and stopped before Caligula. The charioteer saluted and rode away, stopping in front of Ruth. The Praetorian pulled her face down to the ground, fixed the ropes binding her hands to the rear of the chariot, and then hurried out of the arena.

Aulus whipped his horses and the chariot moved off. The cheers of the blood-thirsty mob grew louder as the chariot gained speed. Ruth's thin dress quickly disintegrated as she was dragged from side to side, her head and body bouncing violently over the coarse sand.

After three laps around the *spina,* Aulus stopped his chariot before the Imperial Box. He got out to examine Ruth's body. There was no doubt that she was dead. Her face had been reduced to pulp, and every bone in her body had been shattered, some protruding through her flayed skin.

Aulus nodded to Caligula. Slaves cut the blood-soaked rope from the chariot and using large hooks, dragged Ruth's body out of the arena.

Caligula had given orders that the bodies of all those who died that day would be food for the big cats, as the price of meat was exorbitant. The money saved would pay for the banquet he had planned for that evening. Pleased, he threw down the purse of gold to Aulus and waved him away.

The charioteer climbed back into his chariot and rode around the arena in triumph to the cheers of some of the adoring crowd.

But not all. Those who had heard Ruth's words to Caligula whispered to their neighbours. They were wondering who this Lord Jesus was and why, in His name, she had forgiven Caligula for his cruel treatment of her. She had not cursed the Emperor and had met her death with quiet dignity and courage. She obviously thought that this Jesus was worth dying for, but why? The whispers intensified as they passed along the tiers.

That day, the first seeds of belief in Jesus were sown amongst some of the watching Romans.

Flavius could not stop his tears from flowing. He had never witnessed such bravery. He hoped that the God she believed in would accept her into His Kingdom.

The trumpets blared and the mob went wild as the first gladiators appeared: a Thracian and a Murmillo. The Thracian won easily. There followed many other pairings of gladiators, who all hacked and sliced their way to victory. When the contests were over, the arena was cleared, ready for the main event of the day. It was to be a contest to the death between Rome's favourite gladiator and an unknown, untrained foreigner.

The crowd whistled and cheered as a Provocator entered the arena. The gladiator acknowledged the adoration of the crowd, then stood waiting for his opponent to appear.

The Guards had forced Drubaal to stand at the entrance of the Gate of Life to watch Ruth's execution. Sick at heart, he had wept bitter tears.

"Get out there!" shouted a rough voice, interrupting his grief. Drubaal turned and saw a swarthy man holding red-hot iron rods. "Go into the arena now," the man said menacingly, "unless you want these across your rump." The man waved the irons in his direction.

Pulling himself up to his full height, Drubaal walked out into the weak sunshine. Flavius bit his lip when he saw him enter the arena. He heard the mob's cries of admiration for the colossus, saying to their neighbours that this would be a magnificent contest.

Drubaal was wearing a loincloth, with a wide belt carrying a dagger fixed around his waist. He also wore an arm, shoulder and leg guard. In one hand he carried a net, in the other a trident. He heard the Provocator laugh but, because of the full-faced helmet visor, he had no idea who his opponent was, or how to use the weapons he had been given. If only he had his curved swords, then he might have a chance, but he knew he would never see them again.

When Drubaal had grown to manhood he had feared he would be sold as a gladiator because of his size and strength. The Sheikh had saved him from that fate, but now he was about to fight for his life in a Roman arena. He prayed silently. "Lord Jesus, if I am to die this day, have mercy on my soul."

Suddenly, the gladiator moved towards him. He backed away, then threw the net towards the man's feet, trying to trip him up. It missed. He tried a second time and the net landed to the side. The mob began to whistle and jeer.

The gladiator was incensed. It was too embarrassing. Goading his opponent to put up a fight, he moved in on the Carthaginian and thrust his sword at his uncovered leg, but Drubaal was too quick for him. He swerved to the side and the blade met thin air. This spurred the gladiator on to try to quickly put an end to this farce. He drove Drubaal back with a mighty onslaught of swordsmanship, his sword catching Drubaal's arm a glancing blow.

Despite the pain in his badly-bruised arm, Drubaal continued to jab at his opponent, but time after time, the trident connected with the gladiator's shield and was forced away. He tried to trap the gladiator's sword blade between the prongs of the trident, but the gladiator swung his sword and sliced the shaft in two. The prong-head fell to the ground, leaving Drubaal holding the broken, jagged-edged shaft and the net. With a supreme effort he swung the net around his head, then threw it with all his might. It fell short. Before he could pick the net up, the gladiator bore down on him. Using his shield, the gladiator knocked him backwards onto the sand.

Caligula, concentrating on the unfolding scene before him, did not notice Cassius Chaerea and the two Praetorians slip away from the box.

The gladiator moved in for the kill. He stood over Drubaal, laughing as he put his sword to Drubaal's throat.

Just then Drubaal noticed a slight gap between the gladiator's shield and his torso. He saw that the gladiator's flesh was bare between his loincloth and breastplate, and in a lightning move, he lifted the trident shaft and rammed it through the gap and into the gladiator's midriff. Then he rolled away as the gladiator, roaring in agony, dropped his sword and fell to his knees, which drove the shaft further into his body.

The fickle mob were on their feet, their thumbs pointing downwards, angrily calling for death to the gladiator. Fearing the angry mob, the Editor copied them. Now it was up to the Emperor to decide. The mob looked to the Imperial Box, demanding death for the gladiator and freedom for the brave opponent.

Drubaal knelt by the side of the impaled gladiator and said quietly, "I want to see your face." He lifted the helmet off the gladiator's head and reeled back in shock when he saw Antonius, his face twisted in pain and hatred, staring back at him.

"Put me out of my misery," rasped Antonius. He saw Drubaal shake his head and said, sneering, "Come on you Carthaginian scum, what are you waiting for?"

Drubaal could not kill a helpless man, no matter how badly that man had treated him in the past. He stood up and walked away. As he left, a sinister figure dressed as Charon the Ferryman walked out into the arena. Standing over Antonius, he lifted the massive hammer he carried and brought it crashing down onto the injured gladiator's head. Blood and brains splattered the sand. Slaves dragged Antonius' body out of the arena and through the Gate of Death. His body would also be eaten by hungry animals.

Drubaal stood looking up at Caligula, waiting for his decision.

Caligula was angry. This had not been his plan. He knew that with this gladiator's death he would lose a great deal of income. He rose up from his chair, walked to the edge of the box and looked down at Drubaal, then at the angry mob who were screaming for the Carthaginian's freedom. He had to take his anger out on someone. He turned to face Flavius and said, "You thought it was Aquila who was responsible for your father's suicide." When Flavius did not reply, he sneered, "Before you die, I want you to know that I was the one who accused your father of treason."

Flavius wanted to strike Caligula. His face white with fury, he struggled to free his hands. Seeing his action, a German Guard slapped his face.

Caligula laughed and said, "When Marius told me that your father disapproved of his friendship with me and tried to stop him from seeing me, I thought, how dare a mere Senator dictate to me who I could have as a friend? Then Marius also told me that your father had supported Sejanus. That was all I needed, so I wrote to Tiberius telling him that your father was hatching a new plot against him. The rest you know. It was a pity your father took his own life, I would have enjoyed making an example of him."

Caligula turned back to the mob and raised his hand. Which way should he point his thumb? Before he could make that decision, a Praetorian Guard entered the box.

"Divinity, the young boys who will dance for you at tonight's banquet have arrived. Perhaps you would like to see them rehearse to make sure they are suitable."

"Yes, I would. Let the foreigner and the mob wait, this is more important." Caligula turned to Marius and said, "Wait here, Marius, this will not take long."

The Praetorian and four German bodyguards followed Caligula out of the box.

CHAPTER FORTY-EIGHT

Marius turned to his brother and whined, "I wish I had never told Caligula about our father's dislike of him. It was never my intention for him to die."

Flavius glared at his brother and spat out, "Parricide! I hope you are tormented by the demons of Hades in this life and the next!"

Marius cowered at the curse and hid his face in his hands. Flavius looked down at Drubaal, still waiting anxiously below.

Caligula, his German bodyguards surrounding him, walked along the covered walkway leading to the Palace. He stopped when he came to the boys rehearsing their Trojan war-dance. When they had finished, Caligula said to them, "You are very good. I think you will be most suitable for..." but before he could finish the sentence, he felt a violent pain in his neck. He turned around and saw Cassius Chaerea standing there, his bloodied sword pointing at him. Fearing for their lives, the young boys scattered in all directions

The bodyguards immediately went into action, but more Praetorians, including Decimus, materialised from out of the shadows. The four Germans were easily overpowered and killed. Another Praetorian officer plunged his sword into Caligula's chest. This was the signal for the massacre to begin. Swords slashed, hacked and cut into Caligula from every direction.

The sound of Caligula's screams brought more of his German bodyguards to their Emperor's defence. They poured in from both ends of the tunnel. When the frontrunners saw the mutilated body of their Emperor laying on the blood-soaked ground, they turned on the assassins, but more Praetorians came up behind them, sealing off their escape routes. A furious battle ensued and many Praetorians and Germans were killed.

But not Cassius Chaerea. During the mayhem, Chaerea took Caligula's crown, tore off a piece of his blood-soaked toga and ran back to the Imperial Box. He held up the crown and cloth for all to see and shouted, "The Emperor is dead!"

Marius screamed and tried to make his escape. He reached the entrance to the tunnel and ran straight into Decimus. Decimus thrust his sword into his heart, and he dropped like a stone.

Realising what had happened and worried that the Praetorians would turn on them, the mob began to panic. Desperate men shoved their neighbours out of the way, while screaming women were knocked to the ground and trampled to death in the mad scramble to reach the exits. Hearing the noise, gladiators and animal trainers came into the arena to find out what was going on. Seeing Chaerea holding up the crown, they quickly ran back into the tunnels.

Decimus entered the Imperial Box and saw Flavius struggling to free himself. He went to him and cut the rope binding Flavius' hands to the post, then shouted over the fearful noise of the mob, "The horses are waiting outside for you and your friend." He pointed to Drubaal. "We must ride to Ostia. A ship is waiting for you there."

Flavius looked down at Drubaal. "How can he get out of the arena with all these people blocking the exits?"

"Don't worry about him, he will be taken care of," Decimus replied.

As he spoke, Flavius saw two Praetorians come into the arena and lead Drubaal away.

"What are they doing?" Flavius said frantically.

"They are taking him out through the tunnel the gladiators use to enter the stadium." He grabbed hold of Flavius' arm. "Come on! We must go to the horses."

Flavius did not argue. Brandishing his sword and uttering threats to the mob to clear the way, Decimus led Flavius down the packed public stairway. Terrified, the mob let them through. Soon they were outside the stadium. They ran around to the opposite side of the stadium, where four horses waited patiently for them. Flavius wept when he saw Claudio holding Saturn's reins. Overwhelmed, he rushed over to the horse, mounted up, then turned to Claudio and said, "My eternal thanks, Claudio."

Decimus mounted his horse and whistled. Another Praetorian appeared with Drubaal, now dressed in his tunic, close behind him. Drubaal mounted Draco as the Praetorian mounted the fourth horse.

Claudio took two folded cloaks from one of his saddlebags and gave them to Flavius, who passed one on to Drubaal. Gratefully the two men wrapped the cloaks around their shoulders.

"We will escort you to Ostia as there will be panic throughout the city," said Decimus. His voice held a note of warning.

Decimus was right. The city was in chaos. The Praetorian Guards began to rampage through the Palatine and beyond, killing Caesonia and Julia Drusilla, Caligula's German guards, his favoured dignitaries and his friends. Only Caligula's uncle, Claudius, and his wife, Messalina, escaped the brutality.

The two Praetorians brandished their swords at the people desperately trying to leave the city, forcing them to clear a path. Some did not move quickly enough and were hurled to the side by their horses and trampled by the mob.

When they came to the gate leading to the Ostia Road

the gate guards, overwhelmed by the amount of people trying to escape, were pleased to see two Praetorians and three civilians riding towards them, thinking they had come to help. But the riders kept on going. Knocking the people and guards aside, they forced their way through the gates.

The roads became clearer the closer they got to Ostia. As they neared the port, they saw Decimus' horse suddenly veer to the left. Decimus shouted for the others to follow him. They rode along an unused, overgrown pathway heading towards the coast until, eventually, the sea came into view. They rode down a grassy hill, reaching a cove where a barge awaited them.

Decimus pointed to a ship anchored out at sea. "This is your ship." he said. "And this is the barge that will transport you to it." He silenced Flavius' protests. "I know it is not yet the season for shipping, but the Cypriot Captain has agreed to take you to Cyprus."

"But I have no money, I cannot pay him," Flavius protested.

"Everything is paid for," said Claudio. "My father sent Atticus to see to that. A bag of money has been sewn into the lining of your cloak, it will help you to make a new start."

Flavius was overwhelmed by this generous act. Worried about his mother, he said, "I know my mother is in safe hands with your father, Claudio, but I also know how distressed she will be thinking she may never see me again."

"We'll reassure her that you are safe, and I will look after her as if she were my own mother," Claudio replied.

Flavius smiled. "Tell her I'll see her again when Rome is a happier place." Then a sudden thought hit him. "What about Mary-Farrah?"

"My father has already decided that she will stay with us. She will be cared for and brought up as one of the family."

Flavius nodded, thinking that perhaps she might replace the grandchild Claudius had lost.

The gruff voice of the helmsman came from the barge. "You must come now if the ship is to catch the tide."

Flavius and Claudio gripped arms, then Flavius turned to Decimus and said, "I thank you from the bottom of my heart, Decimus. May the gods' protect you, and above all, stay alive."

Laughing, Decimus said, "I have every intention of doing that. Now get on that barge!"

Flavius and Drubaal dismounted and eased their horses up the gangplank onto the barge. As Decimus watched the barge leave the shoreline, its sail billowing in the stiff wind, he shouted, "Remember, Flavius, courage, strength and honour."

With a final wave, he, his fellow Praetorian and Claudio turned their horses and rode back to Rome.

CHAPTER FORTY-NINE

They had been at sea for several days. Flavius kept a watchful eye on Saturn and Draco, who were penned below the deck. The weather had, so far, been reasonable, but the chill wind made them glad of their cloaks. The Captain, Giorgos, a swarthy Cypriot with a thick black beard and black hair swept back off his face by a colourful bandanna, seemed pleasant enough, but Flavius thought his eyes looked shifty and his smile false.

Flavius and Drubaal kept themselves occupied by playing knucklebones and dice, something Giorgos wondered about, for what wealthy Roman would play games with his slave?

On one occasion, as Flavius leaned forward to pick up his dice, Drubaal saw the gold talisman around his neck. Seeing Drubaal's curious look, Flavius said, "I have worn this talisman since the day your mistress placed it around my neck."

"You must have loved the Princess very much," Drubaal said gently.

"With all my heart," Flavius said sadly. "Now all we have left are memories of her, as with Sheikh Ibrahim and Ruth." He saw Drubaal look away as he tried to hold back his emotions.

Day after day the ship ploughed on through the waves, with no sign of land on the horizon. Their boredom grew, and Flavius wondered how much longer it would be before they reached Cyprus.

One morning a strong wind blew up, making the ship lurch from side to side. Worried about the horses, Flavius went below deck to check on them. Saturn and Draco were whinnying loudly and dashing their hooves on the floor of their pens. Flavius slowly approached them, speaking softly to try to calm them down. Hearing the calm voice, Draco settled down, but Saturn was still restless. He did not like confined spaces, and the ship's movement was making him nervous. He stroked Saturn's neck. The gentle feel of his master's hand quickly calmed him down.

Flavius spent some time making sure the horses were settled. As he turned away from them, he thought he heard a muffled cry, but there was nobody else there. As he put one foot on the stairway, he heard it again. Where was it coming from? Then he realised that the cries were coming from below his feet. He looked around and saw a trap-door half-hidden by a sack. He went over to it, removed the sack and put his ear to the floor. He could hear the sound of groaning. Grabbing the ring in the trap-door, he tried to lift it, but it did not move. With a supreme effort he tried again and this time it shifted. One last pull and the trap-door sprang open.

The stench coming from below was intolerable. Placing a hand over his nose and mouth, he looked down. It was too dark to see, but he clearly heard pitiful groans. Who was down there, and why?

He called out, "I am going to get help."

He did not see a figure come up behind him. He only felt a violent blow on the back of his head. Stunned, he could do nothing as his cloak was ripped off his shoulders with his bag of money still secreted inside. A hard push in the middle of his back propelled him headlong through the trap-door into the darkness below. Semi-conscious, he heard the trap-door slam shut above him. Then he passed out.

Drubaal wondered what was keeping Flavius. Was there something wrong with the horses? He decided to go and check. As he approached the doorway leading below, two burly sailors grabbed him. Caught by surprise, he tried to fight them off, but more sailors came and overpowered him.

Captain Giorgos appeared. "Take him to the cabin and lock him in. Two of you stand guard outside. I do not want him escaping." Drubaal struggled to get free, but there were too many of them.

Flavius opened his eyes and winced in pain. It took a while before they adjusted to the darkness. When they did, he looked around at his surroundings; this place must be a secret area between the lower deck and the bilges. He jumped as a voice nearby said, "We thought you had come to save us. You were our final hope. Now you too are trapped."

Flavius shuffled away from the man. "Who are you? Why are you down here?"

Another voice rasped out, "We are slaves, destined for wealthy Romans in Cyprus."

Flavius realised with horror that this was an illegal slave ship. No wonder the Captain was willing to sail during the winter months; there was less chance of him being arrested, as Roman naval ships were not so active at this time of year. Were he and Drubaal destined for a slave market? He was sure Claudius and Decimus had not known about this.

"How many of you are there?" Flavius asked the man next to him.

"There are twenty of us," the man replied. "Our hands are tied with rope to rings set in the hull of the ship."

Flavius wondered why his own hands had not been tied. He shrank back as he heard violent coughing coming from nearby and knew why the sailors had not come down there. Sickness. Whatever it was, he knew he could not escape from it. What would become of him, of them all?

Time passed, and Flavius knew neither the day nor

the hour. All he knew was that he was dirty, growing weaker by the day, and that the sickness was spreading. Violent coughing, the smell of vomit and increasing groans surrounded him. Would they all be dead when the ship reached its destination? He was worried about the horses, especially Saturn. Were they being looked after? Or left to starve like him and the slaves? The movement of the ship told him the weather was worsening too.

When the storm came, the wind howled like a demon in torment; the waves battered the hull of the ship, threatening to splinter the wood as the ship violently pitched and rolled from side to side. Flavius prayed to Neptune to save them.

But Neptune was not listening.

There was an almighty bang as the mainsail cracked under the onslaught and its top half crashed onto the upper deck, killing sailors beneath it. The helmsman, trying to steer the ship, was hurled into the tumultuous sea, leaving the ship unable to stay on course. The hull of the ship began to buckle under the weight of the sea battering it. A split appeared in the wood and the sea began to pour in, quickly drowning the slaves at that end. The ship was slowly being torn apart. Flavius was desperate to get out before the hull disintegrated.

Just then a crack appeared in the deck above him, and he scrambled away as part of the deck fell onto some more of the slaves, killing them. Seeing a large plank of wood hanging down from the deck above, Flavius pulled on it. Satisfied it would not give way, he began to shin up it.

Reaching an undamaged part of the deck, he made his way to the horse pens.

He stared in disbelief. A section of the upper deck had collapsed onto the pens. Hearing the horses whinnying in fear, he scrabbled at the wood, desperately trying to reach them, but could not get through. He heard the sound of the sea rushing into the pens and heartbroken, knew there was no hope of saving them. He turned and ran to the stairway leading to the upper deck.

All was chaos around him. Sailors were desperately clinging on to the lower part of the mainsail, while others were running to and fro looking for anything to hold on to. Where was Drubaal?

Then he saw Giorgos standing in the prow of the ship, praying to his gods to save him. Flavius approached him and said sternly, "Where is my friend?"

Without looking at him, Giorgos said, "In the cabin. If he is still alive!"

Flavius turned away. Fighting his way through the wind and rain, he reached the now-unguarded cabin. The door was locked, but seeing that it opened outwards he shouted, "Drubaal! Charge at the door. Keep on charging until it opens."

Immediately he heard the sound of Drubaal crashing against the door. He stood aside as it flew open and the Carthaginian appeared. Relieved, Flavius said, "Quickly my friend, we must get off this ship."

The two men jumped together into the turbulent sea

below. On kicking their way to the surface, they saw a part of the deck floating nearby and swam towards it. When they reached it they clung onto it, kicking out with their feet to drive it away from the ship.

When they were far enough away, Flavius looked back. Giorgos was still standing on the prow as his ship broke up under him and slowly sank into the sea. Sick in heart and body, Flavius laid his head on the plank and sobbed, mourning the loss of his beloved horse.

They floated in the sea for two days. At night, Drubaal tried to read the stars, hoping they would guide them to land. On the third day, he narrowed his eyes as he saw a coastline in the distance. He hoped it was Cyprus, as Flavius was sick and growing weaker. He prayed asking the Lord Jesus to help them.

His prayer was answered, for the tide now took them ever closer to the coastline. Close to collapse, Drubaal pushed against the plank, trying to force it towards land. When they were close to the shore, Drubaal lifted Flavius off the plank, gripped him tightly and swam towards the shore. At last, he staggered onto the sand. He laid Flavius down and then collapsed, exhausted, beside him.

CHAPTER FIFTY

Julius was leading the morning cavalry patrol along the coastline on their daily search for illegal activity. He suddenly slowed his horse and raised his hand, ordering his men to stop. What was that on the beach? Taking two men with him, he rode over to investigate. As he drew nearer, he saw two bodies.

He jumped down from his horse and took a closer look. He was shocked when he saw that it was Flavius and Drubaal. How had they got there? He touched Drubaal on the shoulder, and the Carthaginian flinched. Then he put his ear to Flavius' chest. "Praise the gods," he said quietly, "he is alive." He looked up at one of his cavalrymen and said briskly, "Ride to the fort and bring back a horse and wagon. Tell the gate guard it is needed for an emergency." He watched as the cavalryman rode off, then turned back to the two half-drowned men laying on the sand.

He could not take them into the fortress, as he and Pilate were the only ones who knew who Flavius and Drubaal were. Julius himself was fairly new to the Caesarea garrison and Pilate was no longer the Governor. He came to a decision: he would take them to his father's house.

The cavalryman soon returned. Julius and another of his men carefully lifted Flavius into the wagon. It took three men to lift Drubaal and place him beside Flavius.

Julius led the way to Cornelius' house. Martha opened the door, surprised to see Julius standing there. She was even more surprised when he told her to find a spare sleeping mat, place it on the floor at the foot of his bed, then fetch woollen blankets and towels and take them to his room.

Julius' men lifted first Flavius and then Drubaal out of the wagon.

"Put them in there." Julius pointed to his room.

Martha waited in Julius' room for further instructions. She looked on in horror as the cavalrymen carried in an unconscious Flavius, then brought in Drubaal.

"Wait outside, Martha," Julius said, then ordered his men to stay. Supported by two cavalrymen, Flavius was undressed by Julius. Drubaal, held up by cavalrymen, was stripped of his clothes by another. Their naked bodies were vigorously towelled dry, then wrapped in the blankets. Flavius was laid on Julius' bed; Drubaal was laid on the sleeping mat. One of the cavalrymen took their dirty clothes away for disposal.

Julius called Martha back into the room. "Where is my sister?"

Martha led him out into the garden where Julia was sitting on a bench, sewing. When Julius told her what had happened, her thoughts were in turmoil. Flavius was here? And in mortal danger? She had to do something. She looked at her brother and said earnestly, "Let me take care of him."

"You must stay out of my room. I don't know if anything is wrong with Drubaal, but Flavius is very ill, he could have a contagious disease."

"All the more reason for me to watch over him. I can make up herbal medicines to try to bring down his fever." Seeing her brother's worried face, she added, "At least let me try."

Julius knew it was useless arguing with her. He took her hand and said, "Very well. But if you too get the fever..."

Julia smiled and squeezed her brother's hand.

"I have to go. I must continue the patrol." He kissed Julia's forehead, then returned to his men, who waited patiently outside. The cavalrymen took the horse and wagon back to the garrison as Julius and the rest of his men continued their patrol.

Julia knew that the next hours would be crucial for Flavius. She would do everything in her power to help him recover. She went into the garden and picked suitable plants and herbs to make the medicine she needed.

The next day, when his duties were finished, Julius came to see how Flavius and Drubaal were. He entered his room and saw Julia sitting on a couch near to the bed; she was bathing Flavius' forehead with a damp cloth. Drubaal was sitting up on his mat.

Julia looked up at her brother and said, "As you see, Drubaal has made a good recovery, but I am worried about Flavius."

Julius frowned as he saw Flavius tossing and turning in his sweat-soaked bed and heard his laboured breathing. Julia was right to be worried. He looked at his sister, saw the dark shadows beneath her eyes and said, "Have you slept?"

She shook her head.

Drubaal wrapped his blanket around his naked body and got up from his mat. "Let me help you, mistress. I was only exhausted, not ill like Flavius."

Before Julia could reply, Julius said, "My sister will be grateful for your help, Drubaal, but you cannot move around in that blanket, we must try and find a tunic large enough to fit you."

"We have some material Martha was going to make new bed covers with, that should be large enough," Julia offered. "Martha can make a tunic out of that."

Soon Drubaal was proudly showing off his new dark red garment.

Day and night, hour after hour, Julia and Drubaal took it in turns to bathe Flavius' face and body with a cloth dipped in cold water, hoping to reduce his fever. Drubaal would hold Flavius' head while Julia helped him to swallow her herbal medicine mixed with watered wine. As one slept, the other sat watching over their patient, both praying for Flavius' recovery.

Flavius slowly opened his eyes. His head ached intolerably, but his fever had gone. He heard a soft voice say, "At last!" Turning his head, he saw Julia sitting close by his bed.

"Julia?" Flavius was confused. Even more so when he saw Drubaal standing behind her. "Thank the gods, you are alive," he said to the smiling Carthaginian.

Julia placed a hand on Flavius' forehead, relieved to find that it was cool.

"Where am I?" he asked, bemused.

"You are in my father's house."

"How did I get here?" Flavius was shocked when Julia told him about her brother's part in his rescue. "But he placed you in danger," he said, worried for her.

Julia smiled. "It was my decision. Someone had to take care of you."

"Is Julius here?"

Julia shook her head. "Julius and my father are staying at the fortress. I'll send a message to them saying your fever has gone."

"How long have I been here?"

"Five days."

"I cannot thank you enough. You saved my life. I will never forget that."

Julia looked down, not wanting him to know that she would have willingly stayed by his side forever if needed. Hiding her embarrassment, she said, "I couldn't have done it without Drubaal's help. You must thank him too."

Flavius looked at Drubaal. "Thank you, my friend."

Julia stood up and said, "Rest now, Flavius. You must regain your strength. I'll come and see you later. Until then, Drubaal will stay with you."

Flavius' eyes followed her as she left the room. He felt for the talisman. By some miracle it still hung around his neck. Farrah had told him that its powers would save him from death, including by water and the evil eye. It seemed she had spoken the truth.

Flavius stayed in bed for the next two days, slowly regaining his strength. Julia fed him fresh fruit and vegetables, sweet honey-cakes and other nourishing foods, washed down with honeyed wine mixed with restorative herbs.

Julius came to see him. "I'm so glad to see you are recovering."

Flavius smiled, then held out a scroll. "This is to go to Rome, to my stepfather, Senator Claudius Marcellus. It is to let him and my mother know where I am and that I am well. Would you place it in with the communications to be sent from the fortress to Rome? Oh, and please seal it with your signet ring, Julius. I fear that if my seal was seen, this would never reach Claudius."

Julius did not question Flavius. He just nodded, sealed the scroll with melted wax, pressed his signet ring into it and took it back to the fortress.

The early spring weather grew warmer. Wearing a set of Julius' clothes, and wrapped up in a blanket, Flavius was able to sit in the garden for a short time every day. One afternoon, Julius and Cornelius came from the garrison to see him.

"You look much better, Flavius," Julius said, smiling.

"Thanks to Julia and Drubaal," Flavius replied.

"When you feel up to it, will you come to the fort and see your old comrades?" Cornelius asked. He was stunned when Flavius replied that he was no longer a Tribune and why. "Caligula was a monster!" Cornelius replied, disgusted.

"Drubaal told us what happened in the arena. I am sorry for the cruel loss of your friend," Julius said. "You and Drubaal were lucky to escape."

"Without the help of my Praetorian and Senator friends, we would not be here."

Flavius was waiting anxiously to hear from Claudius, hoping he would say that Decimus had survived the severe repercussions that had undoubtedly come after Caligula's assassination.

"As for the slave ship," Julius continued, "we deal with many slave traders during the winter months, it is why we patrol the coastline. It must have been fate that we were patrolling the shoreline that day we found you on the beach."

"Lucky for us that you did." Flavius sighed. "I wish I could have saved Saturn, but he was trapped and I could not get to him. He went down with the ship."

Julius was sorry to hear that. He knew how much Saturn had meant to his friend.

Flavius looked at Cornelius. "The captain of the ship stole all of my money, so I cannot repay you for your kindness."

"Don't worry about that now," Cornelius said. "When you're ready, will you tell us what you've been doing these past few years? You left Caesarea without a word. We wondered why."

Before Flavius could answer, Julia appeared, holding a wine cup. Seeing Flavius' sad expression, she intervened and said, "Let him rest. You can question him some other time."

Her father and brother knew not to argue with her. Cornelius said, "We will come and see you again, Flavius." They smiled at Julia and left the garden.

Flavius was grateful to Julia. He was not ready to talk about Rome at this moment; he had too many bad memories of the place. He returned her smile as she placed the wine cup on the small table in front of him, then watched as she went back into the house.

As the days grew longer, Flavius spent more time outside. Julia would often come and sit with him. He looked forward to seeing her. She was good company and her tinkling laughter cheered him up. But where was Marcus?

The next time she joined him, he said, "When I left Caesarea, you were about to marry Marcus."

"We did marry," she replied sadly. "He was killed three years ago."

Flavius was shocked. "I'll understand if you do not wish to talk about it" he said.

"I want to talk," she said sadly. "Pilate had been told that the Samaritans had planned an uprising at Mount Gerizim, so he sent in the Legions to quell it. There was no uprising, not at first anyway, but because of rough handling by some legionaries, the situation escalated."

Flavius wondered if that was why Pilate had been recalled to Rome.

Julia continued, "I was told that when Marcus tried to intervene, he suffered severe injuries." She sighed. "He never recovered."

"I am so sorry."

Flavius was horrified when she told him how cruel Marcus' parents had been to her. His instinct was to hold her in his arms, to comfort and protect her, just as he had protected her when he had first met her at Pilate's Saturnalia party, an age ago.

He studied her face. The pretty young girl he remembered had grown into a beautiful woman. Her hair shone like spun gold in the sunlight, her smooth skin was unmarked by time and her gold-flecked brown eyes sparkled with unshed tears. He took her hand and said gently, "You have suffered so much, I wish I could take away your sadness."

Julia looked up at him, trying to hide her yearning for him. She had always kept a secret place in her heart for the handsome Tribune.

Flavius looked deep into her eyes and saw her love and longing mirrored there. His heart melted. He leaned forward and tenderly kissed her. Hesitant at first, Julia gradually responded to him. He gathered her in his arms and kissed her again, realising that his feelings for her were now much more than gratitude.

CHAPTER FIFTY-ONE

For the past few weeks, Peter had been staying in Lydda, a town nine miles from Joppa. While visiting the converts there, he had come across a man named Aeneas, who had been bed-ridden with paralysis for eight years. Taking pity on him, Peter said, "Aeneas, the Lord Jesus cures you. Get up and make your bed." Seeing Aeneas standing up unaided, the startled people of Lydda and Sharon believed that Jesus was indeed the Son of God.

One day soon after, Peter received a visit from two men from Joppa with an urgent message for him. They told him that a local woman named Tabitha, known for her acts of kindness and charity, had fallen ill and died. They begged him to return with them to ask the Lord to raise her from the dead. When he heard that, Peter went straight to Joppa with them.

When he arrived at Tabitha's house, he went to the upstairs room, where she had been washed and laid out on her bed. Many widows stood around the bed, weeping. When they saw Peter, they showed him the shirts and coats Tabitha had made for them.

Peter sent them all outside. He knelt down and prayed, then standing over Tabitha, he said commandingly, "Tabitha, arise."

Tabitha slowly opened her eyes, saw Peter standing there and sat up. Peter helped her to her feet, then called in the men and the widows and showed them that Tabitha was alive. The news of the miracle spread throughout the area and many turned to Jesus. Peter stayed on in Joppa for some time, living in the house of a tanner called Simon.

Flavius lay on his bed turning things over in his mind. His bond with Julia had grown stronger. When he held her in his arms he felt not only a longing for her but a feeling of peace and contentment washing over him, something he had never experienced before. He sighed. Farrah had been the passion of his youth and he had only married Claudia to please her father. With Julia he felt a deep and abiding love and knew that he wanted her by his side for the rest of his life.

Now that Flavius had recovered, when his duties at the garrison allowed, Cornelius returned home. He saw Julia's new-found happiness and was concerned that it was due to Flavius. He decided to speak to him. That evening, after dinner, he took him aside.

"I have seen looks pass between you and Julia," he said. "Tell me, have you feelings for my daughter?"

Embarrassed, Flavius replied, "I love her."

"Does she feel the same for you?" Cornelius asked.

"Yes," Flavius replied.

Cornelius frowned. "I know that you are an honourable man, Flavius, but I will not stand by and let her heart be broken again."

"I will never hurt her, Cornelius."

"And if, now that you have recovered, you decide to return to Rome, what then?"

Now was the time to tell Cornelius about his father's suicide, his inheritance being stolen by Caligula and the generosity of his father's friend, Senator Claudius Marcellus. "I married Claudius' daughter; we had a son, but both sadly died," he said wistfully. "The rest you know. I have my own house in Rome, or at least I did, but it would be unwise for me to return there. I am probably still a marked man."

"I'm sorry to hear of your loss," Cornelius said gravely. "You have been through a bad time. Caligula's uncle, Claudius, is Caesar now. Perhaps things will improve."

"Perhaps," Flavius replied, doubting that would happen any time soon.

"I have not seen Julia so happy in a long time." Cornelius added a warning note. "Take care not to hurt her, Flavius."

"That I will never do," Flavius replied. "If I had anything left to give her, I would ask for your permission to marry her."

Cornelius stared at him, but kept his thoughts to himself.

That night Cornelius lay in his bed pondering what he should do about his daughter and Flavius who had both suffered the loss of loved ones. He could think of no one he would rather see Julia marry than Flavius. But by his own admission, Flavius, by terrible misfortune, had been left destitute, with no financial support. Heavy-hearted, he prayed for guidance, then fell into a troubled sleep.

The next morning, Julius, having a few days leave from the army, came home. Later that afternoon, as Claudius was sitting in his room reading from a scroll containing one of the Jewish Scriptures, he suddenly became aware that someone had entered the room.

Without looking up he said, "Is that you, Julius?"

A silvery voice replied, "Cornelius."

Cornelius put down the scroll and stood up ready to challenge whoever had called his name, but when he saw the shimmering light surrounding the stranger, he fell to his knees, terrified.

Keeping his eyes lowered, Cornelius said, "Are you an angel?"

"Yes," the silvery voice replied.

"What do you want with me?" Cornelius asked, afraid.

"Your prayers and acts of charity have gone up to

Heaven to speak for you before God," the angel replied. "Now you must send to Joppa for a man named Peter. He is lodging in a house by the sea with Simon, a tanner."

Cornelius looked up, but before he could question the angel further, the shimmering apparition began to fade. Cornelius blinked. The angel had gone.

Julius was sitting in the garden with Flavius and Julia when Cornelius came rushing out to them. Seeing the look on his father's face, Julius said, "What is it, father? You look as if you have seen a ghost."

Cornelius smiled. "No, but I have seen an angel."

"What?" Julius stopped laughing when he saw the earnest look on his father's face.

"It is true." Cornelius repeated the instructions the angel had given him. "Take Drubaal and ride to Joppa. Andros will take the cart. Hurry please."

Julius did not understand why they had to ride to Joppa to find this Peter and bring him back; he just knew he had to obey his father's wishes. He went to the stables and told Andros, the stable hand, to saddle his and one other horse and prepare the horse and cart. Drubaal was helping Andros to clean the stables. He was startled when Julius said, "You are coming with us."

Soon all three were travelling along the road to Joppa.

It was a hot afternoon. Peter went up onto the roof of Simon's house hoping the breeze coming off the sea would cool him down. He looked down at the waves gently lapping the shore, then looked up at the sky. Bemused, he saw the sky suddenly split open. A large sheet of sailcloth floated down through the empty space and was lowered to the ground by unseen hands. When it had settled, Peter looked into it and saw creatures of every kind: those that walked, crawled or flew.

A voice said, "Peter, kill and eat."

Disgusted, Peter reeled back from it and said, "No. Lord, no. I have never eaten anything unclean or profane."

The voice came again. "It is not for you to call profane what God counts clean."

This statement was repeated three times. Then the sheet with its contents was taken back up into the sky and the split closed.

Had he been dreaming; was it a vision? Peter was puzzling over the phenomenon when he saw in the distance three men riding towards Simon's house. When the men arrived at the entrance to the house, Julius called out, "We are looking for Peter, is he lodging here?"

Seeing that one of the men was a Roman, Peter stepped back, afraid, but a Heavenly voice said to him, "These men are looking for you. Quickly, go downstairs. It is safe to go with them, for it is I who have sent them."

Peter hurried down to the men, puzzled when he saw that Drubaal was with them. He said, "Why are you looking for me?"

"We have come from Caesarea, on behalf of my father, Centurion Cornelius," Julius replied. "He says he was instructed by an angel to find you so he may listen to your words. We have come to take you back to him. Will you come?"

Peter's thoughts were in turmoil. He had been asked to go to a Gentile's house, something forbidden. Yet the Roman said his father had been visited by an angel and the Holy Spirit had told him that He had sent these men to him. He came to a decision.

"Stay here tonight, rest and eat," he said. "Tomorrow, I will go with you to Caesarea."

After they had eaten, Peter asked Drubaal, "Are Ruth and Mary-Farrah in Caesarea with you?" He wept when Drubaal told him of Ruth's martyrdom and said, "My poor, brave girl." Poor John Mark too, he thought, knowing that he would be devastated by this terrible news. Seeing Drubaal's cast-down look he said, "I am certain that she is in Heaven with our Lord." He wiped his tears. "What happened to Mary-Farrah?"

"She is in Rome being cared for by trusted friends," Drubaal replied.

Peter nodded. "I pray that the Lord will be with her."

The next morning, with six Jewish converts accompanying Peter, they travelled to Caesarea. When they arrived at Cornelius' house, Cornelius hurried out to greet Peter. As Peter stood before him, Cornelius bowed to the ground in reverence. Peter raised him to his feet and said, "Do not bow to me. I am a man like anyone else."

Cornelius led him into the house, with Julius, Drubaal and the converts following him. They were joined by Flavius and Julia.

Peter looked at them all and said, "You know that a Jew is forbidden to visit the house of a Gentile, but God has shown me that I must not call any man profane or unclean, so I have come at your request. Why have you sent for me?"

Cornelius told Peter about the visit from the angel, adding, "Now we are anxiously waiting to hear all that the Lord has ordered you to tell us."

Peter was intrigued. How did this Roman know about God and Jesus? He said, "I now see that God has no favourites, but that in every nation the man who fears God and does what is right is acceptable to Him."

Cornelius asked Peter to sit down, then the family, Martha and Andros, sat down around him. They listened in awe as Peter told them about the life, death and resurrection of Jesus.

"We know that He did rise again, because we Apostles saw Him and spoke with Him on several occasions," Peter said. "Before He returned to His Father in Heaven, He commanded us to tell everyone about Him and say that those who trust in Him will receive forgiveness of their sins."

As Peter spoke, Cornelius felt a strange feeling of exhilaration come over him. He suddenly began to praise God.

Flavius felt power coursing through his veins. Bemused, he looked at Julia. Her face was radiant with joy. He saw

Drubaal, head bowed, drop to his knees, while Julius sat utterly still. Martha was weeping as Andros stood, eyes closed and smiling.

Some of the converts who saw this were astonished that the holy gift was being given to Gentiles. Knowing that the Holy Spirit had been received by the listeners, Peter praised God, then said, "Will someone bring me water so I may baptise them?"

Martha immediately went to fetch a bowl of water.

Beginning with Cornelius, Peter baptised them one by one, saying joyously, "I baptise you in the name of the Lord Jesus."

Filled with love and hope, Cornelius asked Peter to stay with them for a while. Peter gladly agreed. Later, Flavius came to Peter and said, "I witnessed the deaths of Stephen of Alexandria and Ruth. Both died willingly for Jesus. I could not understand why then, but now I can. Jesus never hurt anyone, He only helped them. If only the cruel and greedy rulers of Rome were like Him."

Peter placed a hand on Flavius' shoulder. "I firmly believe that one day where Emperors rule now, the Lord will reign forever."

Flavius hoped he was right.

The next day, Cornelius told Peter that Philip was in Caesarea. "I can take you to him, if you wish," Cornelius offered. Delighted, Peter readily accepted.

They found Philip preaching in his usual place. When he saw Peter at Cornelius' side, he was overjoyed. "Peter!" He cried, going straight to Peter and embracing him warmly. "What are you doing in Caesarea?" He was shocked when Peter told him and said, "What will the Disciples in Jerusalem say about this?"

Peter smiled wistfully, "I think they will be angry. I pray that the Lord will give me the words to explain my actions."

Philip smiled at Cornelius. "Welcome, brother." Then he turned back to Peter.

"Peter, will you speak to the people here?"

Peter nodded. Philip introduced the Lord's Apostle to the converts, who listened in awe as Peter told them about his time with Jesus.

When Cornelius and Peter arrived home, they found a sad-faced Julius waiting for them.

"What's wrong, my son?" Cornelius asked, concerned.

Julius sighed. "I am a soldier in the Legions. Sometimes I have to do vile things. How can I reconcile that with following a God of love and peace?"

Cornelius looked at Peter and said, "I too share that feeling."

Peter replied, "The Lord never spoke out against Rome, in fact, He even healed the servant of a Centurion stationed in Capernaum, so impressed was He by the Centurion's faith in Him. So I say to you both, do your duty to Rome but with compassion, and above all, have faith in the Lord and let Him guide you."

Later, with Peter's words ringing in his ears, Julius

rode back to the garrison. After two days he returned to the house, bringing with him a scroll. He found Flavius in his room. Handing Flavius the scroll, he said, "This arrived with today's dispatches."

Flavius read it and then said out loud, "It's from Senator Claudius. He says he is relieved to know that I am safe and that he and my mother are well. He is very proud of Claudio, who has just won his first election and is now a Quaestor. He goes on to say that Mary-Farrah, although still mourning for her mother, with their love and care is slowly adapting to her new life. As for Decimus, he is still a Praetorian now under the new regime."

A smile spread across his face. "Claudius also says that he has arranged for the credit held in my bank account in Rome to be transferred to its branch here in Caesarea." He looked at Julius. "It means I am no longer destitute."

"That is good news," Julius replied, smiling.

Flavius showed Cornelius the scroll. When Cornelius had finished reading it, Flavius said, "Now that I have the means, will you allow me to marry Julia?"

Cornelius smiled at him. "If she wishes it, then you have my permission."

When Flavius asked Julia to marry him, she wept tears of happiness, saying, "Yes, oh yes, Flavius."

Flavius held her close. "Let us ask Peter if he will marry us."

Peter was talking with the Jewish converts when Flavius and Julia approached him. When he heard their request, he smiled and said, "Gladly. Gather the family together."

The family, including Martha and Andros, watched as Flavius and Julia knelt before Peter. Peter said solemnly, "Flavius, will you love and be faithful to Julia all the days of your life?"

"I will," Flavius replied, choked with emotion.

"Julia, will you love and be faithful to Flavius all the days of your life?"

"Yes," she whispered.

Peter placed his hands on their heads and said reverently, "Lord Jesus, bless this union and let Your Light shine upon them. Be with them now and forever, Amen."

The happy couple stood up. Cornelius and Julius smiled as Flavius kissed his bride, while Martha, shedding tears of happiness for her mistress, hurried off to create a wedding feast for everyone.

That night, in the privacy of their bedroom, Flavius removed the amulet and placed it in a drawer. He would never forget Farrah and knew that Julia would never forget Marcus, as they had both played such an important part in their lives, but now he and Julia had to look to the future. He drew Julia down onto the bed and held her in his arms, his longing for her culminating in an explosion of exquisite passion.

Afterwards, Flavius looked at Julia sleeping contentedly in his arms. He had never experienced a love like this, a love so pure and unselfish; a love that would last a lifetime.

The next morning, as Peter was preparing to return to Jerusalem, Drubaal came to see him. "Peter," he said pleadingly, "Let me come with you, let me help you in your work."

Peter looked at him intently. "As you have seen, spreading the Good News of the Lord is dangerous. Are you prepared to face this?"

"Yes, I am prepared." Drubaal replied. Seeing the look of sincerity in his eyes, Peter said, "Then come with me."

Drubaal found Flavius and told him that he was returning to Jerusalem with Peter.

Flavius clasped Drubaal's arm and said, "I wish you well, old friend. I will never forget you."

"Nor I you, Perhaps we will meet again someday."

"I hope so, Drubaal," Flavius said emotionally.

Drubaal was a free man and could go wherever he wanted, but Flavius knew just how much he would miss him. They had shared so much together.

The family said their farewells and watched as Drubaal, Peter and the Jewish converts joined the road leading to Joppa and Jerusalem. Flavius said a silent prayer for them. He had seen how the rulers of Rome treated those who challenged their authority; if the new religion became a threat to their power, he knew they would hunt down and horrifically put an end to those who followed it. He had been through so much these past few years, but he had remained steadfast and undefeated. He would not turn his back on his new-found faith, even though he knew many dangers lay ahead.

He put his arm around Julia's waist and smiled at her. Armed with the love of the Lord, and their love for each other, he knew that he and Julia would face those dangers together.